THE CRY OF A LONE BIRD

ARDAIN ISMA

Ardain Isma

Ardain Isma, born in Saint Louis du Nord, Haiti, spent his formative years on the island before immigrating to the United States. A celebrated essayist and novelist, he is the author of several critically acclaimed works, including *Midnight at Noon*, *Bittersweet Memories of Last Spring*, and *Last Spring Was Bittersweet*. Ardain now resides in Saint Augustine, Florida, with his wife, Maryse.

To the children still living in servitude, to the memory of my dear friend Virgile Pierre-Jean, and to my wife Maryse with our children—Ardine, Ardain Junior, and Ardy—whose love and strength sustain me. And to my beloved Haiti, whose people fight each day for a better life. Hold firm. Don't give up.

Acknowledgments

To all the children still bound by the chains of servitude—may your voices rise, your dreams take flight, and your lives be freed from the weight of injustice.

In cherished memory of my late friend, Virgile Pierre-Jean—steadfast companion, loyal supporter, and fellow traveler on the long road that led to Lone Bird. Your spirit walks beside me still.

To my wife, Maryse, the heart of my home, and to my children—Ardine, Ardain Junior, and Ardy—whose laughter and love give meaning to every page I write.

Pou Ayiti cheri. Pou tout yon pèp k ap goumen pou lavi miyò. Kenbe la. Pa lage.
(For my beloved Haiti. For a people fighting for a better life. Hold firm. Don't give up.)

"When a single voice dares to rise against injustice, it carries the weight of many who could not speak."

— Ardain Isma

Table of Contents

<u>*C h a p t e r   1*</u>

A special one indeed, she winds like a man's pocket watch down this rocky trail overgrown with Spanish moss. She does not seem weary, or if she is, no sign of tiredness appears, especially when the rising sun casts its golden glow on her worried face. She strides forward with relentless steps, covering villages, ravines, and hills with the determination of a modern-day heroine. Her backpack, filled to the brim, does not seem to weigh her down. She moves with the resolve of an intrepid soldier, unwavering in her mission.

Haiti, 1948. Céline Bodin, a girl from uptown Saint Louis, has returned home from Scotland after five years of study. Her homecoming is marred by news that her childhood friend and former servant, Louisinette, was raped, conceived an unwanted child, and was expelled from the only home she had ever known. Determined to right this horrific wrong, Céline embarks on a journey to find Louisinette and bring the man responsible to justice.

******

Despite the mountains looming monstrous in the distance—blue or purple depending on the sun's rays—Céline shows no sign of fatigue. Her ruddy face, tanned to copper, is marked with stone-like gravity. People heading in the opposite direction catch only a repressed smile or a subtle nod when they wave. She doesn't look back; she presses on.

Stains trickle down her floral dress, shadows of salt marking her progress. Her tennis shoes crack apart over the grayish pebbles. Humid and tropical, the morning air mingles with lingering rains and sweat, soaking her golden, straight hair—hair that sets her apart with its Levantine appearance.

By eight a.m., Céline reaches the peak of MònZonbi. The ridge slopes down toward the western bank of the Acajou River. She shields her narrow eyes with one brown hand against the sun's piercing rays. For a moment, she sighs, overwhelmed by the tropical beauty around her. The lime-green décor of hills and valleys steals her heart, so unlike the barren landscapes in the southern provinces. Fresh-smelling mountains, flowering undergrowth, and hazy mornings conspire to create a picturesque vista—one she seldom overlooks, even as creeping fatigue spreads through her aching body.

Sitting to recharge her restless soul, she squirms on a half-rotten log surrounded by wild citronella and tall guinea grasses. The morning dew has vanished. A cool breeze crackles through nearby tree branches, its sudden fury making her heart leap in a frenzied spook as a bird shrieks its cacophonous cry.

Back on her feet in an instant, Céline heads down the winding trail, now bordered by thorny cacti she carefully avoids. The path coils like a snake, and it has been over an hour since she last saw anyone. Only the murmur of crickets and the whispering trees, draped in Spanish moss, keep her company. The eerie silence unsettles her.

At last, she reaches the rocky riverbed. Thirsty, she pulls a water bottle from her pack, half-emptying it with one prolonged gulp. Rolling up her pants, she wades through the river's racing currents. Suddenly, a cow's mooing and the crack of hooves startle her. She darts glances everywhere but sees no one. The sounds fade into the rainforest's murmurs. Resolved to escape the unnerving atmosphere, she hurries on.

Louisinette's parents live east of the Acajou River. That is all Céline knows. Betting that Louisinette's story remains infamous—a tragedy that rippled through the valley—she hopes the villagers will guide her to Louisinette's home. Céline longs to embrace her friend, to pull her from the shadow of despair, to tell her that life, cruel as it may be, twists and turns in ways that can still bring hope. But what words will she find when they finally meet? How will Louisinette react to the sight of her?

For now, Céline pushes the uncertainty aside and keeps walking.

The trail plunges beneath a dense canopy of green foliage, so thick it swallows the sunlight. The forest floor grows dark, as though she is venturing into a subterranean world. But fear does not claim her. Her only motivation is to reach Louisinette before midday.

Her hopes rise when she hears gossipy hens, roosters crowing, and a stubborn donkey braying off-path—signs of life. The canopy opens, and the trail splits into two forks. One leads to the valley floor, and the other snakes toward a ravine lined with cashew apple trees. Beyond the ravine lies a green cornfield guarded by drooping scarecrows in the hot sun.

Optimism propels Céline. But as she rushes toward the ravine, her foot strikes a rock. She stumbles, sprawling against a young breadfruit tree. Woodpigeons explode skyward, and a nearby hound erupts into furious barking.

The barking draws the attention of barefoot children returning with water jugs balanced on their heads. They freeze at the sight of her. Wide-eyed, they drop their jugs and flee into the bushes, crying out in terror. Their reaction stuns her.

They think I'm Simbi, she realizes, recalling the old Haitian tales of the water goddess who haunts riversides, combing her raven hair. Céline watches the children vanish into the banana trees before following their path to a modest courtyard.

The yard's three-room cottage is adorned with wild lilies and tropical flowers. Green okra, lima beans coiling around their poles, cherry tomatoes, and wild-hearted spinach form a vibrant vegetable garden, with local weeds creeping into the backyard.

An elderly, gray-haired woman squats on the front porch, adjusting her hair bound in a white kerchief, its loose edges brushing her rawboned shoulders. She wears a blue *karako* garment, traditional among Haitian women. A large, bulky black scarf, sprinkled with tiny silver stars, is wrapped snugly around her slender waist. She rises, startled by Céline's sudden approach.

"*Bonjou,*" Céline breathes, her voice faint.

The old woman squints. "*Bonjou,* pretty girl," she replies, waving her hand to hush a barking dog. "Lili, shut up!"

The hound whines and retreats but sits alert by the door, growling low. Céline ignores it, unfazed by dogs. Céline lives in a household with several vicious dogs. Bourgeois families often breed these ferocious animals as their primary defense against disenfranchised, wandering homeless individuals. This practice not only ensures peace of mind but also appeases self-guilt and reflects a deep-seated animosity toward those who rebel against the state.

The old woman studies her, bewildered. "What can I do for you, my dear?"

"I'm looking for a young woman, a former *restavèk* named Louisinette. I was told she lives in this area," Céline answers.

"Louisinette? Not sure I've ever met such a person. What does she look like? How does she carry herself?" the old woman inquires.

"It's been five years since I last saw her. She's a slim girl, not tall, not short, and she likes to smile; she also has a strange birthmark on her forehead."

The woman frowns, adjusting her white kerchief. "Louisinette?" she mutters, pondering.

"Absalon!" she calls sharply to a young man in the cottage loft, who is stuffing green mangoes into a basket to hasten their ripening. He leaps down, alighting on the ground. Strong and well-built, his face and clothes are streaked with sweat and dust. His dark features freeze in surprise at the stranger before him.

"Do you know a girl named Louisinette who lives around here?" the old woman asks.

Absalon nods. "I know two of them," he replies with an air of reassurance, prompting Céline to step closer.

"There's a woman who lives at the base of Morne Château. She has three children and is married to a tall, imposing man, like a warrior. She sells bread by the roadside; I see her every Saturday at the seaside marketplace in Berger, selling her loaves." He glances at Céline. "The other is a young woman who was a victim of rape and was expelled from her home in Saint Louis. She now lives near a deep, wooded gorge in Fond Philippe. Remember her, Granny? Her story was the talk of the valley five years ago. She..."

Céline's chest tightens, tears fogging her vision. "Yes, the second one. Can you show me the way?" she asks, her voice trembling.

Absalon hesitates. "Let me wash my face first. I look filthy."

The old woman chuckles. "Sit, my dear. Can I offer you something to drink?"

"Thank you, but I'm fine," Céline says, though unease makes her reluctant to refuse kindness. Before the woman offers a chair, Céline lowers herself to the floor, crossing her legs beside her.

<u>*Chapter 2*</u>

The children who had run away reappear, lining up to greet Céline. Gleeful and wide-eyed, they no longer seem afraid. They have been hiding, playing inside the house, and listening to the earlier conversation. Now reassured, like children everywhere, their fear dissolves into curiosity. One by one, they gather around her, some sitting nearby, others touching her face to ensure she is indeed real.

A chubby girl with slanted eyes steps forward and looks straight into Céline's eyes. "What's your name?" she asks in a quiet and timid voice.

"Céline," she replies, stroking the girl's hair and gently poking her tawny cheeks.

An albino boy edges closer, his gaze unblinking. "Do you live beneath the water?" he asks with an eagle eye.

Céline grins. "YES! I'll take you there if you want me to. In fact, I'll take all of you!" she teases.

"Noooooooooooo!" they shout in unison, bursting into laughter.

The girl leaps backward, eyeing Céline up and down with hesitation and curiosity. "I'll go with you," she stammers, "but not to live in the water."

Céline giggles, amused by the girl's willful expression. Children are the same everywhere: curious, innocent, and ready to embrace the joys and blows of life with unwavering spirit. How useful would these bright, untapped minds be for Haiti?

Will they ever go to school? How cruel, she thinks. A country's best natural resource is human intelligence, yet here it is wasted. The thought pierces her mind as the children bury her in eager hugs.

Ten minutes later, Absalon returns, refreshed and dressed in clean gray trousers and a tight, sleeveless red undershirt with white stripes that accentuate his muscular build. A wide-brimmed, yellow straw hat sits atop his head. He rides a chestnut mare, galloping with grace across the courtyard. His dark eyes flare wildly as he catches sight of Céline. Pulling back on the reins, he makes the horse rear to an abrupt stop, its neigh breaking the silence.

With a dramatic flourish, Absalon doffs his straw hat and bows. "Sorry it took so long. This horse is yours to ride. Mine's tied up in the backyard," he grins.

"It wasn't that long—maybe ten minutes," replies Céline, still tangled in the children's enthusiastic hugs.

"*Ti moun*! Children!" the old woman calls, her voice cutting. "Stay away! This young lady has a long journey ahead." When they refuse to move, she disappears inside and returns holding a leather whip. Her face stiffens with mock anger. The children squeal and scatter like startled birds, fleeing through the back door.

The dog, however, stays at bay, growling near a clay jar in the corner.

"Are we ready to leave now?" Céline asks, eager to return to the trail.

"Not yet," Absalon replies, grabbing a sheepskin saddle pad from the porch. Carefully, he tucks it beneath the saddle and secures the cinch with practiced ease. With the bridle and reins in place, he pats the horse's neck. "It's for you, Mademoiselle," he says with an air of great pride.

"I've never ridden before. How do I get up?" Céline admits, anxiety creeping into her voice.

"Don't worry. I'll help you." Absalon eases her onto the horse, sidesaddle. "Hold the reins to guide her. She's gentle, like a dove."

Once seated, Céline smiles, her confidence returning. She feels regal atop the horse, her posture reminiscent of Catherine Flon, a heroine from Haiti's fight for independence. Between one blink and the next, Absalon vanishes from sight, returning perched on the back of an odd sorrel mule whose tail poufs like dandelion fluff. Waggling his finger, he gestures for her to follow.

Before leaving the courtyard, Céline turns back to wave. "Goodbye!" she calls to the old woman, who smiles warmly. The children, now poking their heads through the cottage window, wave back as Céline throws them kisses.

The sound of hooves clapping against stone echoes as they descend the rocky path leading to the valley floor. The sky thickens with clouds, turning gray and heavy. Sporadic lightning illuminates the distant sky, while a breeze sweeps through the foliage, causing the branches to rustle with considerable force. Masses of billowing clouds block the sun's heat, which Céline welcomes—as long as the rain holds off.

"Are you okay?" Absalon laughs, noticing Céline's serene expression. He assumes she is afraid of the ride, but she is not.

Céline rides in silence, lost in thought. How will she face Louisinette? Shame gnaws at her—her own parents had cast Louisinette out, condemning her to an unspeakable fate. "I'm not an ingrate," she whispers to herself. *Will Louisinette understand?*

The trail continues, winding through valleys blanketed with tropical fruit trees and clusters of royal palms. Villages dot the hills, their tiny mud huts barely visible through the tall grasses. The voices of peasants singing a cappella ripple across the fields, wild and free. The music, simple and unaccompanied, touches something deep in Céline's heart. It reverberates off the mountains, a harmony of labor and life.

After an hour of riding, they reach the end of the rocky trail where a small, pristine river flows. Downstream, half-naked women wash clothes in the shallows, their laughter blending with the rushing current. The horses balk, their snorts puffing steam into the air. Absalon taps their hindquarters, and they edge across, water swirling around their legs.

On the far side, the trail becomes a sandy path leading to the foothills of Morne Château. In a blur, the sound of hooves thuds through the bushes. A giant white horse bursts into view, carrying a young man about Céline's age. He wears a wide Mexican sombrero, an open-collared shirt, and gleaming white trousers. A silver pipe dangles from his lips, and his broad shoulders give him an imposing presence.

Twitching his red-rimmed eyes in surprise, he rears his horse to a stop. He removes his hat and bows to Céline, smoke curling from his lips.

"Bonjour," he sighs in French, his voice calm and deliberate.

"Bonjour," Céline and Absalon reply in unison.

Without another word, the stranger spurs his horse and gallops off, disappearing in a cloud of dust.

"Who was that?" Céline asks.

"No idea. First time I've seen him," Absalon replies.

"He seemed… strange."

"Maybe. But I think he's harmless."

Céline frowns, unsettled. The man's face stirs a memory she cannot place. But she pushes the thought aside. "How far to Louisinette's house?"

"Not far. We'll leave the horses here; it's too steep to climb on horseback. Ready?"

"Yes… but give me a moment," she says, gathering her strength. She knows the moment of truth awaits her. Will she find the courage to ask for forgiveness? Will Louisinette accept her sincerity? Her heart weighs heavy with uncertainty.

The climb is rough, her legs buckling with every step. Still, Céline pushes ahead, preparing to face the inevitable, no matter how unfair it seems.

<u>*C h a p t e r 3*</u>

Exhausted after a painful hike, Céline and Absalon reach the mountaintop, with Louisinette's dwelling somewhere hidden beyond the thick foliage. Céline's optimism rises. After pausing for a few minutes to catch their breath, they resume their trek. Winding down a narrow trail, they see no signs of human life—just the relentless chirping of blue jays feasting on ripe yellow mangoes. Céline's pulse quickens as she notices a giant green snake coiled on a barren branch. She shrieks and clings to Absalon for comfort.

Absalon chuckles, his youthful demeanor unshaken. "You have to make peace with this forest if you're going to pass through. It's their home too," he says with a reassuring smile.

"That thing could swallow me whole!" Céline cries, retreating.

"Not likely. It's just a *Landòmi*. They hunt at night and sleep during the day. Harmless, really—unless you plan to let it eat you," he jokes.

"You're quite the Maestro, aren't you?" Céline grins, shaking off her fear.

Just then, a hawk strikes like a thrown dagger, exploding through the underbrush. Hens burst outward in a storm of wings and alarm-cries, their chicks' panicked chirps slicing the air. Absalon's eyes kindle—not with pity, but recognition. "We're close now," he says.

"How can you tell?" Céline asks, puzzled.

12

"These chickens are tame, not wild. That means houses are nearby."

Sure enough, they soon spot the nut-brown thatched roof of a hut, hidden among verdant trees. Their pace accelerates, emerging into a windswept courtyard. Two teenage girls are seated on a log near a pile of corncobs, peeling off silks for drying. Startled, the girls leap to their feet, eyeing the strangers with a mixture of curiosity and wariness.

"*Bonjou!*" Céline and Absalon call out.

Shock locks their limbs for a heartbeat—then, haltingly: "Bonjou," as if testing whether the word is safe to release.

Absalon steps forward, his tone calm and reassuring. "We're looking for a lady named Louisinette. We heard she lives nearby. Can you help us?"

The girls exchange glances before one disappears into the hut, returning moments later with a shirtless old man wearing knee-length trousers. Absalon is well-acquainted with the drill. While the children know who Louisinette is, custom dictates that they should not reveal an adult's whereabouts. In Haiti, conventional wisdom holds that the true killer of a snake is not the one who chops off its head, but the one who points it out. These simple, homespun village girls, unaware of the strangers' intentions, remain cautious and silent.

With a weathered smile, the man interrupts Absalon before he can speak. "I know who you're looking for," he says.

"Really?" Céline's excitement is palpable.

"Here, follow this little path by the tomato garden. It will take you to the edge of a small Malanga field. Do not cross the field. Instead, turn right toward the ravine. As you do, look to the left. A few steps down, behind a tall mango *monben* tree, you'll find a large courtyard with five houses. Louisinette's home is the last one on the far side of the yard, just above the ravine," the man instructs with confidence, his tone firm yet reassuring.

Céline falters, worry flickering across her face. She glances at Absalon, seeking comfort and guidance.

"Don't worry, my children," the old man adds with a warm smile. "It's not difficult. Follow the path, and you'll be there in one shake of a hound's tail."

With lingering uncertainty, Absalon and Céline continue their journey. As they near the end of the tomato garden, the man calls out once more, his voice carrying over the distance: "Do not cross the ravine! If you do, you've already gone too far. Don't worry—it's easy."

"Thank you!" Céline calls out, waving.

The journey resumes. They slow their pace as the rushing current of the pristine ravine grows louder just a few yards away. The mango tree the old man mentioned comes into view on their left, towering like *MètKalfou*, the Master of Crossroads, standing sentinel at the entrance of the courtyard. Its roots are framed by two lines of rustic, protective cacti.

A pathway, bordered by wild, sweet-scented basil, cuts into the ravine trail, bypassing the mango tree. It meanders forward, splitting into a network of snaking walkways that weave the houses together into the heart of the courtyard.

At last, they reach their destination. Céline's cheerful mood fades into unease, then collapses entirely. Streams of sweat streak her flushed cheeks, and her trembling steps stagger several times as her heart races with the intensity of the moment.

The yard is almost deserted, save for a group of young men absorbed in a game of dominoes beneath the shade of an almond tree. The sweltering afternoon heat has driven most of the settlement's inhabitants into their mud huts, their thatched roofs shielding dirt floors from the blazing sun. A few strides farther, Céline spots a tiny cottage embedded in the hillside at the far edge of the settlement. Its front door is wide open, like the other homes, where awestruck residents lean against their entrances, watching with quiet curiosity.

They watch, hands folded behind their backs, utterly bemused. Their wide eyes follow the wary strangers as they move toward the small house on the settlement's edge. The villagers have never seen anyone like Céline stroll through their quiet enclave. Worried children cling to their parents, seeking comfort, their frightened gazes fixed on the unfamiliar figure. Even the domino players under the almond tree pause their game, their attention drawn to the two strangers approaching from the hillside.

A young woman stands rigid at the cottage door, her mouth opening and closing in silent disbelief. Both hands rest on her supple hips as she watches the visitors with a nervousness that mirrors the tension in the air. Raising a hand to shield her eyes from the glaring sun, she tries to get a clearer view of the advancing mixed-race woman. Memories of a past she has worked hard to forget begin to surface, stirring edginess in her heart. Shaking her head, Louisinette tells herself it cannot be. She is not important enough for such a visitor. Yet, as the figure grows closer, the truth becomes undeniable—it is Céline.

From the shadowy hollow of the pathway, Céline spots Louisinette standing by the cottage door. She recognizes her familiar form: barefoot, dressed in a blue madras and a light-red button-down dress. A long scarf cinches her waist, accentuating her toned, curvy figure. Large, dangling hoop earrings frame her innocent, squared-off face, yet her expression is unreadable—distant, almost indifferent. When Céline glances at the villagers watching her from afar, an unwelcome thought seizes her: *I don't belong here.*

Panting, her chest heaves with a mix of sadness and trepidation as she hastens her pace toward the cottage. Just a few steps from the door, her strength gives out, and she collapses. Absalon rushes to her side, steadying her as she navigates the uneven step-stones leading to the entrance.

"Louisinette!" Céline cries out, tears cascading down her flushed cheeks.

"Céline!" Louisinette's voice tears through the air, her anguished cry reverberating against the cottage walls. The sound is sharp enough to pierce through years of silence.

Suddenly, a stocky man storms from the back rooms, a gleaming machete slicing the air above his head. His fiery, bloodshot eyes and bulging muscles exude the intensity of a soldier ready for battle. But as his gaze falls on the unfolding scene, his aggression melts into confusion. The machete slips from his grip, falling to his side, and his once-defiant stance softens. His jaw tightens as he retreats inward, overcome by the unexpected confrontation.

Behind him, two little boys peek out, clutching his trousers' belt loops for protection. Their wide, fearful eyes dart between the strangers and their father, seeking the safety of his presence while trying to make sense of the scene before them.

Unsure of how to handle their emotions, Céline and Louisinette embrace in a group hug, squeezing tightly, their arms interwoven as they let out a series of high-pitched squeals. The sound is pure delight, unrestrained and cathartic. They cling to each other, unwilling to let go, their cries echoing down to the settlement floor. The commotion draws the attention of the villagers, who, moved by curiosity, begin to gather. An unspoken signal seems to compel them, and they shuffle forward in a procession-like line, their gazes fixed on the little cottage at the forest's edge.

The crowd's collective attention settles on Absalon, his wide, innocent eyes betraying no answers to their unspoken questions. His quiet demeanor leaves them puzzled, offering no explanation for the scene unfolding before them.

After several minutes of tight embraces, Céline and Louisinette pull apart—the separation slow as a peeling bandage. Louisinette steps back inside, leading Céline into the small home. She gestures to a wooden chair by a modest table in the corner. Céline sits, her heart full yet heavy, tears streaming down her face and soaking the collar of her shirt. Her prolonged sobs, high-pitched and unrelenting, are born of mixed emotions—bitter yet sweet, overwhelming yet freeing.

Louisinette, in contrast, remains stoic, though her reddened eyes burn like embers ready to ignite into flames. As always, she suffers in silence, her grief repressed and buried deep. She struggles to conceal, perhaps for the final time, the weight of years spent grappling with her pain.

Growing up, Louisinette had been made to believe her life was fated to be one of precarity, humiliation, and servitude—a *restavèk*, bound to the will of others until her death. She knew too well the cruelty of life, its unrelenting unfairness. For sixteen long years, she bore its burden. Her hopelessness had only deepened after she gave birth to an unwanted child, the result of a violent tragedy that forever scarred her.

"So, how have you been doing?" Céline asks, her voice faltering as she gulps, avoiding Louisinette's gaze.

"Fine," Louisinette replies, her voice clipped.

"I heard what happened while I was away."

"Yeah...."

Louisinette turns sideways, her face pale and distant. Céline can tell she does not wish to relive those haunting moments. For years, Louisinette has carried an unhealable wound, one she no longer wants to reopen. Yet, Céline knows her mission would be meaningless if Louisinette refuses to confront the past, even briefly, so that Céline can offer the apologies she has carried in her heart.

Louisinette, however, seems to have transcended her despair. No longer trapped in the inhuman servitude that defined her early years, she appears to have reclaimed her life, defying the narrow, dehumanizing boundaries imposed on her as a perpetual *restavèk*.

"Louisie," Céline begins with a tender voice, "I know there's nothing I can say or do to erase the pain of what happened to you. Violation of your will is an unforgivable and hideous crime, but what my family did afterward—denying you justice—is another, even crueler wrong. I'm not here to make excuses for my parents' actions. What they did was heartless, but it came from a deep ignorance and prejudice. I'm ashamed of it—terribly ashamed. When I was younger, I was blind too, oblivious to human suffering. It wasn't until I left for school far away that my eyes were opened."

Céline wavers, her voice shaking. "I now realize how fortunate I was to be born into a family that could provide everything I needed. For you, it was the opposite—pure misfortune. You endured a terrible childhood, and I'm here to tell you…I'm so, so sorry for everything you had to endure."

Louisinette turns to face Céline, her expression unreadable. "Why do you feel sorry, Miss Céline? You weren't responsible for what happened to me. You never treated me badly."

"Don't call me Miss Céline," Céline interrupts in a softening voice.

"But—"

"No 'but,' my dear!" Céline interjects, shaking her head with conviction. "It brings back bitter memories. Call me Liline, as you used to—like everyone else at home."

"Okay," Louisinette says with a faint smile. "But, don't feel sorry for things you didn't do. To tell you the truth, I've moved on with my life. It was hard at first, being thrown out like that—the humiliation, the pain. But in a way, my ordeal became my liberation. It made me grow, made me stronger. I'm not afraid of life's struggles anymore. Before I came here, I thought I couldn't survive without your family's help. But I found my way, thanks to good people—and especially Victorin, who has stood by me every step of the way. Now, I can proudly say I have my destiny in my own hands."

"I'm so happy for you, Louisie," Céline says, her voice brightening. "Tell me, is that Victorin?" She nods toward the stocky man standing nearby.

"*Wi*, that's him," Louisinette replies with a soft laugh. "The father of my second son—he's two now."

Céline turns to Victorin with a warm smile. "How are you, sir?" she asks, her voice carrying both pride and a hint of nervousness.

"I'm fine," Victorin replies with a reserved smile, mirroring Céline's warmth.

"And how is the older child?" Céline asks, her voice gentle, shifting her gaze back to Louisinette.

Louisinette's face tightens, her smile fading a bit. "He's the one I conceived during…you know…" Her voice trails off, the weight of the memory filling the room.

"You need no further explanations," Céline murmurs as she leans in to embrace Louisinette. Her friend's body trembles, as though trapped in an icy cavern. The pain is raw and searing, too intense for words. Céline then shifts her focus to the children, who are still clinging to their father's trousers. Dumbfounded and uncertain, the boys struggle to make sense of the scene.

Sensing their apprehension, Louisinette steps toward them with a reassuring nod, her arms open wide like a mother hen sheltering her chicks. The boys, releasing their iron grip on their father, dive into her embrace.

"It's okay, Dubison," Louisinette says, cupping her younger son's chin while poking the soft, creamy cheek of the older one. "This is Aunt Céline. She's an old friend of Mommy's," she explains to her innocent children.

Céline kneels down, her movements slow and deliberate, as she pats the children's tawny, kinky hair. The boys soon relax, collapsing into her arms with a mixture of confusion and acceptance. The moment feels less like a natural embrace and more like a fragile test of trust. Céline, however, wins them over as the children begin to play and sing local Creole songs with her. Their innocent voices attract the curious eyes of neighbors peering from the next yard.

From the gathering crowd, an elderly man steps forward, leaning on a broad-based wooden cane. Stroking his gray hair, he ambles into the cottage, his cow-skin slippers slapping against the hardened dirt floor. His tight undershirt and khaki overalls barely contain his rounded belly, and an unlit silver pipe, filled with dried tobacco, rests between the gaps of his missing teeth.

"My dear, we folks welcome you into our community! From today on, you are one of us, and we're proud to have you," the old man declares, his wrinkled face brightened by a smile. Céline is moved by the nobility of his gesture.

"My name is Délivra," he continues, offering his hand. "I never doubted Louisinette, despite what people in this section said when she arrived here from Saint Louis five years ago." His voice carries the weight of wisdom and authority, befitting his role as the settlement's chief elder.

The crowd listens, their gazes fixed on Délivra. With his palms resting on his cane, he raises his red-rimmed eyes to the group, seeking their approval as his words settle over them. His demeanor is one of quiet dignity, reinforced by the pipe clenched in the corner of his mouth.

"*Wi*, Uncle Délivra!" the villagers cheer in spontaneous unison. Céline, overcome by emotion, throws caution to the wind and pulls the old man into a heartfelt hug. He returns her embrace with a subtle smile that softens the lines of his careworn face. With an effortless grace, he steps back and takes a seat on the edge of an old bunk bed near Céline.

Louisinette stands nearby, smiling, her presence steady and calm as she leans close to Victorin. Meanwhile, Absalon strikes up a conversation with Délivra, soon joined by Victorin, their low voices blending into the warm hum of the room.

The children continue playing with Céline, who walks outside with Dubison cradled in her arms, the older child trailing closely behind. Wandering into the small, tidy yard, her presence captivates the gathered crowd. Louisinette steps out to join her, and the jubilant onlookers erupt in cheers once again. Their excitement bubbles over into a flurry of questions, as they surround Louisinette with curiosity, each voice eager for answers.

Amid the commotion, a reedy teenage girl with a peculiar heart-shaped face dusted with brown freckles pushes her way to the front, positioning herself proudly beside Céline.

"Are you Louisinette's sister?" she asks, her expression a mixture of confusion and intrigue.

"Yes, I am!" Céline replies. "For many years, we lived together in the same house in Saint Louis," she adds with a nostalgic smile.

"How come you look so different?" asks a little boy with piercing eyes, his tiny frame just short of reaching the teenager's shoulder. Louisinette glances at Céline, as if tempted to respond, but she is reluctant, allowing Céline to speak.

"Well, we didn't share the same mother or father," Céline explains. "That's why we look different. But in life, someone doesn't need to have the same parents to be a true brother or sister. Sometimes, siblings who share the same blood drift apart and don't care about each other's hardships. But Louisinette is more than just a sister to me. She was the one I could always trust when I was younger. I had more real faith in her than in my own parents. We shared all our little secrets together," Céline says, her face lighting up with a wide, genuine smile.

The crowd listens with the utmost attention, their curious expressions softening into admiration. After a prolonged time of simple chatter, the villagers gradually disperse, including the elder Délivra, who ambles back toward his cottage near the settlement's entrance.

Céline and Louisinette retreat inside the cozy home as the younger child, now heavy with sleep, rests in Céline's arms. His nappy-brown head nestles against her shoulder, his soft breaths a soothing rhythm. With a sigh full of love, Céline hands him to Louisinette, who carries him to the far corner of the dirt-floored living room. There, she lays him down on a shared bunk bed, tucking him in with the quiet care of a devoted mother.

<u>*Chapter 4*</u>

As the neighbors depart, a much-needed peacefulness settles into the cottage. The home is modestly furnished with only the bare necessities, yet every corner exudes a sense of deliberate care. In one corner of the main room, a three-drawered silver chest stands tall. On top of it lies a white tablecloth, pinned into Granny-style folds to fit the size of the chest, while a crystal vase filled with fresh citronella flowers rests atop it, their fragrance perfuming the air.

In another corner, a medium-sized clay jar filled with cooling spring water promises relief after long, hot days spent in the fields. The dining room features a rustic table surrounded by four wooden chairs, each painted with intricate, handmade designs. On the table lie ceramic plates, silverware, and a small short-wave radio, all set in order in plain view. A cheap designer lace curtain divides the rooms, adding a touch of practicality to the otherwise sparse space.

A full-sized bed sits behind the curtain, its blue-green sheets pooling like shallow reef waters, the fluffy bedspread untouched as dawn sand on Saint Louis Beach. Faded yellow throw pillows with golden tassels adorn it, lending a home charm. A used but sturdy dresser stuffed with household items leans against the wall, while banana-frond mats are rolled up in a corner, ready for afternoon naps or accommodating overnight visitors. Though the cottage is far from luxurious, it radiates a sense of orderliness, a reflection of Louisinette's determination to maintain dignity in the face of poverty.

Céline gazes around with quiet admiration, overwhelmed by a growing awareness of the resilience of those who live on the fringes of society. The evident happiness in the faces of these impoverished yet joyful people stirs a sense of humility in her soul. For the first time, she wrestles with the notion that wealth and extravagance are far from being the true sources of happiness. Materialism, she realizes, often breeds dangerous relativism, an insight inherent in the Haitian proverb: life is a double-edged sword.

Céline, a privileged uptown girl, has lived in the lap of luxury her entire life, but since returning from Europe, a burgeoning sense of humanity has taken root in her heart. Louisinette's plight, for Céline, epitomizes the injustice faced by Haiti's most vulnerable: the *restavèk*. Céline's desire to champion their cause and seek justice often transforms her into an impassioned, even impetuous advocate. She is well aware of the risks—her wealthy parents could easily retaliate by using their influence to punish Louisinette—but Céline feels compelled to stand against the oppressive order of the state. To do otherwise would betray her conscience and her self-appointed mission of social justice.

Meanwhile, outside the cottage, Absalon strolls along the ravine trail with Victorin, who is eager to show him the flourishing watercress garden he hopes to harvest before Christmas. Inside, Louisinette leads Céline to the backyard to show her the property lines, rickety and fenced in by decaying, splintered logs that resemble brittle bone fragments. They pause beneath an apricot tree, listening to the distant laughter and chatter of Absalon and Victorin mixing with the rushing currents of the ravine and the sharp chirps of hummingbirds nesting on the barren branches above.

Amid this serene setting, Céline and Louisinette reminisce about their childhood. They recall sneaking out of Céline's parents' mansion to buy fresco—frozen drinks—from a nearby market stall. They would hurry home, their teeth chattering from the icy sweetness, only to be betrayed by the pink stains on their lips. Céline also remembers accompanying Louisinette to the riverbed to wash clothes, though her mother would often scold her for risking a tan.

However, as the memories resurface, so do darker recollections. Louisinette's cheerful demeanor sinks, her head drooping as her thoughts drift to the traumatic experience that forever changed her life. Céline notices the shift and attempts to change the subject, asking, "Tell me more about your garden. Who helped you plant it—your sons?"

Louisinette sighs, "Who else…Victorin." Her tone regains some steadiness, though her eyes betray lingering shadows. Céline realizes that Louisinette's resilience has allowed her to survive, but the pain she carries remains unspoken—a burden too heavy to fully share, even with those closest to her.

Without notice, the older boy bursts from the house, throwing himself onto Louisinette's lap. Wrapping his thin legs around her waist, he clings to her neck. Louisinette smiles, smoothing his tear-streaked cheeks as he burrows into her embrace.

"What's his name?" Céline asks, her voice soft but trembling.

"Lamizè," Louisinette replies with a bitterness in her tone, the Creole word for misery.

"Why such a name?" Céline whispers, her heart sinking.

"Because he's the perfect example of my misery's worst nature," Louisinette explains, her voice breaking. "He didn't ask to be born, but he's condemned to carry the weight of my pain. I pray every day that he won't inherit the evil lurking in his bloodline." Her body shakes with suppressed sobs.

Céline spreads her arms, enveloping Louisinette and Lamizè in the most comforting embrace she can muster. Overwhelmed by the weight of the moment, she turns her face sideways, resting her cheek against Louisinette's. Holding them tightly, she murmurs, her voice thick with emotion, "It's not only Lamizè who didn't ask to be born. No child has a choice in being brought into this world."

Louisinette's voice wavers as she replies, her resentment tinged with sadness. "I know, but Lamizè's situation doesn't happen often. Those, like me, who live at the bottom of society, they have no defense against the worst this world can throw at them. Misery is a curse, not a destiny. When you're destitute, people see you as nothing but trash. The man who did this to me—he wasn't afraid. He knew he could get away with it."

Céline releases them from her embrace, her arms falling to her sides as she gazes upward, her eyes tracing the vast expanse of the sky. "Misery or poverty isn't a curse," she says, her voice gaining strength. "It's a social condition that can—and must—be corrected. We just have to fight against the barriers that keep so many trapped in abject poverty. With enough conviction and the will to fight, we can change it."

She pauses, her expression thoughtful, before pivoting to a new topic. "By the way, did you recognize the man who hurt you?" Her tone is cautious but probing, hoping Louisinette is ready to share the painful details.

Louisinette stalls for a moment, then gives a gentle nod. "Of course…*wi*…I did. When I saw him coming, I thought he was heading toward the river mouth. I'd seen him there before when I washed clothes at the river's edge."

"Do you remember his name?" Céline asks, her voice a fragile sound.

"*Wi*. It was Monsieur Dalambert," Louisinette answers, her words dripping with bitterness.

"Dalambert?" Céline's voice rises in disbelief. "The man who used to come to our house every Sunday with his newspaper, talking politics with my father?"

"Yes," Louisinette says, her voice tightening as the memories resurface. "That day, he wore blue shorts and a light-beige t-shirt with blue horizontal stripes. I was rushing to finish my laundry because the sun was setting. My head was down as I folded the drying clothes into a pillowcase. All of a sudden, I heard footsteps. I turned around, and there he was, walking toward me, smoking a cigarette. At first, I thought he was just heading for a swim. Then he started talking to me."

"Talking about what?" Céline asks, her curiosity heightened.

"He said he was going to teach a class every afternoon for all the *restavèk* in town and that he would ask your mother to enroll me. I was so happy. I was innocent and didn't know any better. It had always been my dream to go to school, to be smart like you, and to meet other children. I thought Monsieur Dalambert pitied me, that he wanted to help. I trusted him. But then I noticed… I noticed the erection under his shorts. That's when I knew—I was in grave danger. I wanted to run, but I couldn't. I couldn't leave without the laundry basket, full of wet clothes. And I was hoping, praying, that someone—anyone— would come to save me. But no one came."

Her voice falters, but she continues, her tone darkening. "He kept talking, but I stopped answering. My heart was pounding so hard I thought it might burst. Then he touched me. He stroked my neck. I told him to stop. I even threatened to tell my parents. But he didn't care. His face turned cruel, his voice low and threatening. 'You're a fool,' he said. '*Restavèk* have no parents. They only have masters.'

"He became a monster right before my eyes. I tried to move away, but he gave me no chance. He grabbed my shoulders, pinning me down as if I were a helpless hen caught under the claws of a wild *malfini* hawk. I managed to grab two stones— God knows I wanted to hurt him, to smash his... But he overpowered me.

"I screamed, Céline. I screamed, but no one came. He clamped his hand over my mouth, and I couldn't breathe, couldn't fight back. Then he forced my legs apart. It felt like a dagger stabbing through me—my body, my soul. I fainted. When it was over, he stood there, his voice like ice. 'If you tell anyone, I'll kill you,' he said. Then he walked away, wading across the river and disappearing into the banana fields."

Céline is frozen in place, her jaw slackened, her breath caught in her throat. Blinking away tears, she pants, "What did you do after he left?"

"I lay there, wishing I could die. I'd never felt so dehumanized. I didn't care that I was bleeding. I just wanted to end it all because I knew—I knew no one would believe me. I wanted to cry, but I had no strength. For the first time, I truly understood how alone I was in this world."

Céline swallows hard. "And then? What happened next?"

Louisinette sighs, her voice trembling but steady. "After an hour, I realized I couldn't stay there. Somehow, I found the strength to move. I waded into the water to clean myself. The cold—it was like needles stabbing my skin. But I had to stop the bleeding, wash away the…everything. By the time I finished, it was dark. So dark, I couldn't even see my shadow."

"How did you manage to get home?" Céline's words slip out like a secret, her voice thin as a blade of grass.

"I gathered the clothes, stuffing the wet ones into a pillowcase and piling them on top of the dry ones in the basket. But the basket was so heavy—I couldn't lift it. My legs were shaking like fireflies trapped in a net. Then, out of nowhere, I heard a pig behind me. I thought it was a werewolf. My heart almost stopped. I turned around, trembling, but I could only see its silhouette fading into the night. I started moving, pulling the basket along the rocky riverbed until I reached the shallow crossing where the cars used to pass.

"I stood there for a long time, trying to catch my breath. I knew I had to carry the basket to cross the water. It was heavy, but I somehow managed to lift it over my head. Wading through the mossy stones, my feet slipping with every step, I finally made it to the other side. But then—a bat swooped down out of nowhere, and I stumbled against a rock. The basket flew out of my hands and landed in a ditch by the road. I thought everything was ruined, but the wet clothes must have weighed it down because nothing spilled out."

Céline exhales, her heart aching for her friend. "You were so brave, Louisie. But why didn't you take the shortcut? The little path by the river mouth—it would have led you straight to the back gate of the house."

"I couldn't," Louisinette says, shaking her head. "That path was dangerous at night. Everyone said it was where the *lougawou*—the werewolves—and evil men lurked. I wasn't ready to risk a violent death, not after what had just happened. So, I grabbed the basket and hoisted it over my head. I quickened my steps, hoping to get home faster. But the faster I walked, the heavier the pain became.

"When I passed by the main cemetery on the way into town, I heard strange sounds—voices humming and the eerie shrills of birds chirping from inside the huge metal gate by the entrance walls. A long tree branch stretching over the road cracked loudly, as if it were about to break and fall on me. My heart leaped, but I didn't scream. I didn't dare look back. Despite the pain tearing through my body, I forced myself to rush, jog, and zigzag along the croton hedge that bordered the steep walls on the north side of the cemetery. My heart pounded in rhythm with every shaky step."

She pauses, drawing a deep, shuddering breath. "When I finally left the cemetery behind, my fear eased just a little. Ahead of me, I could see small houses, their faint gas lamps casting a soft glow onto the dark road. I slowed down, listening to the voices of people laughing and chatting inside their homes. For a fleeting moment, I envied their happiness. I wished—I wished I could be one of them. But then, I felt it again—the blood trickling down my legs. Heavier now, warmer. I stopped, looking around to see if anyone was watching. There was no one—just two little girls playing near the tiny bridge at Latirolie. When they saw me, they ran. I could still see their skinny frames darting through the darkness until they disappeared into an empty courtyard. The blood wouldn't stop, and I didn't know what to do. I couldn't go home like that."

"God… What did you do?" Céline asks, her voice breaking.

Louisinette's expression darkens, but she continues. "Then, a minivan came fast from the south end of the road. It stopped quick by the bridge to let someone out. The horn blew, and the lights hit me right in the face. I jumped back, scared. When the van drove off, making smoke and dust, I took the small path. It went to the empty yard where the girls ran before. It was quiet there. You could hear the wind in the trees.

"I stood there. Leaning against the back wall of an old house. You remember that house, right? The one where the fishermen used to sell fish? Its door was broken, just swinging in the wind. I didn't go inside. Too scared. I just dug in my basket and took out a white t-shirt. I folded it three times. Put it between my legs, using my underwear to keep it there. It wasn't much, but it stopped the blood from coming out so fast. Then, slow, I made myself move and went home."

Céline nods, the house rising in her memory—blackened timbers against a sunset sky, a scar on her mind's eye. "What happened when you got back?"

"No one saw me when I slipped through the back gate. In the darkness, I made my way to the linen room. I was exhausted—so exhausted that the basket slipped from my hands and crashed onto the table in the corner. The noise was so loud it startled Madame and some guests in the living room. Their laughter stopped, and they started talking low, like they didn't know what happened.

"Madame came to see what had happened. When she walked into the linen room, she saw me—limping, all a mess, my face pale with pain. She looked at me for a moment, but then, like I wasn't even there, she turned around and went back to her guests. She didn't ask if I was hurt, didn't care where I'd been all day. She just went on talking to her guests."

"Really? Oh, gosh! Then what happened, Louisie?" Céline says, her voice breaking as if struck by unimaginable horror.

"So, I went to my little room—the one Madame gave me in the back of the house, where we used to store charcoal. Do you remember?" Louisinette says, her voice soft but laced with bitterness. "After you went away to school, she moved me there.

It had dirty walls and no window. At night, it was cold and blank—so dark and scary, like the tombs of the dead. The bed bugs were everywhere, and my little *nat*—the mat I slept on—did nothing to protect me from their stings. My skin felt raw, like I was lying on rough slate.

"Some nights, the cold was unbearable. I'd feel the chill strike straight into my bones. I'd stop whatever I was doing, crouching on the floor in the corner by the door, wrapping myself tightly in flimsy bed sheets given to me by the parish nuns. And I'd pray—pray for morning to come faster, for daylight to seep through the tiny gaps between the rusty corrugated metal roof and the walls."

Louisinette pauses, drawing in a shaky breath. "There was a dirty little wooden table by the door. Madame never gave me permission to use it—not even for a gas lamp to keep the dark away. Above my head, there was a huge light bulb dangling from a long wire hooked onto the ceiling. At night, it swung in the wind, like the swollen feet of a hanging man on a tree branch after he's committed suicide. I hated that room. It felt like my secret prison, a place where every breath reminded me I was less than human.

"But that night," she continues, her voice hardening, "as much as I hated that room, I found it to be a refuge. My worst nightmare wasn't the cold, or the bed bugs, or even that cursed light bulb. It was your mother turning away, acting like I wasn't there. Her complete disregard for my wellbeing. Those thoughts paralyzed me that night. I didn't know what was going to happen to me."

Chapter 5

Louisinette's horrific recollection is too much for Céline. She turns away, her back bending, feet firmly planted on the ground, and her gaze fixed on the narrow walkway winding toward the ravine. The murmur of men's chatter fades, replaced by the occasional clap of sound echoing from the gorge, a faint reminder that Absalon and Victorin are nearby.

Céline cannot bring herself to meet her friend's eyes, burdened by the weight of what Louisinette has endured. The atrocities inflicted upon her friend were not merely acts of injustice; they shattered every norm of decency, exposing the cruelty of a system that denied Louisinette her humanity. Yet, as Céline wrestles with her emotions, she marvels at Louisinette's strength—a resilience as enduring as a coconut palm rebounding after a storm. Céline's preconceived notions about her childhood friend dissolve. Louisinette is not broken; she is a woman of renewed dignity and unwavering awareness of the injustices she has faced.

Louisinette's ability to survive—her concealed passivity and feigned naivety in moments of despair—shocks Céline. Her meticulous recounting of that harrowing night reveals a sharp intellect honed by life on society's fringes. Céline's face reddens with shame, realizing the privilege of her ignorance. Though she had cherished Louisinette as a child, she now sees the vast gulf between their life experiences. Céline once believed her compassion for the less fortunate made her different from her aristocratic peers, but here in this small, remote yard, she feels the weight of her family's prejudices and the injustices they perpetuated.

Céline struggles to find the right words. She wants Louisinette to heal, to open her heart to trust again, and to move beyond her contempt—not toward her tormentors, but toward the possibility of a future without fear. She worries, though, that such wounds run too deep to be soothed by mere words.

The silence is heavy. Louisinette, shaken by her memories, sits like a child dazed after a nightmare. Her son, Lamizè, has fallen asleep in her lap, his small hands clutching her neck as she strokes his back. Céline stands facing the ravine trail, her red-rimmed eyes brimming with unshed tears. She plucks a budding apricot stem from a nearby tree, rubbing its leaves between her fingers as though threading a rosary, searching for solace, courage, and the strength to preserve their sacred friendship. Words feel inadequate; actions, Céline resolves, must prove her sincerity.

Finally, Louisinette breaks the silence. "Céline, you should go. It's getting dark," she says, her voice steady but distant.

Céline forces a smile. "I was just thinking the same," she replies softly. She turns toward the ravine and calls for Absalon.

"*Wi!*" Absalon's voice echoes up from the gorge, startling Louisinette into a laugh. "Victorin loves to brag about his garden," she says with a faint smile.

Moments later, Victorin and Absalon emerge, hands full of plump purple avocados. Victorin beams as he hands a white bag to Céline. "Thank you," she says with a laugh. "How did you know these are my favorites?"

Victorin replies with simple pride, "The best fruit for the best friends." Louisinette's glowing gaze makes him pause, her admiration plain.

"Would you hold the bag, Absalon?" Louisinette asks, her wide grin lighting up her face.

"Of course, I would!" he replies with enthusiasm, stepping forward to take the bag from Céline, who is still marveling at the luscious purple avocadoes. Together, they head inside for a final chat.

Once inside, Louisinette lays her son beside the younger one, both sound asleep on the bed. Moving with purpose, she bounces into the next room and rushes back, holding a small white rag embroidered with a unique, flowery design. On one side, Céline's name is stitched in fading threads—a relic of childhood bonds and promises kept.

"Look, Liline," Louisinette cries, holding up the rag and pointing to the embroidered, fading name. "Do you remember this piece of cloth?" Her voice is filled with the bittersweet joy of childhood memories. Absalon and Victorin exchange amused glances.

"*Oh, mon Dieu!* You still have this piece?" Céline exclaims, her voice tinged with awe.

"You bet I do! It's the only souvenir I have from you. It reminds me of the night you gave it to me before you left for foreign lands. You promised to return, and I believed you. But when I was forced to leave Saint Louis, I was convinced I'd never see you again. And so, I preserved this rag to never forget you. Every time I go to my wooden chest and see it, you immediately come to mind. Liline, you are the only person who made my childhood a little bit brighter. Those precious moments mean a lot to me."

Moved beyond words, Céline steps forward and wraps Louisinette in a tight embrace, holding her like a mother sheltering her child from impending danger. In that moment, Louisinette's heartfelt revelation reassures Céline. She knows now that she retains Louisinette's unwavering trust—a trust strong enough for Louisinette to recount even the darkest days of her life. This realization rekindles a sense of joy in Céline, a light she carries as she prepares for the journey home.

"We have to get going!" Céline says, her voice buoyant with cheer. Without waiting for a reply, Absalon takes the lead. Céline follows close behind, with Victorin and Louisinette walking a few paces back. Together, they accompany their visitors to the mountaintop.

As they prepare to part ways, Louisinette takes Céline's hand, her grip lingering, hesitant to let go after being forced to confront the trauma she had long buried. Céline meets her gaze, understanding the weight of the moment.

"I'll be back soon," Céline says, her voice soft but resolute. "I believe you and I, we have a very important work to do here on this earth. It's a huge fight to make things right for our people in this country. But what we do, just us, right here in this part of Haiti—maybe if we lead the way—it could show everyone else how to join together, how to make a big change. Together, we could work to stop children being made to work like slaves, and break down other bad ways people take advantage of others."

Louisinette remains silent. Her expression betrays confusion and doubt, unsure how a poor peasant woman like herself could play any role in such an ambitious undertaking. Yet, her eyes soften, reflecting a quiet resignation, as though willing to trust Céline's vision. Raising her head, she gazes out at the valley below, its beauty stretching as far as the eye can see toward the horizon.

"Liline, I'm not sure I understand what you mean," Louisinette admits, her voice tentative, "but if you believe we can make a difference, I'll always stand with you." She turns to Victorin, seeking his silent approval.

Victorin answers with a warm smile, and Louisinette releases Céline's hand. She steps back to her husband, who wraps an arm around her shoulders, offering the comfort and reassurance she needs.

Céline and Absalon descend into the countryside, picking their way along the pebbled trail as they walk downhill toward the trees where their horses are tethered. At the mountaintop, Louisinette and Victorin remain for a moment, watching their visitors shrink into the distance, disappearing beneath the canopy of the forest. With arms entwined, the couple turns and heads home, their figures silhouetted against the vast, open sky.

<u>*Chapter 6*</u>

Gray fog cloaks Saint Louis in an oppressive afternoon stillness. A handful of tenacious street vendors cling to their wares at the marketplace, undeterred by the gloom. Down on Main Street, a solitary *camionette*—the town's lifeline for transportation—tears through the haze, leaving behind a trail of dusty muddiness and confusion. The disoriented locals retreat indoors, seeking refuge from the murk. It is now five o'clock, and within the imposing concrete and masonry walls of Céline's home, anxiety grows palpable.

Céline's departure at dawn remains a mystery to her family. Her father, Monsieur Jean-Foreste, with whom philosophical debates are a breakfast ritual, paces the veranda with increasing agitation. Draped in a green robe, hands sunk into its deep pockets, he draws on his silver pipe, releasing smoke in languid puffs that belie the naked fear gripping his heart.

Meanwhile, Madame Bernadine, Céline's mother, lounges in a rocking chair, gazing out at the beachfront. A tall mixed-race woman in her late forties, she compulsively rocks back and forth, clutching a magazine she does not read. Her owl-rimmed spectacles perch at the tip of her nose. The flipping of pages is mere theater, a facade to mask the swell of anxiety coursing through her. She refuses to engage with her husband, unwilling to confront the issue of Céline's whereabouts.

Madame Bernadine is a formidable presence—a domineering woman who prides herself on never being wrong.

In contrast, M. Jean-Foreste is a mild-mannered and contemplative man who navigates his wife's volatile moods with practiced patience. He avoids eye contact, knowing full well she is poised to unleash her simmering frustrations onto "poor old" him. Her hair is yanked back into a tight bun, but her body betrays no such control—feet slapping the veranda floor as she paces. Her nut-brown face shifts through pale shades of scarlet, her frown deepening the grooves of her wrinkles.

Unable to suppress her growing unease, Bernadine at last springs from the rocker, flinging the unread magazine onto a side table. With the gait of a stalking tigress, she strides toward the back gates. The sea breeze catches her nightgown, making it billow, while loose strands of graying brown hair flutter rebelliously around her face. Her long strides falter as she pushes open the gates, stepping onto the sugar-sand pathway that parallels the shoreline.

In her haste, she trips. One slipper bursts free, flying like a stray fuzzy rocket and burrowing into the sand. She lets out a furious cry, audible to the heavens. Staggering, Bernadine bends to retrieve the errant slipper just as another gust of wind catches her nightgown, lifting it up to her head. The medieval pattern of red, black, and white undergarments she wears is laid bare, clinging awkwardly to wrinkled thighs. Her shriek cuts through the heavy air like a whip, loud enough to alarm the entire coastline.

Back on the veranda, her husband watches in stunned silence, torn between shock and helpless amusement. Bernadine's composure snaps back into place—one breath— before she strides for the gates, her steps punishing the earth. She finds Jean-Foreste standing there, wide-eyed, his conflicting emotions plain.

"I can't believe you saw me fall and didn't rush to help!" Bernadine yells, her voice quivering with rage. The ruddy edges of her mouth convulse, her wavering hands matching the tremor in her voice. The chill of the ocean breeze is lost on her burning indignation.

"*Chérie*, I know what kind of person you are—you always recover. I just don't want to inflame a situation that requires… restraint." Jean-Foreste's voice is polished ice. Bullshit. He closes the distance between them in a heartbeat. "I'm sorry, *chérie*," he croons, the words syrup-sweet—just enough to keep the 'Iron Lady' from reducing them all to cinders.

"…*très stupide* back gates," she mutters, glowering sullenly.

Just then, they glance eastward to see Céline waltzing along the beachside pathway, her soaked pants rolled above her knees, sweat streaking her flushed cheeks. Ruddy in the breeze, she looks utterly exhausted.

"Liline!" her mother cries out. "We've been looking all over for you!"

Céline doesn't respond in words. Instead, she moves closer, kissing her mother's forehead but sidestepping her expected embrace. She heads straight to her father, who smiles and opens his arms wide. When she reaches him, he envelops her in a warm hug. Bernadine steps aside, concealing her displeasure behind a forced, jaded smile.

"You smell like wild grasses. Go inside, take a shower," her mother orders, a sharp edge in her voice. Céline ignores her, continuing to talk with her father, who wraps an arm around her shoulders and leads her to the house. Her mother trails behind, her face a canvas of unspoken grievances.

Twilight descends as Céline and her parents step inside, sliding the glass doors open. Without a word, Céline heads for the hallway, grabbing a towel from the rack as she makes her way to the bathroom. Her father, relieved now, retreats upstairs to the balcony. There, he resumes his routine of pacing while waving at passersby below. Her mother remains downstairs, tending to Céline's dinner to ensure it is warm enough when served.

The house's rhythm has changed since Louisinette's "incident." There are no *restavèk* anymore. Peasant parents, wary of the cruelty their children might endure, no longer send them to work in wealthy homes. Instead, Madame Bernadine employs a housemaid who works eight-hour shifts and lives in a settlement near Morne Miguel. The maid refuses to work overtime, needing to care for her own home. This irritates the Iron Lady, who begrudgingly undertakes some evening tasks herself, earning her a fleeting sense of pride.

After her shower, Céline retreats upstairs to her room, wearied by her long journey. Guilt, an unfamiliar and weighty sensation, gnaws at her soul. She sits on the edge of her queen-sized bed, soul-searching. Her eyes roam her room as if seeing it anew: its neatness, the faint gardenia fragrance, the cherry-wood dresser near her opulent Florentine bed, its built-in bookcases overflowing with French, Haitian, and English novels. In the adjacent walk-in closet, dozens of expensive shoes—some unworn—stand in perfect order beside her old, scuffed tennis sneakers. It is a world of comfort and luxury, starkly contrasting with the rugged simplicity she has just left behind.

In spite of herself, Céline gazes sharply around her room, caught in a strange sense of casual distaste. Two photo albums rest atop her spotless dresser. Drawn as if by an invisible force, she reaches for one and begins flipping through its pages. On the third page, she pauses, her eyes fixed on an aging, yellowed black-and-white photo. It shows Céline and Louisinette standing together near the back gates beneath a cashew apple tree. She lingers on the image, a well-loved photograph that she has often removed from the album to show friends and family.

Louisinette's innocent expression stands out. Her ragged garments, unkempt hair, and wide, radiant smile reflect a peculiar kind of purity. Her thin arm, wrapped around Céline's waist, conveys both affection and vulnerability. Memories of long-ago times flood Céline's mind, crashing in relentless waves against the shores of her wind-swept thoughts. It is difficult, she muses, to control such haunting memories. She places the album back on her dresser and walks toward her double-bay windows, pulling back the colorful silk-satin draperies to look out onto the courtyard below.

The moon rises boldly, casting its silver glow across the distant purple mountains. The cloudless sky holds a lone twinkling star, and a cool breeze stirs the tree branches, creating eerie whispers like the cackles of imaginary werewolves in the night. Céline's gaze shifts to the narrow, gas lamp-lit street and the tiny homes beyond. Poverty's rawness does not escape her attention: decaying walls, rusting aluminum rooftops, and the unmistakable marks of hardship etched across these humble dwellings. As with most provincial towns on the island, wealth and poverty stand as inseparable contrasts.

Beneath the dim glow of the gas lamps, Céline observes malnourished children wandering near their homes. Oblivious to their vexing misfortunes, their wretched conditions wrapped in an odd, innocent resilience, these children seem cheerful, playing hide-and-seek around their modest cottages. The sight stirs something deep in Céline's heart. She recalls her mother's disdain for these shantytown dwellers, whom she mockingly referred to as "estranged neighbors," a term that implied their insignificance. Her mother would never allow them into her bespoke nouveau riche world. And Céline doubts that her well-meaning but detached father gives them much thought either.

She closes the windows, shuts her eyes, and flops face-down onto her bed, her body splayed like a lifeless fish. Lying there, she listens: to the dull thudding of her heart, the rhythmic chirping of crickets outside, the gentle splashing of the fountain in the front yard. Inside, she hears the peaceful snoring of her father in the master bedroom. This night will be a long one, she thinks, her mind too restless for sleep.

The absence of Louisinette in the house distresses her, leaving an emptiness too painful to ignore. Minutes later, her mother steps into the room, standing by the headboard. "Are you okay, little lost princess?" she asks in a tone that blends irritation with faint concern. Céline doesn't answer. Instead, she turns onto her side, staring at her mother with quiet disapproval.

"I thought you were… sleeping… Mom," Céline mumbles.

"You know I don't go to bed early. It's your father who goes to bed at sundown. Don't you hear his snoring?"

"Yes, I do," Céline laughs, a quiet huff of amusement. "I thought he's in bed early for his nighttime reading, not for sleeping."

"Not anymore. Lately, your father spends his nights thinking more than sleeping."

"What makes you think so, Mom?"

"We've been married for more than a quarter century. I know this man inside and out—when he's happy, when he's sad, and when he's faking it."

Céline raises an eyebrow, skepticism flickering in her expression. "Is that so?"

"Yes, Liline. Since you left, he's become very difficult to deal with. He hardly talks to anybody, and when he smiles, it seems forced."

"Didn't you say you know him inside and out?"

"…yes…"

"Then how come you don't know what's bothering him?"

"I have an idea, but I'm not sure."

"Isn't he your husband, the father of your only daughter?"

"I think so. Yes, he surely is!"

"Then you should ask him what's wrong."

Bernadine hesitates. "Liline, right after you left, something major happened in this house…" Her voice trails off, apprehension flashing in her eyes.

"What? Mother?" Céline's voice sharpens, a quiet force.

"Never mind."

"No, Mother. You can't just say that! If it has to do with Louisinette, I already know. But I want to hear what you have to say."

"There's no need to."

"Yes, there is."

Bernadine falters and moves to the edge of Céline's bed, stroking her daughter's long, golden hair. "Liline, you see, Louisinette is no longer with us. Poor girl, I really miss her…"

"Stop it, Mother!" Céline's voice cuts through her mother's sentimental tone like a blade.

"It's true."

"Mother, you can clearly see I'm no longer a child. Where do you think I was all day?" Céline abruptly sits up, tying a blue headscarf over her hair, her African lineage luminous in its rightful place. She meets her mother's eyes with a hard, unrelenting gaze. Bernadine, shrinking under the weight of her daughter's stare, reddens in discomfort.

"Don't tell me you went up into the mountains?" she mutters, sensing her defeat.

"You bet I did! I didn't tell you because I knew you'd object to my trip."

"No, that's not true! I wouldn't have objected. I knew how close you two were."

"And yet you did that to her?"

"Did what?"

"Kicked her out of our house when you found out she was pregnant. You didn't have to tell me—I know everything!"

"It's not what you think! I didn't kick her out! I had to send her home since she couldn't tell me who the baby's father was. You know we are Catholics, and we don't tolerate grotesque behavior like this."

Céline shivers, a cold beyond words seizing her as she searches her mother's face for any trace of humanity. Bernadine squirms under her daughter's towering presence, the weight of it pressing down.

"If it were me, would you have kicked me out too? Not knowing where I'd sleep that night?" Céline's voice wavers but cuts deep. Eyes brimming with tears, she collapses back onto her bed.

It is too much for Bernadine. She sighs, mutters "Good night," and heads toward the door. Just as she reaches the threshold, Céline's thin voice calls out, carrying the weight of resolve. "I met Louisinette today. She told me everything, and I won't rest until justice prevails. That's the only way I can salvage my soul and the prejudices clouding yours and Dad's."

Bernadine freezes, her lips trembling. "But what did she—?"

"Good night, Mother." Céline cuts her off, pulling the sheets over her head and turning away. Defeated, Bernadine retreats to her bedroom, burdened by the chasm between herself and her daughter.

_C h a p t e r 7_

The next morning at the break of day, Céline rises as the distant crowing of a few roosters pierces the dawn's stillness. She doffs her nightgown and takes a shower, droplets clinging to her fresh, sweet-scented face. Her golden tresses puff into huge waves, which the ceiling fan scatters gently over her steaming head. Grabbing a copy of _Le Matin_, her favorite newspaper, from the mahogany-wood stand in the hallway, she strides purposefully out of her room. Passing by her parents' bedroom without glancing in, she descends the stairs, craving her morning ritual of a milky coffee.

To her surprise, her mother is already downstairs, standing by the kitchen table and pouring steaming café-au-lait into a red mug. "Liline, you're already up? I was just about to fix your favorite breakfast," Bernadine greets her with uncharacteristic warmth, her face brightening with hope.

"Thank you, Mommy. I just came down for coffee," Céline replies, her tone cordial, casting a rare glimmer of reconciliation into her mother's mind. Perhaps this morning would be different.

"Here's your café-au-lait. I'm baking your favorite breakfast rolls, too—they'll be ready in just a minute. Since you love organic food, I went to the backyard early this morning to pick you some bananas and yellow cashew apples. I'll have Solitude grill the cashew nuts for you as soon as she comes in."

"Solitude? Who's that?" Céline asks, raising an eyebrow.

"She's our new maid. A nice young lady, very easy to work with."

"I see. I didn't get a chance to ask her name." Céline takes a thoughtful sip of her coffee. "Mommy, whatever happened to Yvon Poitevien, the big cacao exporter in town?"

"That croaker? He's six feet under, last I heard," Bernadine replies matter-of-factly.

"Are you sure? What happened?"

"You think I'd make up something like this? After you left for Scotland, Poitevien moved to Port-au-Prince. About two years ago, news spread that he was killed while on his way to the Downtown District. Apparently, it was a revenge killing—he had tried to outsmart a businessman in a shady deal."

"That's sad. I feel sorry for his children. Three years ago, I saw his oldest son, Jean-Marie, at a student demonstration in London. It was over a big hike in college tuition. Jean-Marie surprised me; we chatted for over an hour before he left. That was the last time I saw him."

"Did you ask about his family?"

"Yes. He said they were fine. I didn't know his father would die a year later. How tragic."

"Poitevien made a lot of enemies, especially because of his zealous support for President Lescot, even when everyone else wanted Lescot gone. Your dad was devastated when Lescot fell. He spent two weeks in bed—that was January, two years ago."

"I remember. It was big news, even in Scotland."

"Your dad supported Lescot, but I preferred Colonel Frank Lavaud, who replaced him."

"What about President Estimé?"

"Liline, I've never liked politics—too much corruption. But I don't care for this current president either. They say he doesn't like mixed-race folks."

"Mother, that's not entirely true. Estimé has many of them in his government."

"Maybe so, but that's what they say," Bernadine retorts dismissively.

"Mommy, remember how Jean-Marie used to like me?" Céline changes the subject.

"Of course! He was so handsome with those big gray eyes and wavy dark hair. His French was perfect, so elegant. I just hope he didn't inherit his father's flaws."

"He was very smart in school, too. When I met him in London, he told me he was studying civil engineering at Oxford."

"Smart, just like his father. Poor man—he just made bad choices."

"Jean-Marie had a friend who used to come with him to our back gates. He was thin and shy, hardly spoke a word, even when I tried to include him in the conversation."

"Ah, yes, Ludovic. The son of Decimus Malbranche, the coffee exporter uptown. You wouldn't recognize him now! He's returned from France—The Sorbonne, I believe—and is built like a brick wall. I've seen him driving his Jeep Wrangler around town, puffing on a silver pipe. The girls from prominent families are all over him!"

Céline does not respond to her mother's comments; her mind drifts instead to the stranger she encountered the previous day at the bottom of the hill near Fond Philippe. A sudden silence descends between them, heavy and contemplative. The stillness is broken by a squeak from the back gates. A young woman enters. She is tall and thin, with a red bandanna draped around her hair. Her blousy yellow dress floats and flits in the morning breeze, and her sandals crack against the pebbled walkway, emphasizing her urgency to get to work.

Halfway across the courtyard, the woman notices Céline and her mother sitting in the dining room, facing the backyard. She quickens her pace toward the wide-open back door.

"*Bonjour,*" she wheezes, winded from running. Céline's eyes linger on her for a moment, noting the dark, sprinkled spots on the right side of her face, as though someone had flicked a paintbrush dipped in tan across her cheeks. Solitude sets down a bag of juicy yellow mango *monben.*

"*Bonjour,* Solitude. How are you?" Céline greets her warmly. Before she can say another word, Bernadine interjects.

"Solitude, Mademoiselle Céline has a job for you today. She wants you to grill these nuts before you go home this afternoon," she announces with a forced, insincere smile. Céline turns to her mother, observing her face without meeting her gaze. A deep ache stirs within her, witnessing how Bernadine struggles to maintain even the facade of a respectful conversation with the maid.

Céline stands, taking the bag from Solitude's grasp. "Come," she says, walking with her into the kitchen. Bernadine remains at the table, throwing a furtive, conflicted glance at her daughter as they disappear inside. Left alone, she pokes at her breakfast, appetite diminished. Her coffee grows cold as she sips it in small, distracted gulps, her mood dampened by the growing chasm between herself and her daughter.

Chapter 8

Madame Bernadine epitomizes the dispirited, spoiled wealthy landowner, undone by a lofty lifestyle inherited from her aristocratic origins. Born and raised in the lap of luxury, she is within a perpetual circle of people who—out of fear of rejection—prefer to tell her what she wants to hear rather than what she needs to know. Her nonchalant, dismissive manner of dealing with her subordinates leaves no room for misinterpretation or spontaneity.

Her creed is clear: everyone who works for her must be slavishly conformist. "You do as I say without objection. I know everything, and you know nothing," she declares, setting the tone for every new hire. It doesn't take long for her employees to realize that her arrogance is difficult to bear. Most roll with the punches, but the moment they save enough money, they leave, forcing Bernadine to start the hiring process anew.

Among her peers in the uptown gathering rooms, however, Bernadine displays a different face. When putting on the airs of aristocracy, her overbearing demeanor softens, giving way to a melancholy form of nobility that is hard to miss. Beneath her polished veneer lies a woman burdened by her own discontent.

Monsieur Jean-Foreste, her devoted husband and Céline's father, is a subdued and thoughtful man. His intellectual demeanor prevents him from expressing overt prejudice. He is the great-grandson of Colonel Bodin, a high-ranking quadroon officer in Toussaint Louverture's Ninth Brigade, based in Port-de-Paix under General Jacques Maurepas. This lineage is a source of pride for him and many mixed-race families in Haiti, who often highlight their roots in the nation's fight for independence.

Tall and muscular, Jean-Foreste's physique reflects his sportive lifestyle. His gray eyes gleam, and his thin, pointed nose curves downward like the beak of a jungle parrot. Almost beardless, he retains a boyishness that delights Bernadine. His youthfulness serves as a bittersweet reminder to his wife, who clings to the fading glow of her own youthful allure while continuing to indulge in the dualistic games of love and aristocratic romance.

Jean-Foreste is well-liked in the exclusive uptown suburbs. Articulate and deliberate, his words command attention. This makes him a respected figure among his peers, especially when he delivers compelling passages from the first volume of Thomas Madiou's *History of Haiti*. Yet his audience, mainly women enjoying fine Creole cuisine and vintage French wines, seems more captivated by his diction and refined mannerisms than by the historical content of his speeches.

Quite an irony! Jean-Foreste himself appears detached from Madiou's accounts of the strategic alliances between black and mixed-race communities, slaves and the enfranchised, who united in their noble struggle for Haitian independence. The words flow from his mouth with practiced elegance, but their essence seems to matter little to him.

An educated fellow, a "man about town," M. Jean-Foreste has mastered the art of hiding his prejudices behind a veneer of charm. A sweet talker, he employs folkloric idioms to captivate and influence those who cross his path. At first glance, he appears harmless—a fervent patriot whose love for the Motherland seems unwavering. Yet behind that disarming smile lies a self-centered and reactionary disposition, concealed but ever-present.

Jean-Foreste is, in many ways, emblematic of Haiti's upper class, shaped by privilege and bound by its contradictions. Sometimes, he sees himself as a victim of his social standing, suffering in silent acknowledgment of its constraints. These complexities are lost on his wife, Bernadine, who lacks his intellectual depth. Her impulsive demeanor and dramatic outbursts serve as a smokescreen for her insecurities, a strategy that works well against Jean-Foreste's aversion to conflict. Yielding to her grotesque whims has become his default response, a compromise that underscores his own moral lethargy.

Jean-Foreste's material success is considerable. He has inherited vast coffee fields, a sprawling sugarcane plantation, and owns a prestigious jewelry store in town. Business has been so prosperous that he dreams of expanding to Port-au-Prince, with plans to open two additional stores. Yet, his ambitions are thwarted by Bernadine's staunch opposition, rooted in her fear of the capital's chaotic life. At nearly fifty, she envisions their future in the comfort of their estates—one in Bodin near Port-de-Paix, and the other in Avignon, France. Jean-Foreste, understanding the futility of pursuing his aspirations without her support, gradually abandons his plans.

The family home is a testament to their opulence. Commissioned twenty-six years ago, the six-bedroom, two-story mansion boasts mahogany hardwood floors, crystal chandeliers, and a sprawling courtyard enclosed by stone walls. The wrought-iron, gold-rimmed gates make an imposing first impression, while a garden fountain cascades silvery water over hibiscus shrubs and multicolored crotons. Red roses frame marble walkways filled with sparkling white gravel, leading to a backyard patio that overlooks lush tropical plants and cashew apple trees. This garden paradise is the stage for their lavish soirées, attended by Haiti's crème de la crème and guarded by three fierce German Shepherds, ever vigilant for intruders.

In this extravagant environment, Céline grows up sheltered and oblivious to the harsh realities of the impoverished world beyond the gates. The perfection of her surroundings belies the inequities that define the lives of those outside her privileged circle.

By ten o'clock that morning, Céline descends from the upper-level balcony, making her way toward the bungalow where her father sits on a bar stool, sipping hot ginger tea while absorbed in his newspaper. Lost in the article, he cannot put it down. Every line pulls him deeper, heightening his emotional engagement.

"The city of Jérémie is issuing an ordinance, ordering all bourgeois from the business community to donate ten percent of their revenues for social projects aimed at helping the city's poor," one passage reads. Jean-Foreste's face flushes a deep crimson, his irritation mounting to a degree unseen in recent memory. "Failure to comply with the rule will result in property confiscation, or even jail time," another line blares. Trembling with indignation, he feels this last statement sending shockwaves through his veins.

"That new Marxist mayor wants to make the rich pay for the wrongs of our country," he growls. Rising from his seat, he smacks the newspaper against the wooden bar with one swift motion, ready to storm away. As he lifts his head to steady himself, his eyes meet Céline's.

"What's making you angry, Father?" she asks.

"Nothing, my princess," he says, smoothing his expression in a gawky attempt to seem calm. He strides into the kitchen to remind Solitude about his favorite dumplings, which must accompany the red bean sauce. Solitude, standing by the kitchen stove with two skinned and headless chickens in her hands, is preparing to make stew. She casts him a fainthearted smile and nods a quick yes, reassuring him that his every culinary whim will be fulfilled.

Céline doesn't follow her father or press him further. Instead, she continues along the pathway, bypassing the bungalow. She strolls down the cool, pebbled path toward the front gates, her thoughts adrift, her movements deliberate. She walks like a young woman in search of her soul. Her attire is a vibrant reflection of her tropical surroundings: Polo jeans paired with a splashy cotton tunic in bold hues of yellow, orange, and red—like a December sunset over the beach. With a gentle push, she unlocks the left side of the gate, stepping confidently out onto Grande Rue, or Main Street.

Raising her parasol to shield her face from the golden rays of the rising sun, Céline turns toward Rue Vincent, which intersects with Grande Rue. The street is alive with pedestrians hurrying to the bustling marketplace. Though Grande Rue runs straight into the main square, Céline avoids it, unwilling to face the choking dust clouds and the overwhelming chaos of the street.

Walking down Rue Vincent, Céline slows her pace to wave at neighbors and old friends. "*Bonjour*, Madame Poitevien," she calls to a middle-aged woman standing on her front porch, hands on hips. Céline does not bother to ask for Monsieur Poitevien, for her mother has already recounted the story of his death in Port-au-Prince.

"*Comment vas-tu, ma belle Céline?*" Madame Poitevien replies with a warm smile spread across her open face. How are you doing, my pretty Céline? She steps closer to exchange a few words, but Céline, already on her way, gives a polite wave before continuing toward the square.

Rue Vincent is a historic street lined with well-preserved colonial houses: double-louvered doors, flared roofs, and shadowy, lowered shutters. Many of these two-story walk-ups have small bricks set between wooden posts, front-facing balconies, and expansive open porches, designed to welcome visitors and shoppers as in Olden Times. Downstairs are bustling businesses; upstairs lie the living quarters.

The street serves as the backdrop for the Fashion District, circling the town square, but Rue Vincent's narrow alleyways house some of the town's poorest residents. It is an obscene irony—squalid poverty thriving in the shadows of extravagance. Céline knows many of the people in these muddy alleys, their plight a sharp contrast to the life she grew up living.

At the edge of the square, a group of scruffy, barefoot boys spot her silhouette and race toward her.

"Mademoiselle Céline!" they cry, their small arms outstretched, their voices full of longing and excitement.

Their wan faces light up with innocent joy as they envelop her, clinging to her legs and offering tiny hands. Their ragged clothes and fragile frames tell stories of daily hunger and survival. Céline drops her parasol, spreading her arms like a mother osprey trying to shield them all, but there are simply too many.

Unzipping her purse, Céline pulls out a handful of Haitian silver coins. Taking the time to place a few coins in each child's hand, she pats their backs and kisses their cheeks. Seeing her as their generous benefactress, the children run and leap in circles around her, their laughter echoing through the square.

Businesspeople who know Céline and her family look on in stunned silence. They whisper among themselves, amazed at the sight of Madame Bernadine's daughter interacting so freely with these impoverished children. "Foreign lands must have changed her," they murmur.

As they reach the square, the children, now jubilant, release Céline and rush toward the fried food and soda pop stands. Céline stands still, watching them spend their small coins, their joy mixed with the desperation of hunger.

Shaking her head, Céline mutters to herself, "What a crime. Denying these innocent children and their families the chance to live decent, productive lives…it's unbearable."

The sun climbs higher, its heat intensifying. Céline suddenly remembers the parasol she had dropped during her fuss with the children. In a flurry, she hurries back to retrieve it, but it is gone. She scans the area, searching for any sign of it, but no one appears to have picked it up. Resigned, she sighs and turns to continue her journey into the square.

Just as she does, a voice from a house across the street calls out to her.

"*Bonjour*, Céline!" shouts a slim girl nearby. Her long, straight hair, textured in the hues of a brushfire, flutters in the warm breeze, cascading gracefully with her movements. Stepping in huge, leaping strides, she shows off her flowing floral dress, catching the late morning sun. Reaching Céline, she hands her the parasol, joyous laughter beaming from her golden face.

"*Merci*," Céline replies cheerfully.

"I was in the backyard when I heard the children laughing. I stepped outside and couldn't believe my eyes—you were surrounded by so many kids! They adore you; it was like they had buried you in their hugs. When I saw you'd forgotten your parasol, I picked it up. Don't worry, I was planning to deliver it to your home later," the young woman says.

"That's so thoughtful of you. Thanks!" Céline responds with a warm smile before turning back toward the square.

She navigates through the bustling market, weaving past street vendors and shoppers who have traveled from across town and nearby rural areas to trade their goods. The midday sun casts long shadows, bearing down on the square's vibrant chaos. Adjacent to the square, the Catholic Church's dome gleams under the blazing light, its circular shadow etched on the cobblestone ground like a grand celestial marker.

On the eastern edge of the square, merchants display piles of golden mangoes. Céline buys half a dozen, tucking the fragrant fruits into her leather purse. These sweet, local mangoes are small but her favorite. Leaving the market, she heads toward a narrow street winding upward to Sou Fò, an affluent suburb perched on a hill overlooking the square and the Fashion District. At the entrance to Sou Fò, the town's two regional Catholic schools—the nuns' and the brothers'—face each other from across the road like cowboys in a duel, their imposing facades an enduring testament to tradition and rivalry.

At the foot of the hill, Céline encounters Fleurie, an oversized woman she knows. A chubby boy dressed in faded blue trousers trails behind her, struggling to keep up. His large, flopping straw hat threatens to take flight with every gust of wind, forcing him to tap it back into place repeatedly. Fleurie marches forward, sweat glistening on her sun-darkened face, her red silk madras doing little to absorb the moisture streaming down her cheeks.

"Hurry, Mondésir! Hurry!" she calls to the boy, her voice a mix of urgency and maternal exasperation. Her quick strides aim to escape the stifling morning haze as she pushes toward the shelter of Sou Fò.

Her white calico dress stirs an old memory in Céline's mind. Fleurie, the woman everyone whispered about, owned a grocery store at the entrance of the square. Céline vividly recalls the days when she and her peers stopped by the store to buy frozen milkshakes—treats as sweet as stolen moments. Yet, despite the allure, she was forbidden to enter. Her parents had filled her childhood with tales of Fleurie's supposed dark nature—calling her a werewolf, a witch, or some other monstrous figure.

"She still wears that same kind of outfit," Céline murmurs under her breath as her eyes catch Fleurie's familiar silhouette. Bowing her head, she shields her face to avoid any eye contact. Though she no longer believes in her parents' prejudiced fabrications, she feels the lingering sting of psychological scars that time and reason have yet to fully heal. Prejudice is a tough weed to uproot, she muses.

Chapter 10

As Céline ascends the hill, a long procession of peasants with burdened burros crosses her path. The animals, their backs sagging under overfilled saddles, trudge forward, their exhaustion betrayed in every faltering step. Oblivious to their suffering, the peasants shout and sing, urging their beasts onward with relentless cries. When a burro strays, a sharp oath and a harsher lash yank it back in line. The scene, monotonous and cruel, troubles Céline's heart.

She waves, trying to connect, but the peasants ignore her. Their focus lies solely on their burdens and destination. Céline recognizes some of them. They are from Fond Boulé, a settlement near Bassin Joseph where her parents own acres of fertile land. Once, these very peasants worked her family's land as sharecroppers.

Near the hilltop, by the Catholic nuns' residence, stands a quaint, white house hidden by the generous shade of a red-flowering tree. Its long branches drape over the open courtyard like an umbrella of nature's quiet protection. Céline, seeking a momentary respite, walks into the yard, closing her parasol as she steps beneath the tree's canopy.

"*Bonjour*, Aunty," Céline breathes, her tone softened by the day's weight as she addresses a short, stout woman sweeping the courtyard.

"*Bonjour*, pretty lady," the woman responds with a warm smile, gripping a broom in one hand while tucking the other deep into her dress's drooping pocket.

After a few minutes of pleasant chatter, Céline continues her walk, passing the congregational schools to enter the serene suburb of Sou Fò. Lines of coconut palm trees frame the narrow streets, their fronds whispering secrets in the breeze. To the east, the once-clear morning skies are now awash with bloated, foaming clouds, casting fleeting shadows that dance around Céline as she walks. Her shadow shifts, tracing the sun's slow descent toward the west. The lively hum of Main Street fades into the background—engines rumbling, horns blaring, and merchants' cries are now mere echoes, distant and dreamlike.

Sou Fò appears deserted. The streets are still, devoid of promenading figures. Yet, behind every fourth or fifth house, Céline catches the faint sound of radios playing low, melancholic tunes. Slowing her steps, she takes in the quiet, sodden sidewalks, still damp from the previous night's rain, which seem to mirror the tinge of unease settling into her mind.

At the end of the street, she pauses to catch her breath, her grip firm on her parasol. A faint rumbling grows louder behind her, and she turns her head, her eyes flickering with curiosity. A Jeep Wrangler, its engine purring, creeps in her direction. As the vehicle approaches, the driver slams on the brakes, the sudden halt breaking the stillness.

"*Bonjour*, mademoiselle!" calls the gentleman behind the wheel, his sapphire-blue eyes locking onto Céline's with startling intensity.

"*Bonjour*…" Céline murmurs, her voice just above a whisper. Her steps quicken, but her heart skips as she recognizes him.

"We met yesterday, behind the mountains. Remember?" His voice rises a notch, ensuring she hears him. His dark, wavy hair gleams in the sunlight as he runs a hand through it with deliberate ease, exuding quiet confidence. Keeping pace with her, he releases the brakes, allowing the Jeep to inch forward.

"Yes, I remember," she replies, a shy note in her voice, raising her parasol a little higher. She steals a glance at him, noticing his trimmed Spanish goatee and the easy smile lighting up his face.

"If I may ask, where are you going?" he ventures, his grin widening with boyish charm.

"I'm going to see a friend," Céline answers curtly.

"Can I offer you a ride?" he asks, undeterred.

"No thanks, but that's very kind of you."

"Why not? I'm just driving around," he insists.

"*C'est gentil*, but I'm almost there."

He persists. "May I ask you something?"

Céline finally stops and turns to face him. "Go ahead."

"Isn't your name Céline?" he asks, his tone softening.

"Yes," she says, her voice a cautious dove.

"Don't you remember me?"

Waxing hesitant, Céline tilts her head. "I think I do."

"What's my name?" he teases.

"Don't you think it's odd to quiz a stranger?" Céline replies, her brows furrowing as she resumes walking, leaving the car idle behind her.

Amused, Ludovic maneuvers the jeep under a large mango tree shading the street. He parks, steps out, and hurries after her.

"Sorry," he laughs, trying to recover from his blunder. "I was just kidding; you're no stranger to me."

"No need to apologize." Céline smiles, her guard softening.

Offering his hand with a gentlemanly bow, he declares, "I'm Ludovic Malbranche."

"I know," Céline says, her smile growing. "You're Jean-Marie Poitevien's friend."

Her hand brushes his, and their fingers intertwine for a moment. A spark of unrestrained cheerfulness erupts between them, and laughter breaks free like a summer torrent. Céline, startled by her own giddiness, quickly pulls her hand away, trying—and failing—to regain her composure.

Ludovic understands her hesitation, a subtle joy warming his features as they begin walking side by side. He shoves his hands into his pockets to stifle his own excitement, while Céline, in an almost unconscious gesture, tilts her parasol to shield them both from the unrelenting sun.

"I love walking in this part of town!" Ludovic declares, his voice brimming with delight.

"Why is that?" Céline asks, tilting her head as they walk.

"It offers a spectacular entry into a fantasy world. Look at the green foliage encroaching on the horizon—it feels untouched, serene. I wish the rest of the country could mirror this beauty."

"That's very romantic," Céline replies, a faint smile flickering across her lips. "But I stopped dreaming long ago." She pauses before shifting the topic. "Well…whatever happened to Jean-Marie?"

"He's doing well. He works for an international agency focusing on Sub-Saharan Africa and married his longtime fiancée. I hear they live in Strasbourg, France."

"What's his wife's name?"

"Emilie."

"You mean Emilie Derenoncourt?" Céline's tone sharpens with familiarity.

"Yes, the very same—with her long, spiky golden hair and that radiant smile," Ludovic confirms.

"I knew he was seeing her! But he always denied it. I saw him once, years ago, in London while he was in college. During our conversation, he didn't even mention her name."

"And you know why, I presume."

"Oh, I do," Céline replies with a sly grin. "He wanted me as part of his collection. But I wasn't interested. He was too polished, too calculated—like he wore his charm as an accessory. That attitude always turned me off, though I never said so. Truthfully, I was more interested in his flawless Parisian French."

She stops for a moment, her gaze drifting into the past. Ludovic watches her, his eyes gleaming with quiet admiration. Then she continues, her voice softer:

"Jean-Marie is the classic son of our bourgeois aristocrats. He believed his class was untouchable, superior to all others. Once, he even cautioned me about befriending our servants, as if it were something that might tarnish me. He was referring to Louisinette, a girl who served in our house. She and I were very close. Actually, I was on my way to see her when I ran into you yesterday, behind the mountains."

Her petite grimace adds an endearing charm to her recollection. Ludovic listens with utmost attention, his piercing eyes softening as his lips curl into a warm grin.

"Céline, I was overjoyed to see you yesterday. I thought you were gone, lost forever from my world."

"You've changed a lot, Ludovic. You were thinner back then," she teases. "Now look at you—strong, built like a warrior. So different from the shy young man who used to stand by my parents' gates, too reserved to speak a word."

"You're right, Céline. In those days, my mouth would dry up. I was completely paralyzed, overwhelmed by your charm. I must admit—you still have that effect on me."

"I thought you shared your roué friend's ways."

"Not at all…never did, never will! I was raised by our housemaid, Méloria. She was an angel to me. My parents were always away on business trips. For the longest time, I thought Méloria was my mother. I couldn't sleep without her nearby. Even now, I still call her *manman*."

Ludovic's voice drops, and a shadow falls over his face. The playful grin that had lit up his features vanishes, replaced by a pensive frown. A deep wrinkle forms between his brows.

"One of the biggest problems with this country is the enormous gap between a tiny minority—people like us—who control more than three-quarters of its wealth, and the overwhelming majority who are left to fend for themselves. After graduating in Paris, I received several job offers. I could've chosen the easy route, living in luxury in a wealthy French suburb like so many of my peers. But instead, I came back. I wanted to make a difference.

"Haiti is like the most beautiful woman—soft-breasted, velvety dark—but the neglect and indifference of her children have pushed her into despair, to the brink of collapse."

Céline remains silent, her lighthearted mood dimmed. Ludovic's candid words strike a deep chord within her, filling the air between them with weighty truth. She begins to see in him not just a potential confidant, but the ideal comrade she might need to fight for justice for Louisinette.

They continue walking side by side, taking cautious steps as the path becomes rougher. Eventually, they reach the eastern edge of town, where the street narrows into a country trail. The last house fades behind them, swallowed by the lush greenery.

"Do you know where you're going, Céline?" Ludovic asks, his tone tinged with light amusement but his face turned toward her with genuine curiosity.

"Not really. I suppose I'm just a wanderer on a spontaneous rendezvous with nature."

Ludovic chuckles, then stops abruptly. "I'm thirsty, Céline." He glances ahead and licks his lips, the motion almost sheepish.

"The river isn't far. There's a spring nearby…if I can remember the way. The water used to be so fresh—"

"Wait, there's a cottage over there!"

He gestures toward a small house nestled in a shaded courtyard just a few steps from the trail. A line of towering mango trees leads toward it, their branches heavy with ripe fruit. The pair quicken their steps, their footfalls rustling lie grass and sending faint echoes through the still air.

As they approach, the movement stirs an old woman from her rest. She pushes open the banana-leaf-thatched door and rubs her tired eyes, squinting at the two unexpected visitors.

"*Bonjour*," Ludovic and Céline utter in unison.

"*Bonjour*," the old woman replies. She stands framed in the hollow of the entrance, her wide-open arms resting on the wooden poles flanking her front door. "How can I help you?" she asks.

"We're thirsty and were wondering if we could have a couple glasses of water, please," Ludovic responds, Céline smiling from behind him.

"Of course," the woman says with a warm, almost childlike glee. She releases her hold on the doorframe, her movements slow but steady, and wheels around. Céline and Ludovic watch as she crosses the room, her bare feet padding on the earthen floor. Next to a low, board-plank bed in the far corner sits a simple clay pot of drinking water. Nearby, a few plastic cups lie neatly arranged on a tiny wooden table. The woman pours water into two cups and returns to the porch. Handing the cups to them, her wrinkled face beams with quiet satisfaction.

The two drink in eager gulps, the cool water soothing their parched throats. "Thank you so much, madame," Céline says, her voice earnest.

The old woman waves them off with a smile as they leave the courtyard, her faded scarf flapping in the breeze.

<u>*Chapter 11*</u>

Guided by the distant rush of the current, Céline and Ludovic walk eastward. Within minutes, the river comes into view, its narrow, winding surface glinting under the sun's gentle rays. They follow its edge, leaving the main trail behind, until they arrive at the foot of a massive boulder, lying like a majestic sentinel on the east bank. Céline folds her parasol, placing it on the sand. Ludovic extends his hand, helping her climb the rock's smooth surface. With one giant leap, he joins her.

They sit in silence, a resting pair of doves. The river hums below them, its melody weaving with the soft rustle of the surrounding trees. Céline brushes a stray strand of hair from her face, her gaze fixed on the shimmering water. Ludovic, leaning back slightly, glances at her, his eyes reflecting a quiet admiration.

For a moment, the world feels still—just the two of them and the river, flowing endlessly onward.

Although tired, Céline maintains her composure, avoiding any comfortable lean on Ludovic. Yet, there is a quiet acceptance of his companionship. "This is elegant and lovely," she murmurs, her eyes tracing the forest's edge on the western bank, where a small serpentine stream tumbles into the mighty river with a soothing melody.

"You bet it is!" Ludovic laughs, his voice tinged with wistfulness. "Have you ever canoed here before?"

"No, I haven't. I wouldn't know where to start," Céline's reply is cool, brushing the question aside like an unwelcome hand.

"It's not difficult. You just need a little strength and skill. I could teach you if you'd like."

Céline chuckles, shaking her head. "Are you serious? Imagine what people in town would say if they spotted us podding down the river together."

A flicker of embarrassment crosses Ludovic's face. "I understand," he says, his voice quieter now.

"It's not just about the gossip, Ludovic," Céline continues, her tone softening. "Canoeing is for something else—it's romantic, intimate. We're still new to each other. I don't think you'd want to give people the wrong idea."

Ludovic's gaze drops to the water, where the river darkens into an indigo blue, then shifts into a shimmering purplish green under the sun's golden rays. "I know what you mean," he finally says, his voice subdued, carrying a hint of regret.

They sit in silence, the moment stretching between them like the river itself. Across the water, thick undergrowth transforms the opposite shore into a marshland where crawfish and catfish thrive. Farther south, lines of royal palms arch skyward, their leaves swaying with the wind. A solitary breadfruit tree, its golden boughs lit like flames in the sunlight, stands defiantly among the palms, its withering branches whispering of resilience and decay.

A sudden burst of movement interrupts the stillness as a flock of vultures soars past, their wings slicing the air. Both Céline and Ludovic turn, watching the birds climb higher, disappearing into the wooded heights on the western bank.

Céline speaks again, her voice cutting through the quiet. "Ludovic, if I follow this river path, where will it take me?"

"You'd be where its mouth empties into the ocean," Ludovic says.

"One day, I'll come back and trace its path all the way to Saint Louis," she replies.

"Let me know when you do!" Ludovic laughs, a warm sound echoing through the still air. "There's a great basin before the river bends and merges with the Saint Louis River. It's magnificent."

"How deep is it?" Céline asks, her fingers absentmindedly tracing an outline down his chest, drawing his attention.

"I don't know its exact depth, but it's very deep—almost impossible to see the bottom. As a kid, I'd dive into the basin from a big rock at its edge. Méloria, our housemaid, used to take me along when she washed clothes there. A bunch of us kids would jump in, scaring the fish away with our splashes. It was the most freeing feeling."

His voice softens, steeped in nostalgia. "Even as I got older, I'd return there, especially in times of doubt. The water seemed to wash away my worries. It cleansed not just my body, but my spirit too. Those moments felt like a baptism into hope."

He pauses, inhaling deeply as he gazes at the royal palms swaying in the distance, his voice tinged with longing. "Every time I think of those days, I grow more certain that this country—our country—will rise again."

Céline, moved by his words, nods. "I believe we share the same dream. Haiti was never meant to perish. I've always felt that the revolutionary spirit of 1804, the one that defeated Napoleon, will return someday. It will unite us all for a new and vital mission."

"And what mission would that be?" Ludovic asks, his tone curious but cautious.

"The fight against neocolonialism," Céline asserts.

Ludovic leans back, considering her words. "That's a far greater challenge than the victory of 1804," he says, his voice measured.

"How so?" Céline's gaze sharpens, her brow furrowed.

"In 1804, we had a clear enemy—slavery—and an undeniable cause. It was a fight for freedom, and everyone felt the urgency to either rise up or perish. Today, the enemy is harder to define, more insidious. Even those living in the harshest conditions don't always see the battle before them."

Céline nods slowly. "You're right. But we can't wait for everyone to wake up. Right here in this town, there are injustices happening every day. One victim, in particular, inspires my resolve."

"Who is it?" Ludovic asks, startled by her sudden intensity. Her fiery determination catches him off guard, igniting a sense of admiration and intrigue.

"When the time is right, I'll tell you," Céline replies, her voice firm, her eyes fixed on the horizon.

Leaping off the boulder, Céline nearly twists her ankle. Stumbling forward, her knee grazes a sharp stone. Ludovic bolts down, catching her in mid-fall. She quickly steadies herself, brushing sand off her clothes, a faint laugh escaping her lips as she glances at him.

"*Merci,*" she whispers, retrieving her parasol and unfolding it to shield them both from the blazing sun. As they cross the river and head westward, Ludovic pauses by his Jeep, parked under a sprawling mango tree. Just then, the sound of hurried footsteps draws their attention.

Two rural policemen emerge, leading a young prisoner between them. Shirtless and barefoot, his muscular chest glistens with sweat as he balances a stack of ripening bananas on his head. His arms are tightly bound behind him with coarse rope, which one policeman jerks like a leash, forcing him forward. The prisoner's head hangs low, his hollowed face a mask of resignation.

Céline's eyes burn with anger. Ludovic snaps a breath. "How much for his bananas?" he calls out.

The policeman holding the rope stops, eyeing Ludovic warily. "I don't know," he grunts, yanking the rope again.

The other policeman, a chubby man with salt-and-pepper hair, steps closer, lowering his voice. "Twenty dollars," he mutters, glancing around to ensure no one is watching.

Ludovic pulls a twenty-dollar bill from his wallet, extending it toward the chubby cop. "Here," he says, his voice sharp. "But release him first."

The policemen exchange glances, then untie the knots binding the prisoner. Céline snatches him to her side, shielding him with her parasol.

"What about the bananas?" the chubby cop asks, pocketing the money.

"We don't want them," Ludovic replies, handing the bunch to the other officer, who grabs it with eager eyes. As they begin to walk away, Ludovic calls out, "One more thing."

The policemen pause, turning back. Ludovic steps closer, his voice low but fierce. "Next time you're looking for thieves, go to Saint Louis or Port-au-Prince. That's where the real criminals live—those fat-bellied politicians stealing millions from the poor while you harass hungry men trying to survive."

The chubby cop fidgets, his hand brushing the pocket where the money sits, but before he can respond, Ludovic spins on his heel, returning to Céline.

"You know who the real crooks are, don't you?" Céline murmurs, a faint smile breaking through her stern expression. She pats the prisoner's back. "You're free to go."

Before he leaves, Ludovic stops him. "What's your name?"

"Henrilus," the man replies, his voice hoarse.

"Don't do this again, Henrilus," Ludovic warns. "Next time, they might kill you."

The prisoner nods and trudges westward, his steps uneven.

Ludovic boards his Jeep, motioning for Céline to join him. She shakes her head. "I'll walk. But I look forward to seeing you again."

Ludovic hesitates, then nods. "*À bientôt*, Céline." He drives off, a cloud of dust trailing behind him as Céline watches until he vanishes into the distance.

"Handsome, isn't he?" The words carry on the wind, a low and whispery voice from behind. "Your boyfriend is a real looker!"

Céline squints in the broad sunlight, raising her parasol to shield her eyes as she searches for the speaker. On a front porch, a white-haired woman leans against a wooden post, her face splitting into a wide guffaw when Céline spots her. The laughter fades as an unspoken understanding passes between them, like a bridge built without words.

"He's not my boyfriend!" Céline gasps, a timid smile creeping onto her lips as if to emphasize her innocence.

The woman rolls her eyes, her expression betraying disbelief, before turning her back and disappearing into the shadowy hollow of her living room. She mumbles something indistinct. Céline, rooted in place, feels her lips quivering with the desire to hear more. What did she say? What does she mean?

Sensing Céline's hesitation, the woman steps back onto the porch, closing the door behind her. With a slight limp, she paces to the street's edge, meeting Céline where she stands silent, clutching her parasol.

"Sorry, I didn't hear what you said," Céline ventures, a wary grin softening her face.

The woman chuckles, her voice rich with experience. "There's no need to apologize. You're a lovely young lady. Every relationship must have a beginning: humble, jolly, merry, and sometimes rocky."

"Really?" Céline tilts her head, curiosity flickering in her eyes.

"You're smart and beautiful. Surely, you know that all nice things in life begin with an unforgettable moment. Love is like wild lemongrass—when it springs, it's difficult to uproot. He may not be the one now, but if you want to give love a chance, this young man, handsome and gentle, could share this amazing journey with you. You just need to place him at the receiving end of your heart."

Céline hesitates, her gaze steady. "Do you know him?"

"Not well, but I know his parents. I hear plenty of good things, and I know this: plenty of girls in town are talking about him."

Céline listens in silence, her face unreadable. After a moment, she steps forward, planting a soft kiss on the woman's sagging, ebony cheek. "*Merci*," she says simply, before turning to leave.

The woman watches Céline walk away, leaning against her wooden fence. Her sharp eyes follow the young lady until she disappears around the corner, her parasol a bright spot against the dusty street.

<u>*Chapter 12*</u>

Since her encounter with Céline, Louisinette has been a changed woman. An invisible weight seems to press on her heart, tightening its fragile strings. Nightmares haunt her sleep, and her days are plagued by a whirlwind of emotions—joy from Céline's visit and dread from the daunting task ahead. She feels unworthy of standing with Céline in the fight against sexual predators, convinced that someone like her—marginalized, dehumanized, and unseen by society—has no place in such a monumental cause.

It is another early Wednesday morning, six o'clock, and the day has already begun. Louisinette rises to prepare for a trip to the marketplace behind the mountains. Her children, laughing and shoving each other in delirious joy, finish their breakfast of fresh goat milk and yucca bread. Outside, her little red-tailed burro waits beneath the chestnut tree, grazing before the long trek to the rural market near Morne Zombie. Louisinette packs oranges and avocados into the saddlebags strapped over the animal's back, patting its side affectionately.

Victorin has already left for the fields to clear a new parcel of land for planting white maize. Louisinette, with her children in tow, makes her way to Dantilia's house. Dubison, her youngest, clings stubbornly to the hem of her purple dress, his small hands gripping the embroidered fringe with all his might. Louisinette bends to lift him, pressing a gentle kiss to his

76

forehead. "Don't worry, *ti chéri*," she soothes, setting him back down.

Dantilia, a neighbor and close friend, still clad in her nightgown, stands waiting on the porch, her arms open wide. Thin rays of sunlight streak across her gingered face as she moves to greet them. The children hesitate, their eyes darting between their mother and the neighbor. "Go on," Louisinette urges. "I won't be long, and I'll bring sweets when I return." She pulls Lamizè into a final hug, holding him tightly as tears well in his eyes.

The boys drag their feet toward Dantilia, who with a soft voice coaxes them onto the porch. They turn to wave one last goodbye, their thin brown hands raised high as their mother walks away. Louisinette's heart aches, but she doesn't look back. There is no time for second thoughts. She returns home to fetch the burro and her merchandise, steeling herself for the long road ahead.

Within minutes, Louisinette is on her way, taking a back road toward the ravine trail to avoid facing her children, who might still be lingering on the neighbor's front porch. She rides gracefully atop her groaning burro, her posture regal, like a Haitian queen. A flowery haircloth frames her face, accentuated by the glint of prodigious silver hoop earrings.

Her mind churns with restless thoughts as she journeys toward the mountaintop marketplace. Saint Louis looms in her imagination, a place she has avoided since the tragedy at the Bodins'. The thought of moving there, of immersing herself in Céline's fight for social justice, feels both daunting and inevitable. "I'll kill you if you dare tell anyone!" Dalambert's guttural threat echoes in her mind, a haunting refrain that invades her waking hours and dreams alike. She can still see him disappearing into the shadows, the shallow river swallowing his hateful figure.

"Can Céline truly protect me if Dalambert comes after me?" she wonders, her heart pounding in rhythm with her mounting fears. Her husband's reaction to the idea of moving to Saint Louis troubles her. What would happen to her children if she were harmed—or worse? These questions terrify her, but the fiery memory of Céline's determination rekindles her courage. Louisinette feels an unfamiliar yearning: a need for justice, not just for herself but for others like her. It is an itch only the balm of fairness can soothe.

Lost in thought, she is startled to realize she has already passed several settlements. The village of Cazalie lies just ahead, and the hollow gorge of Morne Zombie looms near. Vendors on horseback and mules hurry past, their voices rising in cheerful bursts as they greet one another. Louisinette waves, her thoughts elsewhere, her mind refocusing on the practical task ahead. Selling her goods is of the utmost importance today.

Lifting her gaze, she spots the hazy outlines of market-goers milling about the ridge. Their distant voices blend with the chirps of unseen hummingbirds, creating a strange harmony. A renewed energy courses through her veins, propelling her forward. But standing in her way is the final obstacle—a rocky incline her burro must climb to reach the marketplace perched atop the ridge.

Gripping the reins, Louisinette steels herself. The mountain road is treacherous, but she presses on, her resolve unyielding. Each step her burro takes mirrors her own determination: slow, steady, and unstoppable.

The little burro seems to dread the painful ascent, braying in defiance as it plants its hooves rooted on the rocky trail. Louisinette leaps down, her patience wearing thin, and lashes at the beast. But the burro remains unmoved, its stubbornness as unyielding as the jagged mountain path.

Just then, a bulky middle-aged man appears, balancing a heavy sack of mangoes atop his bald head. Trailing behind him are three small children, their weary faces etched with fatigue and frustration. The smallest child, a skinny boy with fiery, irksome eyes, spots Louisinette struggling with her animal.

"Papa, let's help this lady!" he shouts, his voice ringing with urgency. The man sighs, setting down his load with a thud. He gestures to his eldest, a shy, diminutive child, to keep an eye on the mangoes before striding over to assist.

"Mademoiselle, hold the leash while I strike the beast from behind," he instructs with a firm but kind tone.

"*Wi, Mesye.* Yes, sir," Louisinette replies, a faint smile flickering across her face. She steps to the side, keeping a tight grip on the leash. As the man scolds and prods, the burro grudgingly begins to move, its hooves scraping against the pebbles as it trudges up the slope.

Halfway up the mountain, the man stops, waving goodbye. "*Bon chans*, Mademoiselle," he beams before returning to his children and his mangoes.

"*Mesi anpil, Mesye.* Thank you very much, sir," Louisinette calls after him, her voice brimming with gratitude. She tightens her grip on the leash, leading the burro onward.

At last, she reaches the ridge, where the marketplace sprawls before her, alive with vibrant activity. Sellers and buyers from Saint Louis and as far away as the village of Bonneau, nestled along the foothills of Morne Vent near the town of Anse-à-Foleur, crowd the area. Their voices mingle with the rustling of goods and the occasional bray of livestock. Louisinette wastes no time. She unloads her burro, tying it to a young mango tree near the entrance, and spreads a pink-red sheet over some banana leaves on the ground. With practiced efficiency, she arranges her fruits: avocadoes in a neat pile, mangoes grouped in lots of three to prompt quick sales.

Her goal is clear—to sell every last piece before sundown. The hum of the marketplace envelops her, a bustling symphony of commerce and community.

*****

Like the street vendors around the main square in Saint Louis, Louisinette has learned to play fair at the food market. She knows losing a few pennies or giving away an avocado for free won't ruin her day's profits; it might even mean a meal for someone who might otherwise go hungry. This quiet act of generosity reflects an unconscious heroism, a belief that life gains meaning not only through survival but also through acts of kindness—small but significant gestures that ripple through her community.

Today's trip, however, feels different. By midday, the last avocado is sold, and the mangoes are gone within hours. Joy floods her ebony features as she marvels at her success. For the first time, she feels like the luckiest vendor in the marketplace. Clutching her tiny leather purse bulging with coins and Haitian gourds, she imagines the smile on Victorin's face when she steps onto their porch. She envisions placing a kiss on his weathered lips before proudly sharing the good news.

Like most Haitian mothers managing a household, Louisinette knows such moments of bliss are fleeting. Daily needs loom large, and money never stretches far enough. Though she has become a master at prioritizing and budgeting, there is always something missing—a disappointing sale, a sudden price hike, or an unforeseen emergency often throws her plans into disarray.

As the midday sun beats down, her joy begins to wane. A wave of anxiety washes over her as she realizes she cannot return home without buying essentials: a bar of soap for washing linens, cooking oil and salt for their meals, toothpaste, and two shirts for the boys. Her heart sinks as she counts her dwindling coins. With a frown, she walks to the north end of the marketplace, muttering, "*A la mizè pou lave kay tè!*" Mopping a house with a dirt floor—it's a thankless task, she thinks.

By the time she finishes shopping, only three gourds remain. Resigned but grateful she could manage the essentials, she unties her burro and begins the rocky descent home. The thought of Victorin's understanding brings a small comfort, even as exhaustion weighs heavily on her. Stroking her burro's neck, she whispers, "Victorin will understand."

Chapter 13

Halfway through the trip home, near Ofou—a small settlement of thatched cottages walled by palisades and nestled on the banks of the Acajou River—Louisinette decides to make a brief stop. Her cousin Dorcélia, recovering from a knee injury, lives here. Ofou, hidden behind tall trees along the foothills, is a place Louisinette rarely visits. The settlement is on the opposite side of the mountain where she resides, and its isolation feels both physical and symbolic. She is reluctant to go, but familial duty pulls her forward.

The path to Dorcélia's home is narrow and winding, curving around dense lines of sugarcane that rustle a whisper in the breeze. Louisinette dismounts her burro, tying it to an orange tree just off the path. As she approaches the modest courtyard of her cousin's cottage, muffled voices catch her attention.

"We're not goin' to Saint Louis, to live with strangers!" a young girl's anguished cry pierces through the stillness, making Louisinette freeze mid-step. She presses herself against the muddy wall of the nearest hut, heart pounding as she listens.

"Unless you want to starve to death," comes the guttural reply, the voice of their mother breaking under the strain of unspoken agony. "Do you know how much it hurts me to see you both go hungry night after night? To have nothing but tears to offer you in the morning? It cracks every bone in my body."

"Then let us stay, manman. Let us starve here with you," one of the girls pleads, her voice quivering but firm.

"No!" The mother's voice bursts out sharply, ricocheting through the air like a whip. Then, it softens, crumbling into a low, trembling hush. "I can't do that. I'm your mother. I brought you into this cruel world; it's my duty to see you live. Even if I never see you again, I know you'll have a chance. Madame Laurimaire and Mademoiselle Martine… they're good women. You'll be safe with them."

The mother's words falter, her voice trailing into a faint sigh. In her heart, she knows the truth. Laurimaire and Martine, like many nouveaux riches, see vulnerable children as tools to advance their social standing. Rumors persist that they send these children to the upscale suburbs of Port-au-Prince, where they are exploited, neglected, or worse.

The weight of her own words collapses upon her. "Oh, my babies…" the mother chokes out, her anguish spilling into shrieking cries of despair.

From her hiding place, Louisinette trembles, tears welling uncontrollably. Memories of her own suffering rise to the surface: the cold nights, the threats, the lingering sting of shame. "I'll kill you if you dare tell anyone!" Dalambert's guttural warning echoes in her mind like a relentless phantom.

The hut's back door creaks open. Louisinette quickly retreats toward the path, wiping her tears and steeling herself as a woman steps out.

"*Bonsoir*," the woman says, her voice weary but warm.

"*Bonsoir*," Louisinette stammers, trying to compose herself.

"Are you Dorcélia's cousin?"

"Yes, I am."

The woman glances over her shoulder. "She's not here. She traveled to Saint Louis this morning and hasn't returned yet."

Two girls take cautious steps out of the house, their fiery ebony eyes scanning Louisinette with suspicion. One is taller, her slender posture betraying malnutrition, her wiry limbs trembling as she moves. The younger one clutches her sister's hand, her purplish eyes sparkling like glass beads in the fading light. Both wear faded blue dresses and scuffed sandals, their tiny frames shadowed by despair.

Taking a position near their mother, the girls cling to her torn and wrinkled calico skirt, their tiny hands quivering as they beg to stay. Louisinette, stepping closer, begins to gently stroke their well-coiffed hair, styled into tight little pigtails adorned with bright, multicolored barrettes. The girls' glassy eyes widen with fear, their desperation etched into their innocent faces. They seem to believe Louisinette is the one who has come to take them away, to deliver them to their new mistresses in Saint Louis. Finally, the younger one bursts out, her voice cracking, "I don't wanna go, manman. Please, I'm begging you."

"Go where?" Louisinette asks, feigning confusion, though she knows the heartbreaking truth.

"I'm sending them…to stay with a relative in town," the mother replies, her voice a thread of sound as she averts her eyes, looking east toward the mountains.

Louisinette's gaze sharpens. "If they're going to stay with a beloved relative, why are they so scared?" Her tone is soft but pointed.

"They…they've never met them before," the mother stammers. "They're just frightened of something new."

"Maybe they have a point," Louisinette says, her voice gentle but firm. "Children need to be raised by their parents, not by—strangers."

The mother flinches, her face clouded with doubt. "What's your name?" she asks, studying Louisinette's face as if searching for recognition.

"Louisinette. And yours?"

"Anatine," the mother murmurs. A flicker of realization crosses her face. "Are you the one people talked about a few years ago? The one who…who…"

"Yes," Louisinette interjects calmly, meeting Anatine's gaze. "And I presume you know why."

A wave of discomfort washes over Anatine, her hands fluttering as if to halt the conversation. Louisinette presses on. "Even if these people are your relatives, how can you be sure they won't hurt your daughters? These kids are your flesh and blood, a part of you. I know it's hard to raise girls in this country. But don't you think there might be another, safer way? Sending them to Saint Louis is a gamble—one I'm all too familiar with. You've heard my story. You know the risks."

Out of nowhere, a tall woman on a buckskin palomino mule storms onto the scene, the animal braying sharply, its tail stiffening as it bucks against its leash. The woman's dark-gray garment and loose black turban flap in the wind as her piercing eyes sweep over everything like a hawk studying its prey. Her movements are calculated, cold. Her arrival feels like an ominous shadow falling over the family.

The girls clutch their mother's calico skirt, their faces pressed into the fabric, trembling. The woman dismounts with a heavy thud, jerking the mule's leash as it zigzags in place. She lashes it with a quick flick to silence its protests. Standing taller than any of them, her presence is as unyielding as the mountain trail.

"*Bonsoir*," she grunts, her voice rough and commanding.

"*Bonsoir*…Georgette," Anatine replies, a shiver in her voice.

Georgette strides forward and grabs the older girl's arm. The child fights back with all her strength, kicking wildly. The mule seizes the moment to bolt, snapping free of the leash. Georgette curses under her breath, her grip loosening as she chases after the mule. A passerby retrieves it and hands it back to her, but not before Louisinette steps closer, her voice rising.

"Anatine, this isn't right. These are your children, not livestock. Look at how terrified they are! If she treats them this way in front of you, imagine what she'll do when you're not there!"

"I know…" Anatine muttrs, her voice cracking. She turns to Georgette, who waits, her foot tapping, tugging the mule's leash. Anatine utters something inaudible, and Georgette mounts her mule and heads toward the river, leaving the girls wailing in anguish.

Louisinette, heartbroken and furious, confronts Anatine one last time. "Do you realize you may never see them again? These beautiful children—your own flesh and blood—might end up as servants, cocottes, or worse. Do you really want that?"

Anatine doesn't respond. She kneels to wipe the girls' tears, murmuring empty reassurances about visiting them in Saint Louis. The girls cling to her out of desperation, their tiny hands shaking as they wave goodbye to Louisinette.

Unable to bear the sight, Louisinette mounts her burro, her chest tight with sorrow. As she fades into the dense foliage, she hears their cries echo behind her, the weight of their pleas settling deep in her soul.

At the water's edge, Louisinette peers across the river and spots Georgette sprawled atop her mule under a fig tree, waiting. Panic rises in her chest. She hastily pulls her burro into the foliage, hiding out of sight. Minutes later, the sound of footsteps crunching through the leaves jolts her. From between the trees, she sees Anatine's silhouette leading her daughters to the riverbed.

The girls no longer resist. Shoulders slumped, faces blank, they shuffle like prisoners resigned to their fate. Louisinette's heart aches as she watches their small, fragile bodies moving forward, burdened by a cruel reality they cannot yet comprehend.

From their side of the bank, the girls peer across the mighty Acajou River, where it bends around its rocky bed. The jolly voices of children swimming near the river basin waft toward them, mingling with the chatter of cheery parents washing clothes at the river's edge and the splashing of silvery young mullets congregating in the shallows. For this fleeting moment, the girls feel a violent urge to shed the burdens of their reality, to race downriver and join their fellow Haitian children in what seems like infinite merriment. But their fleeting hope is crushed by the weight of their mother's firm grip. They know they will never belong to such a world again.

Anatine's shivering hands hold theirs as they wade through the cool, gurgling water in silence. At the far bank, the girls let go, their hands falling limp at their sides. They do not look back. Louisinette sees the truth in their hollow eyes: their childhood, their innocence, their love for life—all extinguished in one devastating moment.

Georgette emerges from her hiding place and mounts her mule with practiced indifference. Anatine lifts each girl and places them in front of the tall woman. Without a word, Georgette strikes her mule and gallops off, disappearing into the towering trees. Anatine stands frozen, her arms hanging limply at her sides, her vacant eyes fixed on the fading figures of her daughters.

The wind rises, whipping against her weathered body. Her legs buckle, and she collapses to the ground, shaking with a mixture of shame and despair. She remains there for several moments before dragging herself across the river and vanishing into the verdant grove, her head drooping as though the weight of the world has crushed her spirit.

Louisinette watches from her hiding spot, fury and sorrow roiling in her chest. Rage bubbles to the surface—she imagines grabbing Anatine, shaking her, and hurling her into the river. How could a mother do this? How could she abandon her children to such a fate? But an internal voice reminds her, soft but unrelenting: *She's a victim, too.*

Tears spill down Louisinette's cheeks as she struggles to reconcile her anger with the painful truth. She sobs, her whole-body quivering, trying to release the searing pain lodged in her soul.

When Anatine finally disappears from view, Louisinette retakes the trail. The weight of what she has witnessed presses heavy on her heart, but she pushes forward. There is no time to wallow—she must get home, and she must prepare for the fight Céline has promised.

<u>*C h a p t e r   1 4*</u>

After her memorable promenade in eastern Saint Louis, Céline returns home buoyant with renewed strength and hope. In Ludovic, she has found the companion she longed for—a partner with shared values, charm, and unwavering resolve. His presence fills her with the determination to confront Dalambert and others like him. For the first time in years, she feels a spark of true possibility.

Back on the balcony, Céline watches pedestrians along Main Street, her gaze unfocused. The earlier oppressive heat has given way to a refreshing salty breeze, and the slowing traffic lends a tranquil rhythm to the afternoon. Below, Solitude busies herself in the kitchen, preparing cashew nuts with an eager attention to detail. Céline's warmth and respect have made an impression on Solitude, who treasures her kindness as a rarity in this household.

"Mademoiselle, dinner's ready! Come get it while it's warm; or if you want, I'll take it upstairs to you," Solitude calls, her voice bright as it floats up the stairs.

"I'll be down in a few—no need to bring it up," Céline replies, her attention held captive by a bulky man trudging along Main Street toward her house. His tinted glasses conceal his eyes, but his deliberate strides suggest purpose. A wrinkled newspaper swings in his left hand while his right rests in his pocket. The sunlight glistens on his bald forehead, emphasizing his muscular frame under a thin white undershirt.

As the man nears the edge of Rue Vincent, Céline leans forward, tension creeping into her limbs. Before she can make sense of his approach, a voice rings out from a shoe store nearby. "Hey, you! Over here!" A slim woman with unkempt hair and a gap-toothed smile gestures at the man, interrupting his steady progress.

"Monsieur Dalambert!" a woman's regal voice calls from across the street. Dalambert doesn't stop but flashes a grotesque smile—his decaying teeth gleaming behind greasy, cracked lips.

On the balcony, Céline freezes. Her legs tremble as though they've lost all strength. She stumbles from her chair and bolts downstairs, nearly colliding with Solitude in the kitchen.

"Lock all the doors!" she gasps, clutching her chest. "Now!"

"What's wrong, mademoiselle?" Solitude's eyes widen, alarmed.

"Just do it! And hurry!"

Without hesitation, Solitude rushes to lock the front gate while Céline slams the back door shut, pulling down the curtains. They retreat to the center of the house, sitting at the foot of the stairs. Céline grips her knees, her breaths shallow. Solitude watches her, fear creeping into her own heart.

The pounding starts—a fist hammering against the wrought-iron gates. The sound reverberates through the house, relentless. Céline grips Solitude's hand. "Don't move," she whispers. Minutes drag, each knock a brutal assault on the door until silence. Céline peers through the blinds to see Dalambert storming off, his broad back retreating toward the square.

"Never open the door for him," Céline says in a firm tone of voice. "Not if you're here alone."

"But…why?" Solitude stammers, her voice rising in confusion. "I've seen him here before."

Céline's face darkens. "I'll explain later. Just trust me."

Solitude frowns but nods, following Céline to the kitchen. "Did you grill the cashew nuts?" Céline asks, attempting to shift the conversation.

"Yes, mademoiselle. But eat your dinner first—it's getting cold."

Céline forces a small smile and sits at the table. As she piles rice, beans, and chicken onto her plate, she glances at Solitude. "Do you live nearby?"

"Not really. It's about a forty-five-minute walk. That's why I leave early."

"That's far. Why don't you take a *camionette* home?"

Solitude sighs. "I can't afford it."

Céline pauses mid-bite. "I'll cover the fare from now on."

Solitude's eyes widen. "Thank you, Mademoiselle."

"Don't tell my parents," Céline breathes.

"I won't. Madame's words to me are few, anyway," Solitude says, her tone low.

Céline nods, as if confirming something she already suspected. "And my father?"

"He's always busy with work. But last week, he was in a good mood. I made him *pisket* with white rice—his favorite. He gave me five *goud* and said it was delicious."

Céline smiles, but her mind remains clouded by Dalambert's return.

Without a word, Solitude heads into the kitchen and returns with a porcelain bowl of nuts, placing it on the table. Céline pushes aside her untouched dinner and begins eating the nuts, her mind elsewhere. Solitude walks to a small room near the kitchen, untying her apron. The sound of Céline's crunching fills the silence.

"Mademoiselle Céline, it's getting late. I need to leave before the werewolves catch me wading across the Saint Louis River," Solitude jokes, her laughter light and airy.

"You'd better get going," Céline replies. She unzips her purse and hands Solitude fifteen *goud*. "Take a *camionette*. At this hour, the fare might be lower."

"*Merci*, mademoiselle," Solitude beams, tucking the money away. She unlocks the back door and steps out into the night.

Céline is left alone in the cavernous house. The last rays of sunlight bleed into the horizon, shifting from yellow to crimson before dissolving into the thick gray clouds gathering above. Twilight descends with a tropical intensity, but for Céline, the evening feels heavy, oppressive. Dalambert's grotesque smile looms in her mind, a haunting specter. She cannot shake the thought of Louisinette and the unspeakable violation she endured.

Céline shoves the bowl of nuts away, appetite gone. Taking it with her, she climbs the stairs to her bedroom, where she leans against the bedpost, restless and uneasy. Peering through the window, she watches as darkness settles over the quiet street. A dim streetlamp near the gate casts a pale glow onto her face before she draws the curtain shut with a quick motion. Alone, the weight of the evening presses harder.

"I hope Solitude makes it home safely," she whispers into the stillness, sliding under the covers. But sleep eludes her. Thoughts of Dalambert claw at her mind, intertwining with flashes of Ludovic—his confident smile, his gentle touch, his boyish charm. Against her better judgment, his image softens her turmoil, stirring a bittersweet ache she cannot suppress.

"This man wants to set my heart on fire," she mutters, half in exasperation. But she knows she's lying to herself. Ludovic's goodbye lingers in her thoughts, an unshakable memory that makes her chest tighten.

"Can I mix love with the fight for justice?" she wonders aloud. "What will Louisinette gain if Ludovic becomes part of my life? Will he truly stand by me when I tell him about the crime?"

The questions tumble through her mind, leaving her more uncertain. She stretches out on her back, hands behind her neck, her golden hair spilling over the pillow's edge. A fleeting sense of longing takes root, not enough to ease her despair, but enough to hint at the possibility of something more.

Squeaking noises from downstairs jolt Céline into reality. Startled, she jumps out of bed, her heart racing. "Mother?" she calls out.

"Yes, it's me, Céline. Where are you?" Bernadine's voice echoes up the stairway, followed by Jean-Foreste's footsteps.

Céline steps to the top of the stairs, her reverie disrupted. "I thought you were out of town," she stammers.

"How could we leave without our princess?" Jean-Foreste teases, his laughter warm and hearty.

Bernadine brushes past him, her tone brisk. "I saw the dinner table. You ate so little of your food, Céline. I told Solitude to keep it warm for you."

"I ate some nuts instead. Solitude grilled them for me before she left."

"Nuts before dinner?" Bernadine scoffs, shaking her head as she strides toward the master bedroom. Céline trails behind, finding her parents settling in—their familiar routines as comforting as they are exasperating.

All three are now in the master bedroom. Céline sinks into a double sofa on the opposite side of the king-sized bed, facing her parents. Jean-Foreste, dressed in shiny navy-blue pajamas, leans against the headboard with a book in hand, his bare feet resting on the antique Tabriz Persian rug. Bernadine paces to the corner of the room, pulling her bedclothes from the mahogany wardrobe. She flicks on the gold-trimmed ceiling fan, its blades whirring with a low hum in the evening air.

Above the bed hangs a framed portrait of Bernadine and Jean-Foreste in their youth. He is dashing in a crisp white suit and black bowtie, while Bernadine's cheetah-print dress and bold jewelry exude glamour. She leans against him, his arms encircling her trim waist.

"Papa, you never age!" Céline gushes, gesturing toward the portrait. "I look at you now, and it's like nothing has changed."

Jean-Foreste chuckles. "No fundamental differences, eh? But there are a few."

Bernadine turns, holding a pink nightgown. "The differences are real, believe me," Céline says, cutting her off with a grin.

"I knew you'd say that," Bernadine retorts, shedding her outfit to reveal her softened, time-worn figure. "I've been talking to your dad about a new diet. A friend uptown swears by it."

"And does this diet lead to the Fountain of Youth?" Céline teases, trying to suppress her laughter.

"It might not take me there," Bernadine replies with a mock sigh, "but it will bring me back to where my love started."

"Where's that?"

"In L'EsterDéré, near the mouth of Rivière-des-Barres."

At this, Jean-Foreste's head snaps up. He sets his book down, his face lighting with amusement. "You've got it wrong, *chérie.*"

"What do you mean?" she asks, a teasing glint in her narrowing eyes.

"We didn't meet in L'EsterDéré. It was in Madame Marcel's backyard. You were chatting with Eugenie and Ilna. The moment I walked up, you froze, and I had to coax you into shaking my hand."

Bernadine raises an eyebrow, smirking. "Perhaps, but it was in L'EsterDéré that we shared our first kiss."

"And where was I during all this?" Céline interjects, feigning indignation.

"In outer space!" her parents chorus, bursting into laughter.

"Papa, I went up to Sou Fò today," Céline says, changing the conversation.

"So, what did our wandering daughter see in Sou Fò today?" Jean-Foreste teases her.

"It was...strange," Céline murmurs, her tone shifting. She recounts the unsettling emptiness, the deserted streets, and the faint hum of a radio playing Christian music. Her parents exchange glances, their amusement fading as they sense Céline's unease.

"Well," Bernadine says, smoothing her pink nightgown, "it's that time of year. People shelter from the heat."

"Maybe," Céline says, her gaze distant. "But it felt like something more."

"When we left Derrière Rue this evening, we met Dalambert," Jean-Foreste says, his tone edged with concern. "He said he came here to bring me an important document earlier this afternoon. He told me he knocked on the front gates, but there was no response. He said he saw you on the balcony, but when he reached the front, the gates were sealed."

"Really?" Céline questions, her heart thudding. She hesitates before deciding to lie. "I was here, and I swear I heard nothing. This man, he still comes here?"

"Yeah, every so often…why?" Her parents exchange puzzled glances, their curiosity piqued.

"Nothing…" Céline mumbles, springing to her feet and strolling out of the room."

In the kitchen, she pulls open the fridge and grabs a ripe mango *Jone*. She sits at the dinner table, biting into the fruit, but the sweetness turns bitter on her tongue. Dalambert's towering figure, his icy gaze, floods her mind, stealing away her appetite. In frustration, she hurls the mango into the trash, its flesh splattering against the can's rim.

Her fingers drum the tabletop as her thoughts churn. She must keep Dalambert away from the house, yet fear paralyzes her. Would her parents even believe her if she told them the truth? Or would they dismiss her concerns, justifying his actions as insignificant because Louisinette was a *restavèk*?

Her anxiety crescendos. She rises, pacing to the refrigerator, yanking out a bottle of Haitian Barbancourt rum. From a nearby cabinet, she retrieves a silver-lined cup, filling it to the brim. A sharp squeeze of lemon completes the drink. Céline gulps it down, the sour sting biting her lips. The alcohol burns its way through her, dulling her fear but not her anger.

Desperate to erase any evidence of her indulgence, she washes the cup and stashes the rum back in the fridge. Her legs unsteady, she stumbles up the stairs. Exhaustion and intoxication weigh her down. She collapses onto her bed, her body limp and fully clothed. As her consciousness fades, her fears remain, coiled and waiting in the depths of her troubled dreams.

<u>*Chapter 15*</u>

Since they last met, Louisinette has not heard or seen anything further from Céline. That one dramatic visit, however, was enough to turn her entire life upside down. Nowadays, she is consumed by trouble, haunted by disturbance, and unable to get her mind off her horrifying, wretched past.

Added to this nightmarish condition is an inability to share her ordeals with anyone. She dreads the prospects of letting her beloved husband know how she feels, tempted to call out to him many times, especially at night as she buries her face in his gentle side. But her lips freeze solid, and she falls mute.

She fears that Victorin, the only other person with whom she could talk about such a sensitive matter, might misunderstand, or even shun her. Haitian men are inherently *macho* by nature; their actions are sometimes unpredictable. She chooses silence over confiding the graphic details of her rape to Victorin, fearing it would only worsen the anguish she already suffers at home, despite needing his moral and emotional support.

Nonetheless, she sees her loving husband as her most sincere companion and soulmate. When she met him five years ago, she told him she was not searching for a "care provider," or someone driven by sympathy for her deplorable condition rather than the honesty of shared love. So, she only gave Victorin a brief, token account of her story, so broadly drawn and vague that it could do no harm to his feelings. Now, beyond her newfound thirst for revenge against Dalambert, her biggest challenge is winning over and firing up Victorin for their righteous struggle for justice.

Will her husband be as committed, as eager and ready as she is, to making any needed sacrifices to achieve her ultimate aims? Or will she position herself on a collision course with Victorin, risking losing the husband, life, and home she has worked so hard to maintain?

Her sexual drive has substantially dwindled since Céline's visit; through the shadow of each man she encounters, including her husband, she hallucinates the awful face of Dalambert lurching to get her. Therefore, her every day is consumed by fear, nervousness, and hatred.

It is now Friday, and dusk is falling. The sun has already sunk beneath the sky-high mountains. A lone bird tweets from a young mango tree in the backyard, provoking a frenzy of clucking from a flock of gossipy hens, roosting on the branches for another tropical night. Standing in the shadows of her back door, Louisinette sticks her head out to survey the yard. Peeking, she notices the last red-orange-yellow rays of the setting sun locked in their final struggle against nighttime. Her thoughts still tangled with the weight of unspoken truths, Louisinette moves to the small table and lights the gas lamp. Its warm glow flickers over the bare walls, but it cannot pierce the shadow gathering inside her heart.

Victorin has not shown up yet from his daily job at the farm. She knows every Friday he works just a half-day. He returns home at midday to rest, eat and be ready for his Friday night *djouba*, a popular, rustic festivity among peasants in the mountains. Tonight, though, his absence felt like a crack in her fragile world.

The children have taken their baths, resting for the night on their little bunk beds, cross-legged and butt-naked, eating yucca pudding out of an aluminum bowl. Louisinette ensures they stay there, away from the dirt floor. However, she is growing more restless.

"Where is Victorin?" she murmurs, pacing the floor, her voice a faint thread over the rising hum of crickets. The question hangs in the air, unanswered, as her gaze drifts toward the horizon, searching for any sign of him. Her sandals crackle underfoot at each step she makes, hair spilling from a blue headscarf. Her loose headscarf shifts as she paces, her movements driven by unease, strands of hair escaping like her untamed thoughts. The soft fabric of her white nightgown clings to her trembling form, a pale silhouette under the dim glow of the gas lamp.

Unable to wait for her man within the frame of the cottage, she eases the door open, stepping outside as her white, puffy nightgown floats like clouds in the evening breeze.

In gigantic strides, Louisinette makes her way to the steppingstones leading to the main trail. Her eyes scan the country road as darkness descends, swallowing the remnants of twilight and the serene hues of the crepuscule. For a few moments, she stands motionless, her heart pounding in rhythm with the whispers of the lime-green foliage swaying in the night breeze. She listens, every nerve attuned, hoping the quiet stillness will deliver the tender sound of Victorin's familiar footsteps rushing up from the gorge.

Disappointment floods her chest as no such sound comes. Just as she turns to slink back to the cottage, the clatter of hooves and muffled human voices break the silence. Her heart surges with renewed hope. "Victorin!" she calls out, racing back to the shadowy road.

"No, Madame Louisinette, it's just us!" two young men yell as one, guiding their cow down the ravine trail for overnight grazing.

Startled but recovering in an instant, she steps closer to them. Her simple heart settles as she recognizes one of the boys holding the leash: Jean-Michel, the son of a friend from the foothills.

"Jean-Michel! I thought it was Victorin. He left early this morning at the first crow of a rooster, and I've been waiting for him," she says, her voice becoming gentler as she comes closer.

Jean-Michel chuckles. "Dad hasn't come home, either. He said he was helping clear a maize field in Morne Lecturne. Probably the same place your husband's at."

Relieved, she smiles, shooing the boys along. "Hurry now and get home!"

Reassured, Louisinette jogs back to her cottage. Inside, she finds her two boys sprawled on the floor, playing with the empty aluminum bowl from earlier, their shirts smeared with traces of yucca pudding. Upon spotting their mother, they leap back into bed, their giggles full of innocent naughtiness. But their antics leave a mess of tangled bedsheets and two little faces in need of cleaning.

"Lamizè! Didn't I tell you to watch after your brother? You're the older one—you should know better!" she scolds.

"Sorry, Mommy. He doesn't listen!" Lamizè defends himself, his eyes pleading for forgiveness.

Sighing, she shepherds the boys outside to the makeshift bath-stand, a simple flooring of three wooden planks. Under the cool evening air, she scrubs their faces, feet, and little behinds until they sparkle. Back inside, she tucks them into bed, their snores filling the small room like clockwork.

After a moment, Louisinette retreats to a low chair in the far corner, waiting for Victorin. The quiet allows her mind to wander, reflecting on how much her husband means to her and wondering how she could ever survive without him. Resting her bushy head against the wall, she drifts into a fitful sleep. But every time her eyelids fall, the cruel face of Dalambert invades her dreams, chasing away any peace she might find.

An hour later, the back door creaks open. Louisinette jolts awake as Victorin limps inside, his shirt caked in muddy-red dirt from Morne Lecturne.

"What happened?" she asks, rushing to his side.

"I stubbed my foot on a tree trunk near the ravine trail," Victorin replies, wincing but managing a faint smile.

"Let me see!" She crouches, examining his swollen leg. Her probing fingers make him wince.

"Ow—easy!" he protests, catching his breath.

"Sit down. I'll get some hot water, rubbing salt, and a clean rag. But first, you need a bath. You smell like a wild goat!" she teases, grinning as she guides him to a chair.

"Yes, Nurse," he quips, slinging an arm around her shoulders and stealing a sloppy kiss. She laughs, her giggle a mere murmur, a rare and welcome sound in their humble home. Peeling off his dirty shirt, she prepares to nurse her husband back to health.

"Stay put. I'll heat your food and get water for your bath," she says, sprinting outside to light the cook fire, her movements quick and full of purpose.

*****

Later that night, they lie sprawling abed, lined up alongside each other. Victorin is weather-beaten and dog-tired, but his throbbing foot stops him from falling asleep. Louisinette, her head laid upon his naked chest, her restlessness mirroring his, her churning mind seeking shelter from the demons invading their solitude. The quiet of the night is broken by Louisinette's soft and hesitant voice.

"Honey, I've been thinking I have to go to Saint Louis soon," she murmurs, lowering her voice to avoid awakening the children.

"Whatever for?" Groaning, he pulls her closer to his heart.

"I need to see…Céline."

"I've been thinking about it, too." His tone is warm but less serious than hers, his hand wandering through her curls. He tousles her hair, loosening her headscarf and letting her locks scatter about the skimpy pillows.

She sighs, holding his hand. "Since the last time she was here, I haven't been able to get a good night's sleep. It's like she opened a door I tried to lock forever. All the bad memories of my younger years, especially what was done to me almost six years ago, have come rushing back."

Victorin's fingers still, his brows furrowing. "If you go to town, how do you let Céline know you're there?"

"I'll find a way."

He stares hard at his wife, his expression a mix of worry and resignation. "When do you plan to go?"

"This coming Wednesday."

"You know I hate the idea of you traveling alone," he says, his grip tightening around her. But he exhales, a long breath, knowing her mind is already made up. "Just promise me you'll be careful."

"Hey, I told you when we met that you're not my caretaker. Don't worry, I'll be all right. Besides, you need to rest your foot.

You'll be home for a while, so I won't need to ask our neighbor to watch the kids."

With a reluctant stare, Victorin nods; that is all Louisinette hopes for, to begin activating her game plan. With that, she shuts her eyes, straining to sleep amidst a world of nightmares, injustices, and daily wrongs, as Victorin wraps his ever-loving arms around her.

<u>*Chapter 16*</u>

At ten o'clock in the morning, the golden sun balloons, clawing its way toward its zenith, flexing its vaulting strength over Saint Louis. Yet, the relentless heat cannot pierce the exotic garden of the Bodins' estate, where fruit trees cast cooling shadows over the backyard and the bungalow.

Solitude sits by the kitchen table near the open back door, her low chair creaking as she leans forward, peeling lima beans for the afternoon meal. The soft thuds of each bean falling into a stainless-steel bowl punctuate the tranquil morning. The discarded shells pile in a nearby wastebasket, rustling under her swift movements. Her calico dress, worn but clean, swishes against her ankles as it cascades to the floor. Breezes, gentle but persistent, tease the tattered brim of her straw hat. Tied by a thin cotton string, it grazes her shoulders, but Solitude—unbothered—keeps her focus on her task.

A knock breaks the quiet. It comes from the back gates—firm, unexpected, and insistent. Solitude stiffens, her hands pausing mid-motion. Madame Bernadine and Monsieur Jean-Foreste are away at their jewelry store, busy haggling with customers in search of treasures. Upstairs, Céline sits on the balcony, engrossed in a novel as her rocking chair sighs a creak in the rhythm of her movements.

The knocking continues. Solitude hesitates, uneasy about leaving her task to face the unknown visitor. She recalls Céline's warning about Dalambert and feels her apprehension rise.

Gathering her courage, Solitude places the lima beans aside and hurries upstairs.

"Mademoiselle," she says in a hushed, urgent tone, "someone is knocking at the back door. Should I go see who it is?"

Céline looks up from her novel, her expression shifting from curiosity to mild concern. With a sigh, she rises, leaving the book open on the seat of her chair. "No, wait," she says, brushing off her skirt. "I'll come with you. I'm curious to see who's knocking at this hour."

The two women descend together, their steps quickened by growing anticipation. As they near the gates, Céline's anxiety ebbs when she peers through the gate-hole. Standing on the other side is Ludovic, his impeccable posture illuminated by the blazing sun.

"Ludovic," Céline breathes, her voice dropping into a playful, timid purr. A warm smile blooms across her face as she unlatches the gate.

"Bonjour," she says, her tone soft yet tinged with delight.

"Bonjour, mesdames," Ludovic greets them with a slight cough and a charming grin. He stands tall and composed, dressed in a tailored dark blue suit. A cotton necktie, well knotted, completes his polished look, while his black shoes gleam as if reflecting the very sunlight.

A touch of color rises in Céline's cheeks as she takes in his stylish presence. She steps back to allow him in, giving Solitude a light nudge aside.

"This is Solitude, our new housemaid," Céline says, introducing her companion.

Ludovic nods with courteous charm. "Enchanted to meet you, dear Solitude," he says, his tone rich with warmth as he regards her with an admiring glance.

Solitude, flustered but delighted, offers a shy smile. "Me too, monsieur," she replies before retreating to the kitchen, her chores pulling her back into their steady rhythm.

The pair strolls toward the bungalow, where Céline invites Ludovic to sit. However, the gusting wind over the courtyard disrupts any chance of a relaxed and constructive chat. She gestures toward a guest room near the patio. Ludovic, cheerful, follows her inside.

Once there, he removes his tailored jacket—a checkered black-and-ivory wool creation with gleaming ivory buttons—and drapes it over the headrest of an armchair. The Christian Dior label, embroidered in cursive with neon-blue thread, catches the light at the edge of his sleeves. A subtle trace of Vent Vert cologne lingers, blending with the airy ambiance of the room.

"Why are you so dressed up in the middle of the week, strutting about under the blazing summer sun?" Céline teases, her gaze locking onto his magnetic eyes with the intensity of a curious interrogator.

"It's nothing extraordinary. I just came from a funeral at the Catholic church—for an old and dear friend," Ludovic replies, loosening his necktie. Rolling his shirt sleeves past his elbows, he crosses one leg over the other and faces Céline with an easy smile. Moments later, Solitude enters with a large bowl of roasted cashew nuts, offering them with a polite dip of her head.

"That's so kind of you, Solitude!" Ludovic says, his voice full of warmth, grabbing a hearty handful and tossing the nuts into his mouth with the glee of a carefree commoner. Céline, amused by his antics, picks a few herself, sliding closer for a more relaxed sharing of the bowl.

"You know, there's something more important than roasted nuts I'd like to share," Céline says, her tone low and deliberate. Her posture shifts; in a single fluid motion, she angles her poised figure to face him directly.

"What is it, my dear?" Ludovic asks, his curiosity sparked.

"It might not mean much to you, but it's been weighing heavily on me since I returned from Europe. I believe I can trust you to help me sort this out."

"Of course, Céline. You can count on me. Tell me what's troubling you."

Setting the bowl of nuts on a nearby cherry lamp table, Céline inches even closer, as if seeking a tangible sense of security in his presence. Her voice softens, laden with hesitation. "Remember I told you about the young maid who used to work here? The one I mentioned I was visiting behind the mountains when we met on the country road?"

"Yes. The injured lady. I recall you saying she had suffered terribly."

Céline pauses, her gaze distant for a moment before refocusing on him. "She was raped. That assault left her pregnant. When my parents found out, they threw her out of our house."

Ludovic's face tightens in disbelief. "Did your parents know she was raped?" His voice is steady, but a trace of horror lingers beneath it.

"No," Céline admits, her words dropping like lead. "The truth is even worse. The man who violated her...was one of my father's closest friends."

Ludovic recoils slightly, his eyes searching hers for answers. "And no one knew?"

"No one. Not for five years," Céline utterers, her voice trembling with the burden of suppressed rage. "The rapist, the girl, and I were the only ones who knew. It was her courage that broke the silence when I visited her last week, after such a long pause. And now…I can't ignore this. She's seeking justice, and I've vowed to help her get it."

"You're right. But who is this disgusting man, this rapist *pig*?" Ludovic demands, his voice tinged with disbelief.

"Laurent Dalambert."

"What?" Ludovic reels back, his expression a mix of shock and disgust. "That pompous fraud? The man who struts around with a book in hand, preaching justice as though he's the moral compass of this town? Unbelievable!"

"But it's true," Céline replies. "The real question is: how do we make him pay?"

"Dalambert," Ludovic growls, "is a filthy, monstrous hypocrite. To bring him down, we'll need to rally the community. This has to be a public fight."

"That's what I've been thinking. But I can't do this without somehow hurting my parents."

"Well," Ludovic begins, a bit cautious, "your parents aren't likely to support you going to war over a *restavèk*, especially when the target is one of their oldest friends. Are you sure you're ready for this?"

"Oh, I am!" Céline declares, her eyes burning with resolve. "I know how they'll react at first. They'll be angry, maybe even humiliated. But once they see my determination, they'll have no choice but to stand with me—or risk isolating themselves from everything decent. This fight is bigger than their social circle."

Ludovic considered, a look of contemplation on his face. "You're right. But don't underestimate the resistance. This is class warfare, Céline. People like our parents don't think justice belongs in the streets. They see activism as something for the poor and uneducated, not for people like us."

Céline's jaw tightens. "That may be so, but justice for Louisinette can't wait for their approval."

"I agree," Ludovic replies. "If we want justice for Louisinette—and it's Louisinette, right?"

"Yes."

"Then she must play the central role in this fight. Without her visible involvement, we'll struggle to gain support. People won't trust us."

"I was planning to involve her, just not so soon..." Céline hesitates, her voice trailing off.

"What were you expecting to do? Convince Dalambert to confess and repent?" Ludovic asks, his tone sharp and incredulous.

"No! Never!" Céline retorts, visibly shaken. "I want nothing to do with that man."

"Then we need to act without delay," Ludovic insists. His eyes flash with determination, signaling his full commitment. "Louisnette has to be involved from the start. Otherwise, this fight will never gain momentum."

"You're right," Céline concedes, her voice steadying. "I'll go to the mountains this Friday to speak with her. But it won't be easy."

"What do you mean?" Ludovic leans forward, his focus unwavering.

"She has a husband and two young children," Céline explains. "I don't know if her husband will support her joining a fight like this. And let's face it: there's always a risk. If anything happens to Louisinette, her family will pay the price."

Ludovic's face darkens as he absorbs her words. "The risks are real," he admits. "But so is the urgency. We can't let fear paralyze us. Justice demands action."

Céline agrees, her resolve deepening. "I'll find a way to convince her—and her family. We have no other choice."

"I understand where you're coming from. When I said we needed Louisinette, I didn't mean to place her physically at the forefront of the struggle. However, we must utilize her name and her words. That will be enough for the people in town to identify with our cause. My biggest question is whether she has a total willingness to seek justice."

"Yes, she is…I'm sure of it! Though I'm uncertain she's quite prepared for a fight just yet. We'll see. I know for a fact that righteous anger still lives and breathes in her heart. I could feel her pain gathering in the agonized emotions of her voice as she told me her story. One cannot see or hear her tale of teenage woe without feeling for her," Céline replies, her voice firm with conviction.

"Would you like for me to go with you on Friday?" Ludovic asks.

Céline pauses, her expression shifting into a thoughtful pout. "I don't think it's necessary."

"It'd be a wonderful opportunity to introduce me to her. That way, I won't be a total stranger when she comes to town."

"Okay," Céline concedes after a moment of reflection. "But we have to depart early, and I'd rather walk this time instead of riding on horseback like before."

"Sounds like a plan," Ludovic agrees, a soft smile lighting up his face.

Shaking hands, the two share a few more moments of easy conversation. In the end, Ludovic stands, grabbing his fine, tailored jacket and folding it over his arm. Céline rises as well, accompanying him to the gates. There, they exchange a warm hug goodbye. As Ludovic's figure recedes down the street,

Céline lingers for a moment, watching him until he vanishes from view.

She strolls back to the canopy, her steps slower, contemplative. Sinking into the lounge chair, she lies back, hands folded behind her head, staring up at the swaying branches above. The interplay of resolve and affection swirling in her heart is not lost on her. Justice for Louisinette looms ahead, but Ludovic's presence adds an undeniable, complicating layer to her thoughts.

Ludovic's gentlemanly fashions, his solemn expression of frankness, and his proud, graceful bearing—these immaterial qualities, intangible as they may be, are steadily stealing Céline's heart. She lies supine, dreaming as if imprisoned by her own feelings. *Love is such a complicated enterprise*, she muses, her mind circling the paradox of yearning and restraint. The fear of compromising her virtue at such a critical time, when her focus must remain on seeking justice for Louisinette, clashes with the undeniable pull she feels toward Ludovic—a man she knows just a little yet cannot seem to ignore.

She tells herself there is a fine line between true love and the circumstantial infatuations that sometimes masquerade as it. Holding her ground against Ludovic's charms, she decides, is the best way to safeguard her independence. Yet the submissive and peremptory effects of love, as she has observed in others, chill her to the core. They fill her with a mounting sense of dread, a fear of losing herself to the monopolizing emotions that deepen hearts with a careless sadness—a solitude she has long recognized in the eyes of her friends and old classmates in town.

Seeking calm, her thoughts drift to the long journey ahead with Ludovic, a trip that will take them alone through forest-covered hillsides, pristine creeks, babbling rivers, and enchanted valleys. It could be a romantic adventure, the kind that stirs hearts and etches memories. Yet she feels herself fighting a two-pronged battle: resisting the wave of emotion Ludovic ignites in her while keeping him close enough to help her secure justice for Louisinette.

The idea of balancing these conflicting goals makes her feel mischievous, even sly, toward someone she suspects she is falling for. *But that's not who I am*, she fusses inwardly, proud of her moral grounding. Ludovic, with his keen intellect and unyielding strength, is no easy match for the treacherous game of love and courtship. *What if our relationship doesn't last, should I decide to surrender to his charms?* she wonders, a thread of doubt tugging at her resolve.

"I'd rather cherish forever a love song that may never reach its climax than risk losing my soul in an everlasting nightmare," she bursts out aloud, the words reverberating into the quiet air.

The echoes of Céline's voice seem to blast past the wind itself, only to remind her of Solitude's quiet presence in the kitchen nearby. Realizing she might have been overheard, Céline turns sideways on the lounger, resting her head against the spread-eagled seat, feigning to be sleep-talking.

Having never surrendered her soul to anyone before, she is daunted by the pull Ludovic exerts over her. The lines between companionship and intimacy blur when she is with him, as indistinct as the thickest morning fog. "If it were only the two of us on this earth," she grunts, adjusting her position, "we could reach out and touch the sky. We could live free from all forms of injustice that hover like shadows over this world."

Lost in thought, she fails to notice Solitude' soundless preparation of the dining table. It is only the clinking of silverware that jolts her from her ever-deepening trance.

"Solitude! I'm sorry; dinner's ready, right?" Céline asks, spreading her arms as she stretches and reenters the room's hallowed shadows.

"*Wi*, Mademoiselle Céline. I made sure you got your favorite dish."

"And what is that?" Céline asks, a hint of curiosity softening her voice.

"Cashews, of course, and chicken stew!" Solitude laughs, her glance bright as a lifted spoon.

"But you already gave me roasted cashews earlier," Céline protests, a hint of amusement in her voice.

"That wasn't served with lima beans and white rice. Besides," Solitude replies with a knowing grin, "I watched; you didn't eat it. Your friend did. Take a look at the lamp table."

"So, you've been eavesdropping on us?" Céline teases, an eyebrow raised.

"No, why would I do that?" Solitude retorts with mock indignation. "I was too busy getting dinner ready. Your father may show up any minute…he'll explode if the meal isn't ready. You know that, don't you?"

"I do," Céline admits, her tone softening again. "But for some reason, I don't have much of an appetite."

"What a dilemma! Maybe it can't be explained," Solitude remarks, her gaze shifting a bit, adopting an air of noble, peasant wisdom.

"What do you mean by that, Solitude?" Céline asks, amused by her maid's cryptic reply.

"When love steals a girl's heart, it sometimes takes her appetite with it," Solitude responds, her tone light yet teasing.

"Where are you coming from with this?" Céline laughs, half surprised and half amused.

"No place, Mademoiselle Céline!" Solitude replies, laughing along. "But right here, in this room, I can see the coyness in your demeanor, the way your eyes squint when you're near him. He's a fine young man—good-looking and well-mannered. You really have good taste."

"Really?" Céline erupts into uproarious laughter. She had not expected such remarks from Solitude, though they seemed to spill from her lips with surprising frequency. This interaction, like many others, reinforces Céline's growing realization: maids and *restavèk* are far from ignorant or dull. They observe, draw conclusions, and navigate the world with a wisdom often underestimated by others. Once again, Céline feels reminded that poverty is not an immutable curse but a social condition that demands change. She is also becoming more aware of the need to guard her gestures and emotions when near Ludovic.

Rising from her couch, Céline saunters into the dining room. She pulls out her chair and gazes at the table, laden with platters of Creole dishes. A tingling joy spreads through her, a gratifying pleasure as she prepares to savor the delicious food at this sumptuous table.

*****

Later that day, just before the sun sets, Céline makes her way uptown to visit Aunt Marguerite, her godmother. Crossing the bustling square en route to Derrière Rue, where Aunt Marguerite resides, Céline passes Chez Toussaint, the town's public elementary school. Along the way, she observes lines of wooden houses propped on posts and palisades, their corrugated metal roofs glinting in the waning sunlight. Children on both sides of the street chatter, laugh, and play games, their high-pitched voices mingling with the clatter of a vibrant evening. Some sit on highchairs on wide, open porches, their legs swinging idly as they watch the commotion.

Derrière Rue, narrower and shorter than Grande Rue, is the perfect place for an evening promenade. Tall royal palms cast shadows that stretch across the unpaved street, while shrubs of fragrant red hibiscus line the edges, adding a dash of vibrant color to the fading day. No vehicles pass by; the pedestrians have complete ownership of the street.

Céline walks with an elegant assertiveness that seems to command the attention of passersby. She wears a knee-length skirt paired with a crisp, white pleated short-sleeve shirt. A thin blue shawl drapes around her neck, adding a touch of grace. In one hand, she carries a folded parasol purse, her eyes fixed forward on the lively street scene.

Without warning, a shirtless boy astride a sorrel horse rushes past her, in full gallop. The horse's hooves clap against the red street pebbles, raising clouds of dirt and nearly knocking Céline's purse. Yet, unfazed by the commotion, Céline strides on, her poise unshaken—a serene elegance Ludovic has found so captivating.

Just before she reaches the gates of Aunt Marguerite's house, Céline spots Jessie Rosier, a dear friend from her school days with the Catholic nuns in Soufò. Jessie, lounging on the front porch of a friend's house, notices Céline as well. Their eyes meet, and Céline quickens her steps, rushing toward her. Jessie leaps from the porch and bounds over to greet her. They throw their arms around each other, laughing with unrestrained joy.

Arm in arm, the two friends make their way toward a vacant lot that buffers Aunt Marguerite's courtyard. Jessie's golden tan glows in the soft afternoon light, accentuating her natural radiance. She stands medium-tall—black heels, sharp as midnight, lifting her stride into sonnets. Hazel eyes. Brows— two brushstrokes. The light fractures into her laughter. She is dressed in an ivory-colored skirt embroidered with crimson patterns, complemented by a cerise bodice. The pin fastening it is tucked away, its color blending with her flawless complexion. A sensual smile graces her scarlet-painted lips, completing the picture of effortless elegance.

"How are things?" Céline asks, her voice laced with an impish giggle.

"Fine! I can't complain," Jessie replies, overjoyed. She pauses to beckon a young man lingering by Aunt Marguerite's back gates. He strides over, swift and sure, his well-built frame showcased in a starched white shirt and a crisp black bowtie pinned at the collar.

"Is he your charming prince?" Céline teases, a playful twinkle in her eyes.

Jessie giggles, brushing off the comment. "No, he's the president of CARLSS." She turns to the gentleman, who retrieves a thick leather wallet from the back pocket of his blue trousers.

"*Je suis* Jean-Claude," the young man announces with a warm smile, handing Céline a business card.

Her eyes scan the card: "*Club Artistique Littéraire et Sportif de Saint Louis (CARLSS)*"—the Artistic Athletic and Literary Club of Saint Louis. "Why are you both dressed to the nines on a weekday afternoon?" Céline asks, her curiosity heightened.

"We're hosting a presentation at the *Salle d'Oeuvres*," Jessie explains, her tone turning serious. "It's a play written by Jean-Mara Edouard, one of the best writers in the club."

"What's the title of this masterpiece?" Céline presses, ever inquisitive.

"*Quand la Pauvreté Disparaîtra un Jour,*" Jessie and Jean-Claude answer in unison. A Day When Poverty Becomes History.

"And when does this earth-shattering event start?" Céline grins, her playful demeanor undeterred.

"In a couple of hours," Jessie replies. "Most of these people passing by now are headed there."

"Let me visit Aunt Marguerite first," Céline says, nodding toward the gates. "I'll catch up with the crowd later. I hope to make it before the curtains rise."

"See you there!" Jessie calls out as Céline strides away, her parasol purse swinging with each step.

<u>*Chapter 17*</u>

On the first knock, a smiling young woman unlatches the gates, allowing Céline to step into a sprawling courtyard, lushly landscaped with a meticulously tended tropical garden. The woman, bare from the waist up, wraps herself in a white, fluffy towel, her feet slipping into clear plastic thong sandals. Freshwater droplets cascade down her square face and along her jawline, trickling over her firm, chocolate-toned shoulders and chest. She seems to have just stepped out of the shower.

Céline follows her along a gravel-paved walkway that winds through vibrant beds of crotons and crimson vincas. Further along, a miniature vineyard stretches beneath a canopy of dense green leaves, heavy clusters of purple grapes dangling tantalizingly toward the ground. The air is perfumed with the woven fragrances of citrus blossoms, as the final streaks of sunset dissolve behind the mountains. Every detail of the garden reflects masterful craftsmanship, creating a breathtaking sanctuary that captivates all who visit.

Though Céline is in a hurry, she cannot resist pausing beneath the verdant trellis of the vineyard. Drawn by its beauty, she plucks a cluster of grapes, savoring the burst of sweetness as one rolls between her lips and into her mouth. But the moment of delight is fleeting. The rhythmic footfalls of passersby echoing from the street outside remind her that she must not linger too long. She risks missing the much-anticipated play at the *Salle d'Oeuvres.*

Turning her attention back toward the house, she looks for the young woman who had opened the gate. The woman has vanished into the shadows of the interior, leaving the back door ajar. Céline moves toward it. Just as she is about to step inside, Aunt Marguerite appears in the doorway, her arms outstretched in a warm, theatrical greeting.

"*Bonsoir*, my dear!" Aunt Marguerite greets, her arms outstretched. Céline melts into the embrace, as if pouring fragrant oil into those welcoming arms. Their interlaced warmth rekindles memories of weekends spent with her beloved godmother, filling her heart with a bittersweet nostalgia.

Together, they stroll to the middle of the courtyard, where Aunt Marguerite pauses to pluck a sticky, bushy branch from a citronella plant she recently cultivated. She hands it to Céline with a knowing smile.

"You remember your favorite tea leaves?" Her hands settle on her sprawling hips, which overshadow her straightened, flat buttocks.

"Of course, I do," Céline replies, inhaling the soft, citrusy fragrance with a contented smile.

Time has reshaped Aunt Marguerite, her aristocratic bearing softened by age. Her belly and splayed feet lend her a matronly air, but she carries herself with the haughty poise of uptown Saint Louis women—an air of nonchalance that dismisses those she deems beneath her social standing. To women of equal class, however, she offers a warmth and attention befitting their shared pedigree.

A blue headscarf made from thick, grease-free Persian lamb wool drapes around her salt-and-pepper hair. Gold earrings brush against her honeyed, round face, making a delicate clink. Over her lavender button-down dress, she wears a silky black apron tied at her waist, an ensemble designed to camouflage her plump figure.

Céline's visit lifts her spirits, and her voice brightens. "Louise!" she calls, glancing toward the back door. When no reply comes, Aunt Marguerite's expression hardens, her forehead etched with irritation. "*Louise, oùestcette petite insolente?*" Where is that little impertinent girl?

With a guttural, sizzling French laced with biting profanity, she strides toward the back door.

"*Wi*, Aunt Margo. I was in the bedroom fixing my hair," Louise responds, pushing the door open as she hurries outside. "Aunt Margo" is the colloquial title bestowed on the formidable matron by most in town, a blend of familiarity and reverence.

"Didn't you hear me calling?" Aunt Marguerite snaps, her tone sharp enough to cut through the evening air.

"No, the door was closed," Louise replies, her gaze drifting north to avoid direct eye contact.

Blushed with brown powder, her youthful face sets in quiet defiance. She continues fixing her thick, dark hair with deliberate focus, undeterred by Aunt Margo's reprimands. Her burgundy taffeta dress with white horizontal stripes pairs faultlessly with clock-patterned pantyhose, adding a touch of sophistication. Despite her poised appearance, Louise radiates an unspoken resistance, making it clear she has no patience for slavish compliance.

Chuckling, Céline understands; but the smile on her face gives Aunt Margo little comfort as she continues her eccentric scolding. "You look really nice tonight," Céline compliments Louise, as if looking for an easy way to water down Aunt Margo's bursts of anger. Louise says nothing, making a little nod of acknowledgment. "It seems like all the young people in town have only one rendezvous tonight," Céline continues.

"*Yeah*…there's a play at the *Salle d'Oeuvres*," replies Aunt Margo. "Don't you hear the chatting, their footsteps outside in the street?"

"I met carloads of them on the way here. I also met Jessie, one of the organizers of the play."

Pursing her lips, Aunt Margo turns her attention to Louise. "Go inside, bring a plastic bag and stuff it with as many oranges as you can carry. *Hurry!*"

But Céline, putting out a gentle hand, halts her.

"No, Aunt Margo. I'll be back tomorrow to get them. Louise has to go. She's already dressed. I myself must leave; Jessie's invited me. Finish up please, Louise. I'm waiting for you so we can go together."

Louise dashes off, running straight to the back door. Aunt Margo and Céline remain outside, but Marguerite cannot hide the anger and embarrassment still lingering on her face. For four years, she has been ruling Louise's life without any signs of inquietude, and in exchange for her total obedience and seeming acceptance of such dehumanizing conditions, she offers the "gratitude" of bestowing upon her a little, tidy room and some second-hand clothes while expecting her to forever serve, both blindly and happily.

Absorbed by her clannish and arrogant lifestyle of upper-crust Haitian women, Aunt Margo does not realize that her world is changing. Unwitting and unacquainted with these changing realities, she is bewildered by the new talks and gossips going around town, especially among the elite during their lavish gatherings—talk of revolting *restavèk*, their hard-headed attitudes, their rejection of conditions they nowadays deem unacceptable to them.

Céline would like to explain to her godmother the complexities and the unpredictable reactions of marginalized and disenfranchised groups in society. A sudden urge to tell it all to Aunt Margo grips her mind. She wants to tell her that the plight of *restavèk* everywhere is only one and indivisible, coated in one color: darkness. A little gray here and there, but the dark alley stands endless, promising no light at the end of the tunnel. It is their indifference of this constant reality that is now triggering such half-awakening and common consciousness— stemming from their shared hardships in poverty, their grief, their joy, and their unspoken hope for a better future. Louisinette's ordeal flashes across Céline's mind. Then she remembers Ludovic's thoughts about the unrepentant souls of those who live in the exotic shades of utter luxury. So, she refrains herself. "I have to go, godmother," she mumbles.

"Aren't you waiting for Louise anymore?" Aunt Margo asks, a deep frown of unbridled disappointment moving across her wrinkled face.

"There she is!" Céline replies. Louise stands by the back door, dressed in that sparkling taffeta outfit, black purse clutched in one hand. You could witness on her face a sense of liberation, especially as she is headed to a venue where decent, outspoken advocacy on behalf of people like her will be put on artistic display before the general public.

Drawing closer, Céline hugs her godmother while kissing her goodbye. She walks to the gates, asking Louise to follow her. Just before she unhinges the latch, Céline recalls her long trip to Louisinette's place in the morning. She wheels around.

"When I said I'd be here tomorrow, I actually meant Sunday. Tomorrow, I have to see a friend out of town, and it'll be late when I come home. See you this Sunday!" she waves as a cheery farewell.

"I'll be waiting with your favorite rice pudding on the table," Aunt Margo sighs. Hands on her prodigious hips, she stands leaning against and among the vines, showing off her normal, dry sense of dominance.

Céline walks out as Louise trails behind. Outside they run into a dressed-to-the-teeth youthful horde, heading to the *Salle d'Oeuvres*, where in wistful longing their hopes for a better tomorrow will rise again. The throng of young women marches side by side down the dusty street, while Derrière Rue is on the verge of being submerged by the playgoers. Along with the tapping of footsteps, there is the chatting, smiling, and laughing of holly-jolly young folks, bemused by their own merriment.

When they reach the town's main square, Louise moves east toward the *Salle d'Oeuvres*, joining a group of *restavèk* going in the same direction, while Céline hurries home in the opposite course to get ready.

Chapter 18

About half an hour later, the front gates of the _Salle d'Oeuvres_ are completely overwhelmed. Every approach leading to the venue swells with eager crowds, a symbolic convergence of Saint Louis's youth with the spirited _restavèk_. Together, they seem to form an overdue alliance, unified in their desire to confront and rectify the wrongs committed by generations before them.

Controlled by the Catholic Church, the _Salle d'Oeuvres_ is a century-old edifice perched on a sparsely wooded hillside. The slope descends to the back gates of the church and its residential quarters. Constructed of ruddy clay bricks, the building offers an illusory air of Gothic elegance from afar. Its main entrance, a pair of unpainted, knotty double doors, swings open and is propped apart by large boulders on either side to resist the gusting winds sweeping through the hillside.

The roof, rusted corrugated metal like most of the town's modest homes and cottages, underscores its humble nature. Lacking modern amenities like air conditioning, the building relies on six rickety windows—three on each side—forever open to invite fresh air inside. Inside, backless wooden benches, rough and worn, provide seating for the arriving attendees. Eyes cannot help but draw to the stage at the front, where a pair of long, white flannel sheets hangs as makeshift curtains, concealing the set until the grand unveiling.

No vehicles can access the *Salle d'Oeuvres* directly, and its location is accessible only by three narrow alleyways. The main path extends from the town's central square, weaving through the courtyard of the church and onward to the venue's front gates. The two opposing back alleys link the affluent suburb of Sou Fò on the hilltop to a rocky trail that extends from Derrière Rue. These paths merge into a singular entry point, funneling streams of people eager to witness the evening's event.

Outside the building, three dense rows of dark, solemn faces stretch endlessly into the evening haze. At the front gates, a robust young man with a stiffly muscular frame stands, an imposing figure flanked by two young women dressed in matching blue overalls and red caps. The trio work without stopping, collecting tickets from eager playgoers, but the swarming masses soon overwhelm them. The *Salle d'Oeuvres*, bursting at its seams, has become the evening's prime destination, forcing the organizers into urgent action to prevent chaos.

With mounting urgency, the organizers instruct the gatekeepers to halt admissions while they deliberate a solution to the escalating situation. From the front porch, Father Bernadin, a Canadian Jesuit priest and head of the church's youth league, observes the restless, swelling crowd with growing alarm. Impatient youngsters, fearing exclusion, begin to surge toward the gates, threatening to break through.

In a single leap, Father Bernadin darts inside, heading backstage where he finds Jessie, the impresario and mistress of ceremonies; Jean-Mara, the playwright; Jean-Claude, the choreographer; and Ludovic, all huddled in a crucial strategy meeting.

"Father Bernadin!" they call out in unison. "We need your help!"

"You need a solution now, or this will spiral out of control," he warns, his lofty forehead furrowing with concern. His white soutane billows in the early evening breeze—a defiant flutter of order against the gathering storm.

"That's what we're trying to figure out, Father," Jessie replies, glancing at her watch with growing apprehension as the play's scheduled start time approaches.

"Why not let them into the courtyard?" the priest suggests, adjusting the buttons on his long cassock. "We can broadcast the play outside."

"That's it!" Jean-Mara exclaims. "We'll set up loudspeakers by the double doors so they can hear the dialogue and follow the action."

"We could also add a second performance," Ludovic proposes, his voice steady but his expression tense. "This play is too important to be remembered as the Evening of the Great Blunder."

"That's brilliant!" the group agrees.

Acting with speed, Father Bernadin returns to the gates, instructing the ticket-takers to allow the crowd in—just a few dozen at a time. The throng pours into the courtyard, but the rush soon becomes chaotic. A young girl stumbles and falls, narrowly avoiding a headlong collision with the pebbled path. Father Bernadin dives to her rescue, scooping her up just in time. The commotion rattles the gatekeepers, who abandon their posts as the crowd muscles its way through.

Within minutes, the *Salle d'Oeuvres* is completely packed, while the courtyard remains teeming with anxious attendees. With haste, twin loudspeakers are set up outside the entrance. Ludovic, a charismatic problem solver and close ally of Jean-

Mara, strides with confidence into the courtyard, gripping a microphone. His commanding presence cuts through the tension, preparing the crowd for a compromise that promises an unforgettable evening.

"Please, be patient! Everyone will get a chance to see the performance. CARLSS has decided to hold two sessions tonight. When Jean-Mara wrote this play, he had all of you in mind, believing no change can ever take place without your full participation. Remember, when poverty is finally uprooted like a blasted weed from this land, you will be the first to bear the fruits of economic and political freedom.

"So, let's show the rest of the country that Saint Louis's youth are indisputably the well-disciplined agents of change. This play will soon travel to other towns. Can we demonstrate to the world that *les Saint Louisiens* are the best-organized and most visionary of groups?" Ludovic's commanding voice resonates through the speakers, carrying his fervor to every corner of the crowded venue and beyond.

"YYEEEAAAHHHHH!!!" the crowd erupts, their cheers reverberating like thunder through the air.

A calming hush settles over the courtyard, where those awaiting their turn now sit cross-legged on the hard, pebbled ground, their restlessness transformed into quiet anticipation. Inside, the play is moments away from beginning. As Ludovic hurries backstage, a familiar voice catches his attention. Turning, he sees Céline waving at him from her seat in the front row, her radiant smile lighting up the dimly lit theater. Louise sits beside her, glancing around to take in the animated crowd.

"You didn't mention any such play before!" Céline teases, rising from her seat as though ready to follow him.

"Come with me," Ludovic replies, extending a protective hand to guide her toward the stage steps. "Louise, hold our spot," Céline calls over her shoulder, clutching her purse.

"What about your seat?" Louise protests. "It's impossible to get another one!"

"Don't worry about it. If someone takes it, so be it."

With one nimble step, Céline joins Ludovic onstage, and together they disappear behind the curtains. Backstage, Jessie and Jean-Mara are fine-tuning the actors' last-minute rehearsal. Ludovic and Céline wait nearby, their presence eventually catching Jean-Mara's eye. Pausing the actors, the playwright raises a hand to address the duo.

"Jean, this is the gorgeous girl I've been telling you about!" Ludovic announces with pride, giving Céline a light nudge forward.

"I can see why," Jean replies with an approving smile, his gaze for a quick moment breaking from the task at hand. The actors exchange curious glances, eager but patient.

"You made it just in time," Jessie beams, her enthusiasm infectious as she greets Céline.

"Barely," Céline responds with a laugh, glancing at her watch. "I was almost stuck outside. Thank goodness I was one of the last ones let in before they locked the doors for this first performance. You'd better wrap up this rehearsal before the crowd becomes unmanageable."

Jessie turns to face Jean-Mara and Jean-Claude, waiting for their signal to open the curtains. Jean-Mara holds his ground, front and center, exuding an air of wit and resolve. A witty young man in his early twenties, he blends cleverness with a penchant for dry humor to make his point. Ludovic admires his forthrightness and the way he wields his pen like a sword.

Jean-Mara's owl-rimmed glasses frame his squared-off face, perpetually accompanied by an unlit mahogany pipe wedged in the corner of his mouth. His disheveled hair and trench coat thrown over a white undershirt complete the look of a bohemian intellectual. Beneath his khaki trousers, scuffed shoes peek out, adding to his unpolished charm. Though soft-spoken, every word he utters strikes with the precision of a cannonball on a battlefield.

Beyond the curtains, the audience stirs with growing impatience. Jessie steps forward to address them, her voice clear and commanding.

"Mesdames et Messieurs, we deeply apologize for the unexpected delay. Your overwhelming response fills our hearts with gratitude. I know you've waited long enough. So, without further ado…" She pauses, then exits with a graceful smile as four actors stride onto the stage. The curtains pull wide open.

Céline's heart skips when the stage lights flare. A wave of self-consciousness washes over her, knowing she isn't part of the play. With Ludovic at her side, she retreats to the backstage shadows, where the light cannot find them. Jessie, Jean-Mara, Jean-Claude, and the rest of the offstage cast join her, awaiting their cues.

Onstage, two drummers perch on low chairs, gripping their instruments between their knees. Shirtless and clad in rolled-up blue trousers, they pound out a rhythmic samba, their hands a blur. The room fills with the raw, pulsing energy of the beats.

A young woman bursts onto the stage, her movements fluid and hypnotic. Her blue miniskirt and crimson t-shirt ripple as she sways, her bare feet gliding with grace. Silk scarves shimmer around her neck, catching the light like radiant coins. She waves two Haitian flags in each hand, their red and blue hues blending with the motion of her spinning hips and fluttering arms. Her

Afro puff, dyed a rich brunette, frames her fierce, focused expression.

The drums roar like wild mules braying on an open valley floor. The dancer twists her waist, her hips dipping and shifting in spellbinding rhythms. As her lithe movements quicken, the crowd claps in sync with the drums, sending ripples of excitement through the room.

Backstage, Jessie can no longer contain herself. She springs to her feet, her excitement infectious. Leaning toward Céline, her face glows with unrestrained joy. Céline watches in silence, captivated by the scene unfolding before them, her heart swelling with pride for the vibrant artistry of her community.

"Who is this girl?" Céline murmurs, her curiosity piqued.

"Elvanette, a sister from uptown," Jean-Mara answers, pride gleaming in his tone.

"She has the talents of a pro!" Céline chuckles, her eyes fixed on the stage.

"You mean like Toto Bissainthe?" Ludovic suggests with a sly smile, his arm sneaking around Céline's shoulders. He inches closer, as though preparing to plant a kiss on her lips. But his boldness falters when Céline slips from his embrace, moving to join Jessie, who stands a few paces away.

"Another blunder," Ludovic mutters under his breath, frustration flashing across his face.

"What's that, Dodo?" Jean-Claude asks, glancing curiously at him.

"Nothing…I was just, uh, analyzing Elvanette's moves. Quite amazing, eh?" Ludovic replies, masking his awkwardness with a casual tone. He avoids further commentary, his face a practiced mask of composure.

Jean-Claude opens his mouth to speak, but Jessie interrupts. "Close the curtains," she commands, pointing toward the stage.

Jean-Claude obliges, pulling them shut just as the dance ends and Elvanette steps offstage with the drummers in tow.

Attention shifts backstage. The cast gathers for a final pep talk. A tall, ebony-skinned girl with a cylindrical face framed by golden hoop earrings stands poised, as though anticipating something extraordinary. She is the most extroverted of the group, her impulsive energy leaving no room for doubt about her patriotic fervor. Even the boys hold back, waiting for her to make the first move, their own restless energy dissolving as the charged atmosphere engulfs them.

This is Ginette, Jean-Mara's cousin, who hails from the hollow of Morne Desgranges on the northern fringes of Saint Louis. A fearless actress on a mission to deliver a knockout performance of artistic brilliance, she exudes an undeniable magnetism. From afar, she is a vision of midnight beauty—her starry eyes captivating, her lithe limbs an exquisite balance of strength and grace. Every young man in the audience feels the pull of her allure, an almost primal craving stirred by her presence.

The curtains reopen. Ginette strides onto the stage, her presence an unyielding force. She halts at the microphone, standing tall and composed, her bearing regal. The audience hushes, captivated by her unshakable poise and the promise of her words.

Her crisp white t-shirt, emblazoned with the CARLSS logo, clings to her form, accentuating her commanding frame. A vibrant scarf wraps snugly around her waist, anchoring the flowing tiers of her gypsy skirt. She moves with a sensual, feline grace—each step deliberate, each sway of her hips calculated to mesmerize. In the back, Céline watches with bated breath, a flicker of doubt crossing her mind.

Will Ginette's elegance and magnetic presence overshadow her message? Céline wonders. Yet, as Ginette raises her head, her starry eyes glimmer with purpose. The room is hers, and her words—pure, potent, and revolutionary—are about to strike with the force of a hurricane.

The towering feminine figure fully grasps the gravity of her mission. As the Messenger of the Prime Hour, she understands the critical importance of delivering a flawless message. Harnessing all her artistic and political power, she begins:

"Poverty is the most vexing singularity in human history. It is a despicable prison, reserved for the vast majority of our countrymen, where they are held in outright subjugation and disenfranchisement."

Ginette's voice, rich and operatic, echoes to the rafters, laced with palpable indignation. One hand rests firmly on her hip while the other extends toward the audience, as though she yearns to lead them toward the promise of freedom and democracy. She continues:

"It is a prison that confines nearly eleven million of our people, trapping them in a relentless cycle of despair. And yet, we fail to see it for what it is. An imaginary veil clouds our vision, blurring the truth. This veil is so thick that it obscures the enemy who wove it—this sinister web designed to entangle us forever.

"We grow up within this suffocating veil, blind to our human rights: the right to quality education, equitable healthcare, and a fair-paying job. We are conditioned to accept that we were born to live, multiply, and die in poverty. We are told it's 'normal' for thousands of our children to have their youth stolen from them—to be dehumanized as *restavèk*, enslaved in servitude, while millions of us avert our eyes in shameful indifference.

"This apathy leaves these children vulnerable to heinous exploitation—rape, prostitution, beatings, and forced labor. How can Haiti ever be free when so many of her children remain shackled, caged, and condemned?"

Crushingly loud, the crowd erupts in a thunderous, "NO!!!"

"Can Haiti truly be free when her beloved children are forced to live in modern-day bondage?" Ginette's voice rings out again.

"Noooooooooooo..." the audience responds, the sound reverberating through the hall like a tidal wave.

"But this veil has offered us a historic opportunity," Ginette continues, her tone shifting to one of hopeful resolve. "By holding us together, it forces us to take a second look at our shared existence—to notice our strengths and reflect upon our differences. Differences that are shallow, skin-deep, and easily reconciled. Remember, a veil is just a veil. It can be pierced, broken through, and ripped apart. And when that day comes, our thirst will not be for revenge but for justice—for becoming active, productive citizens who reclaim their rights to human decency and dignity. It's time to tear the veil!"

Spellbound and transfixed, the young faces in the audience glow with emotion. The truth cuts deeply, hurting and thrilling at once. Down in her seat, Louise's eyes glisten with tears. Chanting in the familiar Haitian way, she raises both hands high. "Let's rip the veil now!" she cries, her voice quivering yet steady, as Ginette finishes her speech and strides confidently backstage.

In the back of the hall, a group of young men and women bursts into animated discussion, their energy electric, their words alive with intellectual fervor. Suddenly, a well-dressed man with robust features rises from his seat. Adjusting his red-and-blue beret, he sweeps his gaze across the room.

"What do we want?" he shouts, his voice full of immeasurable pride.

"Ripping the veil!" the entire audience roars in unison.

"When do we want it?" the man demands, pounding his chest like a rallying drumbeat.

"NOW!" the crowd screams feverishly, their collective cry shaking the very walls of the hall.

Meanwhile, the show unfolds with unrelenting intensity. Each act brims with passion, each dance choreographed with precision. The night becomes an unforgettable milestone, leaving its mark on all who bear witness—a debut that will be remembered for generations to come.

At the end of the play, the crowd, amid thunderous applause, disperses to the carefree tune of Manno Charlemagne's good old classical folk song:

'M'applenyen yon mizè,
Pèsòn pa vleachte-l...
Vyesoulye-m chire,
Rechan-y mwenpachiman,
Se nan-w vè tafia
Mwensanti-m byennere."

I'm auctioning my misery,
But no one wants to bid…
My old shoe is torn,
My shirt is wrinkled
Only in one grog of rum
That I find comfort and peace of mind.

Louise takes command of a growing group from the uptown area, all dazed yet energized by this latest, staged dose of revolutionary fervor. Backstage, Céline stands motionless, quivering with emotion. Words escape her. Before this electrifying night, she had never imagined witnessing such a fervent, inexplicable thirst for justice. Overwhelmed, she steps toward Jean-Mara, embracing him in a heartfelt, patriotic hug.

"This is extraordinary," she whispers, her voice trembling with admiration. "Thank you for creating this masterpiece."

Jean-Mara, stoic but clearly moved, nods in acknowledgment. The raw energy of the night pulses through Céline's veins, leaving her exhilarated. She realizes how deeply young people in marginalized societies understand their precarious positions and their readiness to change the course of their destinies. For the first time, a spark of genuine hope takes root.

"Haiti has a chance," Céline sighs softly, almost to herself.

"Haiti what?" Jessie coughs, turning to her. She had been too preoccupied with the bustling backstage to notice Céline until the word "Haiti" catches her ear.

"Nothing…just saying Haiti's not lost. There's hope!" Céline replies, her tone light but brimming with conviction.

Jessie, who has poured her heart into the production, chuckles in acknowledgement. "You bet there is."

"Listen, Jess, it's getting late. I have to go. See you soon!" Céline waves to her friend and the actors, who are busy, getting ready for the second performance. Meanwhile, the attendees from the first session spill out as the waiting crowd begins filing in to take their seats.

As Céline strolls toward the exit, she notices Ludovic immersed in a spirited discussion with a group of politically charged young men. Their animated debate about other plays and revolutionary productions seems to epitomize the energy of the night. She calls out a casual farewell, but before she can reach the entryway, Ludovic strides after her—long legs eating the distance—catching her at the threshold.

Cupping her hand, he looks into her eyes. "You've got to get home, too. Remember, we leave early tomorrow?"

She gives her head a slight tilt, a playful smile gracing her lips. "Don't worry, I haven't forgotten. Now, get some rest too, my midnight egret."

"As you wish, my eglantine," he responds, bowing a little in mock submission. But before he can say more, Céline turns and slips away, weaving through the thinning crowd. By the time she reaches the double doors and disappears beyond the towering walls of the church, Ludovic is left standing there, the lingering warmth of her hand a bittersweet reminder of her fleeting presence.

$Chapter\ 19$

It is eight o'clock in the morning, and the myriad settlements east of the Acajou River are stirring to life. It's Saturday—market day. Along the main trail, long lines of elated mountain folk descend into Saint Louis. Their goal: to converge on the bustling downtown square, adjacent to the Catholic Church, where every household item can be traded or sold.

The cool morning breeze mixes with brazen sunshine, creating a lively and soothing atmosphere for these mountain communities. The air hums with the chatter and laughter of peasants on foot or mounted on donkeys, mules, and horses. Hooves clatter rhythmically against the dirt path, raising clouds of dust that go unnoticed amidst the cheerful bustle. Everyone is determined to reach the square before the sweltering midday heat dampens their spirits.

Inside her cottage, Louisinette sits on a low chair by the front porch, waving to neighbors as they pass on their way to Saint Louis. Her children play in the backyard, their laughter blending with the sounds of the morning. Victorin has left early to tend his vegetable garden across the ravine trail. For this rural family, it is another simple day in the rhythm of peasant life.

Yet, Louisinette's mind is far from idle. Her thoughts swirl around Céline and the burgeoning fight for justice—not just for herself but for everyone who has suffered under the cruelty of men like Dalambert. While she believes in Céline's mission, doubts linger about her own strength as a central figure in such a righteous struggle. Still, she has not remained passive. Over the past few days, Louisinette has ventured across the mountain and valley, speaking with battered women—victims of rape and brutality. In a low-key manner, she has with firmness begun to rally local female support, planting the seeds of a collective resistance.

By nine o'clock, two boys appear at Louisinette's front door. Their tired expressions reveal they've trekked a long distance across the mountain. Beads of sweat stream down their jet-black cheeks. One, a muscular, bow-legged boy with disheveled hair, clutches a large papaya in his right hand, a palm-frond sack slung around his neck. The other, a wiry lad, wears a straw hat to shield himself from the sun. Shirtless, he is dressed in patched blue jeans held up by a rope knotted at his waist.

"Madame Louisinette!" calls the muscular one, dropping the hefty fruit onto the steppingstones as he stumbles forward, his eagerness unmistakable. His companion lingers by the walkway, a yard from the front porch.

"What is it, Manuel?" Louisinette asks, her brows furrowing with concern.

"We just saw that wealthy, pale-lookin' lady who visited you last time," Manuel stammers, uncertain if he's delivering important news.

"Where?" she demands.

"At the bottom of the hill. She's walking with a man. He's tall and kind of looks like her. Must be rich, too."

"Have you seen this man before?"

"No, ma'am."

Daurélien, the slender boy, eager to contribute, steps closer. "Folks in the valley say they've seen that man before," he whispers, wiping sweat from his hollowed face with a large, dry banana leaf he's picked up from the ground.

"Are you sure, Daurélien?" Louisinette presses, her voice sharp with curiosity. Without waiting for a reply, she springs from her chair and hurries toward the main trail, aiming to catch sight of the figures on the hilltop. The two boys follow closely, their curiosity now heightened as well.

Just before reaching the trail, Lamizè appears from inside the house. "Manman!" he shouts, raising his arms in the air, his small face etched with fear. Dubison, her younger son, follows a step behind, his creamy cheeks streaked with tears. Both boys seem convinced their mother is leaving them behind. Louisinette stops her frantic climb to the mountaintop and turns back to gather her children.

The two young messengers step in to help. Daurélien extends his arms to lift Dubison, but the child squirms away, darting instead into his mother's embrace. Meanwhile, Manuel hoists Lamizè onto his narrow back, carrying him playfully. Together, they set off along the trail.

By the time they reach the mountaintop, Céline and Ludovic are nearing the peak. The pair rests under a custard apple tree, gazing down at the valley as they catch their breath before continuing their climb.

Spotting them from a short distance, Louisinette turns and calls out, "Liline!" Her voice carries both relief and joy.

"Louisie!" Céline responds, jumping to her feet and rushing toward her friend.

Manuel locks Dubison in a bear hug as the child twists like an eel, all giggles and futile wriggling. Louisinette rushes toward Céline, and the women collide on the trail just shy of the summit—an embrace that feels stolen from time. Around them, the children's laughter spirals into the thin mountain air as they tussle with Manuel and Daurélien, their small bodies all tangled limbs and grass stains.

"What happened to you?" Louisinette gasps, pulling back to study Céline's face. The older boys and children remain rooted in their playful battle, the summit's breeze carrying their shrieks like sparks from a fire.

"I wanted to make sure that the next time we met, I'd have something meaningful to share with you," Céline says, grasping Ludovic's hand and presenting him to Louisinette. "I've brought a good friend—he's here to help us in this fight. His name is Ludovic." She adds with a humble smile, "Don't worry; he's as committed as we are."

"Nice to meet you, Lu…dovic," Louisinette stammers nervously.

"Nice to meet you, too," he replies with a warm laugh.

Dubison and Lamizè hide their faces in their mother's flowing, billowing garment. Though they seem to recognize Céline, they remain wary, stealing hesitant glances at the two strangers. Manuel and Daurélien giggle, their laughter soft. Manuel rubs his eyes, shielding them from the bright morning sun, while Daurélien studies the couple, his gaze sharp and probing, as though trying to discern their motives.

"Hello, boys!" Céline greets them, her voice bright.

"Good morning, madame," they respond, their voices respectful yet shy.

Frowning slightly, Ludovic steps forward, offering a firm handshake to each of the older lads. Before Céline can ask about their presence, Louisinette takes charge, pulling the boys forward by their hands. "This is Manuel, and this is Daurélien. They're my cousin Claudette's sons. She lives over in Jean-Claire, just on the next hill."

Taking the lead, Louisinette signals everyone to follow her back to her house. As they approach the settlement, Manuel and Daurélien wave goodbye and head south toward the ravine trail. "See you soon, boys!" Louisinette calls after them. "Tell your mom I'll stop by later," she shouts to their retreating figures.

The boys, now reaching the embankment, hear Louisinette's voice echoing through the empty gorge. "*Wi,*" they call back before disappearing into the emerald canopy.

Back in the settlement, a few curious neighbors, who have remained home on this bustling market day, keep their eyes fixed as Céline and Ludovic trail Louisinette down the walkway toward her cottage. Radiating joy, Louisinette ushers them inside, offering cups of tea and thick slices of traditional Haitian bread. Ludovic grins, rubbing his stomach to signal his hunger. Céline nods in agreement, her own stomach growling. Louisinette hurries outside to prepare the food, her boys eagerly following.

For a short moment, the visitors are alone in a storage room next to the back porch. Outside, Louisinette is busy fanning the cook fire into life, her heavy breaths carrying through the open door as she rushes to prepare the tea. Céline and Ludovic sit together on a rough log facing a thatch-covered window. Through it, sunlight beams on banana leaves swaying in the yard, their shadows dancing against the blue ridge of Jean-Claire, where Louisinette's cousin Claudette lives.

"We should've bought some cassavas and avocados at that little stand in Basen Tounen," Céline murmurs, her voice soft with reflection as she gazes out the window.

"You're right," Ludovic replies, leaning toward her. "We were too focused on getting here before the midday heat." He takes her hands in his, his gaze lingering on her face. Words of love bubble up, but he falters, caught in the intensity of the moment. Instead, he leans closer, his lips brushing the edge of her trembling flushed neck.

The back door creaks open, breaking the spell. Céline and Ludovic freeze, their faces inches apart, her parted lips still quivering. Louisinette steps into the room, kettle in hand, her expression caught somewhere between amusement and embarrassment.

"Sorry for interrupting," she says with a shy smile.

"No, it's not what you think, Louisie," Céline stammers, her cheeks flushing as she pulls away.

Louisinette moves past them, unfazed, retrieving an aluminum kettle from the silver chest in the corner. As she pours steaming anise tea into the kettle, its sweet aroma fills the room, enveloping them in its comforting warmth. Céline, eager to dispel the awkwardness, leans toward her friend.

"Can I have a few leaves to take home later?"

"Of course," Louisinette replies with a grin, opening a small cabinet to fetch three ceramic cups. Carefully, she places them on a wooden tray, then retrieves fresh bread swirled with peanut butter. She turns back to Céline, her face glowing with pride.

"Liline, I know peanut butter was always your favorite. I had this batch custom-made for you two weeks ago. I told myself that if you didn't come, I'd take it to Saint Louis to surprise you."

Céline's heart swells as she watches her friend, a sense of admiration blooming in her chest. Despite everything Louisinette has endured, her generosity and resilience shine brighter than the morning sun.

Out of nowhere, the children come racing from the backyard, leaping and sprawling onto their unmade bunk beds.

Despite the enticing aroma of food prepared by their mother, they remain disinterested. Louisinette steps away momentarily, returning with a quilt, which she spreads over a long, wide banana-frond mat she's laid upon the packed-dirt floor. She arranges peanut butter sandwiches on a wooden tray, placing them atop the quilt-covered mat, inviting everyone to join her in an intimate, rustic meal.

"This is wonderful! Did you prepare all this?" Céline marvels as she and Ludovic settle on the mat. Turning to Louisinette, Céline asks with a playful glint in her eye, "Louisie, do you remember our *twa-de*—peanut butter on cassava—from Madame Virgile's grocery store?"

"How could I forget?" Louisinette laughs, her voice tinged with nostalgia. "I was the one risking everything to go buy it at sundown. And that tall boy, Harry, who had a crush on you—he'd always try to follow me, hoping for just a word from you."

"You girls are fearless. Weren't you ever afraid of running into werewolves?" Ludovic teases, his grin widening. Although he doesn't believe in such creatures, the mysterious jungles of Haiti, much of which remains unexplored, lend an air of plausible uncertainty.

"No," Louisinette replies confidently. "Werewolves don't exist. But I was scared of meeting madame along the way," she adds with a sly smile.

"Madame! Who was that?" Ludovic bursts into laughter, genuinely curious.

"That's how the housemaids referred to Mother," Céline explains, her tone softened by memory. The mention of her mother, however, triggers a surge of melancholy in Louisinette. She pours herself a cup of anise tea, the fragrant steam swirling upward as she takes a small, contemplative sip. She tears off a piece of traditional bread and dunks it into her cooling tea, nibbling at it, lost in thought.

"I'm sure you know why we're here today," Céline says, her broad smile fading into an expression of unwavering seriousness.

"Yes, of course," Louisinette replies, a bit hesitant. "But I don't know what I'm supposed to do."

"We don't have all the details worked out yet," Céline reassures her. "Ludovic and I came today to begin planning how we can hold that monster Dalambert accountable for what he did to you."

"Thank you for helping me." Louisinette leans over to give Ludovic a small, grateful hug.

Ludovic clears his throat, his demeanor shifting to one of solemn earnestness.

"Louisinette, we need your help," he begins, fixing his gaze on her. "Without your voice, folks might just think we're troublemakers, or even say we're turning against our own kin."

"How so, Monsieur Ludovic?" she asks, her brow furrowing.

"We need you to be the face of this fight. No one will believe in our cause without you," he explains. "Céline and I were wondering if you'd consider relocating to Saint Louis for the time being. It would make it easier for you to be more active."

"The city?" Louisinette's laugh is a door slamming shut. "I will never go back to living there. I left Saint Louis for good."

"We're not asking you to go back for good," Céline interjects, the words wrapped in velvet—but the hook still glints beneath them.

"Even if I wanted to, Victorin would never agree," Louisinette continues, her voice wavering a little. "And I think he's right. Believe me—I want justice. I think about it every day."

"So, what's the solution?" Céline asks, her tone tinged with urgency.

Louisinette rests her chin on her hand, staring into her teacup. She is pensive. "I have a cousin who lives near the clinic in Desgranges. She might be willing to help, but I can't promise anything. She's very protective and might be hesitant once she knows the full plan."

"Protective can be good," Céline muses, though there's a flicker of concern in her eyes. "As long as she doesn't block our efforts."

"Guess what? I been workin' on that already," Louisinette says, frowning while wiping her hands on her apron like she's scrubbing away doubt. "After your visit, Céline, I been talking—down in the valley, up the hills, wherever women gather at river rocks or coconut presses. Quiet-like. Men don't sniff it out. Told the wives: 'Share if your man's got a gentle ear, else keep it close as ripe mango hides its seed.'"

Céline jumps to her feet, her excitement impossible to contain. "Do they agree to go to Saint Louis?"

"Not all of them," Louisinette replies. "But many of them agree to go. A few of them are free today since it's a slow market day. If you want, I can take you to meet them."

"Fantastic!" Ludovic shouts, his face lighting up with enthusiasm.

Louisinette scans the room, her gaze softening as she notices that the children have drifted into a peaceful late-morning sleep. Dubison's small hand clings to his older brother's shoulder, his rosy cheeks illuminated by golden beams of sunlight streaming through the cracks in the nearby window. The tender tableau is almost sacred, a moment of tranquility that stands in stark contrast with the challenges Louisinette has faced.

Céline and Ludovic rise in silence from the mat, their movements deliberate to avoid disturbing the scene. They slip onto the front porch, where tall citronella plants blend well with a delicate tangle of saffron-colored *flèdizè* (ten o'clock flowers) framing the tidy pathway outside the main door. Ludovic cannot help but marvel at the care evident in every detail of Louisinette's surroundings. Her home is a testament to her meticulousness, a quality that seems almost instinctive. He reflects that this precision must have been honed during her years of service to the gentry—a bittersweet skill shaped by necessity but now a source of quiet pride.

Meanwhile, Louisinette retreats to her bedroom. A few moments later, she emerges wearing a simple yet elegant floral dress with capped sleeves adorned with pink rose embroidery. A pair of low-heeled blue sandals complements her outfit, accentuating her unpretentious beauty. There is a quiet determination in her posture as she steps onto the porch, her smile calm yet purposeful. The shift in her demeanor signals to her visitors that she is prepared to face the day ahead.

Still, there is a flicker of nervousness in her steps as she approaches Céline and Ludovic. Her voice is steady but tinted with hesitation as she says, "Stay here for a moment while I fetch Crizo, my neighbor's daughter, to watch the children." With that, she turns, her floral dress catching the morning breeze as she walks toward the next house, ready to enlist the help she needs to ensure her children's safety during her absence.

<u>*Chapter 20*</u>

A short moment later, Louisinette returns, and the group sets off eastward, their path weaving through lush prairies and pristine ravines. They traverse groves of bananas and towering breadfruit trees, the air alive with the chatter of hummingbirds, blue jays, and other vibrant songbirds. After a half-hour of walking, they emerge onto an expansive savanna of parched farmland. The barren landscape stretches as far as the eye can see, a severe divergence from the lush greenery they had passed earlier. Two solitary coconut palms stand in the middle of this arid expanse, like lonely sentinels, their withered, brown fronds swaying in the hot breeze, their trunks scarred and gray.

Louisinette takes the lead, but Ludovic cannot hide his unease. The stark shifts in the landscape—from the rich groves irrigated for coffee crops to the dry, untended farmlands—underscore the deep inequalities of the region. These fertile groves belong to the wealthy members of the Planters Association of Saint Louis (PASL), an elite club Ludovic despises, even though his father is a prominent member. His resentment deepens as they climb a steep mountain road leading to the remote village of Jean-Claire.

At the summit, they encounter an elderly man with a pack of goats and three yellow hounds. He greets them warmly before descending with his animals. Pressing on, they approach the sleepy village, where avocado trees loom above untamed yucca gardens. The grass-clogged pathways wind like streams between the overgrown plots, but the natural beauty of the valley below seems to abandon this rugged corner of Saint Louis.

As Céline and Ludovic tread carefully through the weedy path, they take in the desolation around them. Windowless huts with crumbling mud-brick walls line the way, their only support coming from weathered palisades. The absence of verdant shrubs, hammocks, or domino tables—common signs of life in rural yards—is jarring. In their place, emaciated children with distended bellies and sunken faces wander aimlessly, their hollow eyes bearing witness to relentless hunger.

At the village entrance, the pathway branches into a network of smaller trails, each leading to a porch. A cluster of elderly villagers stands nearby, their arms crossed as they cast wary glances at the newcomers. Recognizing familiar faces, Louisinette waves. The elders respond with tentative greetings, their voices thin, their expressions a blend of joy and apprehension. Céline and Ludovic wave as well, though their gestures are met with subdued stares, reflecting a quiet but palpable mistrust.

At last, the group arrives at a fenced-in courtyard containing two homes. One is a long, dilapidated shack with slanted mud-brick walls that seem to lean precariously. The other is a modest cottage, its small, well-placed windows peeking out over a stick fence. Lemon grasses line the air with their fragrant aroma, and a tidy plot of watermelons grows near a cluster of tropical plants shaded by pigeon-bean trees. Louisinette leads them to the cottage, its relative neatness a small beacon of hope in an otherwise bleak environment.

From the doorway, the treeless mountainside offers a breathtaking panorama of the Fond Philippe Gorge, where the Acajou River surges with relentless energy, its waters glinting fiercely under the sun's rays. A tall woman emerges from the house to greet them. *"Bonjou,"* she says, her voice as warm as the midday air.

"So happy to see you!" Louisinette gushes, her face bright with genuine affection. Hands planted on her hips, the woman radiates an almost regal presence amid the austere surroundings, her nut-brown complexion lending her the appearance of a Creole queen wrapped in resilient dignity.

"Me, too!" Louisinette enthuses as she steps forward to make the introductions. "These are the friends from Saint Louis I told you about," she adds, motioning Céline and Ludovic forward.

"I got your message about an hour ago," Claudette replies, her tone brisk yet welcoming.

"Where are the boys?" Louisinette asks.

"Manuel and Daurélien went to gather the other women," Claudette replies, before shifting her stance to introduce herself. "I'm Claudette, single mother of four children," she announces, her proud, self-possessed smile for a moment banishing the hardships of her environment. A silken blue headcloth drapes loosely over her glossy bouffant hair, and her red-orange skirt has an elegant fall to her knees, paired with a crisp white t-shirt that accentuates her slender frame.

"Nice to meet you!" Céline and Ludovic say as one, their smiles mirroring her own. Ludovic adds, "I'm Ludovic, and this is my dear friend Céline."

Claudette widens the doorway, stepping aside to let the visitors enter. She gestures toward a couch-divan situated in the far corner of the well-kept cottage. The room, a testament to ingenuity and care, features smooth concrete floors reinforced with sisal fibers and brightly painted low-density concrete walls, creating an ambiance that is both humble and inviting.

"Please, have a seat," she says. "May I offer you something to drink?"

"Water, please," Céline and Ludovic reply both at once.

"Where are your other children?" Céline inquires, glancing around the tidy room.

"It's market day, even if not many people are going. They went to town early this morning with my younger sister," Claudette explains.

Claudette crosses the room to a green cabinet and retrieves four clean plastic cups. She fills them with water drawn from a clay jar, a staple in every rural home. Fresh drinking water, a rare and precious commodity in these parts, is carefully stored in these jars to ensure it remains cool and pure. Claudette moves with practiced efficiency, handing the cups to her guests before sitting with them, her calm demeanor masking the quiet strength and determination that defines her.

"We're leaving soon for Fond Philippe," Claudette sighs, handing water to her guests, who drink it down in single, eager gulps.

"What for?" her cousin asks, eyebrows lifting in surprise.

"That's where we expect to meet most of the women who are interested," Claudette replies.

"I see," Ludovic murmurs. Céline, her eyes still roving over the surroundings, says nothing at first. But after a moment, she hesitates and asks, "I thought you sent the boys to fetch the women?"

"Yes, in a rendezvous with Lavanie," Claudette clarifies, her tone brightening. "She's the motivated lady who's been secretly organizing the interested women in the valley." Walking over to the front window, she draws the curtains wide with a theatrical flourish. "Come see," she calls, waving her water cup as if casting a spell.

Rising in unison, the visitors move with childlike eagerness to the window. Claudette gestures toward clusters of houses scattered along the east bank of the Acajou River. Some are roofed with corrugated tin, their sharp edges glinting in the relentless sunshine. To the east, the land rears up, culminating in the peak of Morne Château, its slopes dotted with tidy cottages nestled among tropical undergrowth and squared-off sweet potato gardens.

Farther beyond the ridge of Morne Château, layer upon layer of mountains climb into the sky, each more imposing than the last. Some appear skeletal and barren, their once-forested slopes eroded into pale, cracked remnants—a testament to the toll of human activity and the relentless making of charcoal. Others remain lush, vibrant lime-green sanctuaries, untouched by man's destructive hand. Among these, Morne Zombie stands out, its blue-green ridge extending toward the heavens, evoking an almost mystical aura in its untouched splendor.

Céline stares at the breathtaking vista, a world both alien and entrancing to her. "Beyond those faraway mountains…yet more mountains," she whispers, her voice rippling like a soft tremor, drawing the others' attention. Turning back, she adds, "I think we'd best get going before midday."

Without saying a word, Claudette leads the group down a narrow, winding dirt road that snakes its way to the sandy riverbed of the Acajou. Here, along the lush banks, the atmosphere transforms, the vivid green foliage appearing radiant enough to obscure the squalid poverty lingering in the hollow gorges around Jean-Claire.

The group halts together, standing ankle-deep in ivory-colored sand, their eyes fixed on the river. Uncertainty lingers about whether crossing it will lead them directly to Claudette's boys. In the distance, the mournful caws of scattered crows punctuate the air, mingling with the misty hum of songbirds flitting about the meadow that lies beside the majestic river, its serpentine path stretching downward.

The sun climbs to its zenith, its scorching heat descending upon them. Louisinette gestures toward a mango tree at the edge of the bank, suggesting they rest there until Manuel and Daurélien return with the valley women. Taking Céline's hand, she walks with her characteristic nimbleness, leading the group to the shade of the sprawling tree. Beneath its thick canopy, they huddle together amidst the verdant undergrowth, their anticipation growing as they await the boys and their companions.

Céline shifts closer to Claudette, her voice dropping to a gentle murmur. "What happened to the father of your children?" she asks. Ludovic leans in slightly, his furrowed brow betraying quiet concern.

"It's a long story," Claudette replies, her voice shaded with weariness. "One I don't care to share in full right now. But I'll say this—he left when my younger child was just a year old. That was seven years ago. It was…an abusive relationship."

Her gaze falls, and tears well up in her eyes. She tilts her head back, letting it rest against the soft, yielding trunk of the mango tree. Her billowing dress pools around her lap as her hands encircle her knees, clasped tightly as if holding herself together.

Céline reaches out, a natural reaction, her touch light and comforting. "I think I understand," she whispers.

Claudette nods faintly, her voice shaking. "That's why, when Louisinette approached me last week about organizing the valley women to fight for our rights, I didn't hesitate. It's time— time for Haitian women to demand the respect and fair treatment we deserve, every single day." A tear escapes, trailing down her cheek. She brushes it away with the back of her hand but cannot hold back the flood that follows.

Céline tries to console her, but her own heart feels heavy. Never before had she imagined the lives of the women beyond these mountains to be so fraught with untold stories, deep-seated pain, and unspoken tragedies. Yet here, amidst the sorrow, she perceives a glimmer of hope—an awakening. In this moment, Céline realizes that the struggle for justice binds women together, their collective faith inextricably linked to the fight for human dignity.

Under the mango tree, an unexpected silence blankets the group. No one utters a word. Only the rustling branches above are heard, shifting and colliding when the wind weaves through the canopy. In a sudden motion, Ludovic stands, stroking his goatee. "I think I heard footsteps," he murmurs, shielding his eyes from the sunlight with one hand. The others immediately rise, craning their necks and scanning their surroundings, ears straining to locate the low hum of voices mingled with an unmistakable rhythm—the steady patter of approaching feet.

Chapter 21

Moments later, faces materialize through the dense underbrush on the opposite bank of the river. Claudette quickly recognizes most of them as merchants from nearby settlements, residents of the valley-floor communities en route to Saint Louis. Some ride on mules or donkeys, their beasts of burden plodding at a consistent pace, while others tread the rugged trail on foot. Among them are the familiar traders of Fond Philippe, nestled deep in the hollow of Morne Madrier, alongside itinerant vegetable sellers from fertile hamlets like La Pierre, Boucan Carré, and Nan Monben. Yet, despite this bustling procession, there is no sign of the anticipated women. Disappointment etches itself onto Louisinette's youthful face, her worry deepening into sharp lines as she whispers, "Where could the boys be? They must've gotten lost."

She is still voicing her concern when Manuel suddenly bursts out of the underbrush, shirt flapping open as he sprints toward the riverbank. His movements are frantic, as though driven by an urgent purpose, and his gaze is fixed on the rushing waters. He seems oblivious to the presence of Louisinette and the others until Claudette steps forward, her voice cutting through the wind. "Manuel!" she calls, stepping into the sunlight and waving. His head jerks up, first spotting his mother and then noticing the group concealed within the protective roots of the mango tree. Relief breaks over his face, and he waves them toward him with exuberant energy.

"Where's Daurélien?" Claudette shouts, her voice raised above the roaring crescendo of the river.

"He's with the women at Lavanie's house!" Manuel yells back, his smile broad despite the beads of sweat trickling down his brow.

Their moment of relief turns to swift action. Splashing through the river's shallows, they navigate the slippery, moss-covered rocks with care, bracing against the powerful current. Reaching the opposite bank, they follow Manuel as he darts ahead, disappearing into a maze of tall, swaying guinea grass. The group presses forward, weaving through the dense greenery in his wake. After several minutes, they emerge into an open field where a meandering country trail stretches out before them, promising the next stage of their journey.

Fresh logs newly cut lie on the ground, mutilated bodies after a savage bout of ferocious warfare. In the far end of the field, a dozen men pour sweat, hard at work scratching, scraping, and clearing several acres of land. Their sharp machetes screech and sparkle in the sunlight. Forming two rows, much like warriors in military formation, they are singing a popular island folksong familiar to most farmers in the valley:

Kouzen, adye he!
Nèg anba pa travay tè o,
Nèg anba pa travay tè o. (bis)
Lè lapli tombe n'a va jwenn dlooooo!

Cousin, what a life *oh!*
Negroes from the south don't work the land,
Negroes from the south don't work the land. (2 times)
When the rain comes, we'll get water *oh-oh-oh!*

Their song echoes like a beehive of querulous sounds, music forever running through the veins of these men—a kind of battery power, needed to recharge their energy. Without warning, a brisk wind gust whirls, sending the dust dancing upward in intensely brown clots of clouds. Pulling her parasol from her daypack, where she has kept it folded, Céline buries her nose underneath it to stave off the invading legion of stifling dust. Ludovic chuckles in a teasing manner, knowing his dear friend is duly baptized, making her entry into the world of the disenfranchised.

A shared urgency to quicken their pace overtakes the group, the weight of anticipation heavy in the air. Overhead, the faint promise of a drizzle begins to gather; soon, the land will succumb to the customary rains of this region. The last glimmers of dew flash before vanishing under a gray canopy, while the incoming drizzle transforms into a steady rain, drenching everything in its path.

At the farthest edge of the field, the trail dips into the bed of a shallow creek. Startled by the travelers' approaching noise, flocks of wild fowl rise from the branches of a sprawling elm tree, their wings beating against the thick air as they flee southward. They settle in the shelter of a young sapodilla tree, chirping and clucking in a discordant symphony. Manuel, ever playful, snatches up a jagged shard of rock and hurls it in a sweeping arc toward one of the birds. Luckily, his aim is poor, and the bird flutters away unharmed. Laughter ripples through the group, lightening the moment and evoking a shared sense of relief for the spared creature.

Nearing the creek's edge, Manuel makes a sudden turn to the right, guiding them down a narrow walkway lined by a cactus fence. The path winds toward a large, enclosed courtyard about a hundred yards away. Circumventing the fence, they come upon Daurélien astride a dingy white mule just outside the gates of a modest three-room cottage.

Sweat-soaked and glowing in the late morning haze, Daurélien strikes the mule's sides with exaggerated vigor, urging the animal forward. Beneath a spreading grapefruit tree, heavy with ripe, golden fruits, Manuel helps him tie the mule's leash. Daurélien dismounts in a single agile leap and strides to the gates, unlatching them with a purposeful flourish.

"What took you so long, Manuel?" he asks, his tone swelled with reproach, his gaze sweeping over Claudette and her companions.

"I didn't know Manman had company," Manuel replies, a bit defensive before stepping aside to hold the gate open for the adults.

They enter to an awe-inspiring sight: over a hundred women, standing in disciplined silence, snap to attention without delay. Their collective energy is palpable, their unwavering salutes directed at Claudette and her visitors.

"Manman, these ladies are losing their patience. They thought you weren't coming," Daurélien whispers, showing the urgency of the moment.

Claudette, unfazed, steps into the center of the courtyard, her presence commanding and unbendable. Her visitors hover near the sidelines, including Louisinette, who appears overwhelmed and uncertain among the unfamiliar faces.

"*Honèrespè, la sosyete!*" Claudette's high, clear voice rings out, offering honor and respect to her gathered sisters.

"*Honèrespè!*" the crowd responds in chorus, their voices echoing with the power of solidarity.

"By the grace of God, we are here today," Claudette continues, her voice brimming with fervor. "I have never been this happy before! I feel truly blessed for two reasons. First, I never imagined so many of you would show up, especially on market day. Second, I have the honor of introducing my visitors—important people from Saint Louis who deeply understand and relate to our struggles. They are here to stand with us in this fight for women's equality!"

Breathless, Claudette ascends the cottage's raised front porch, motioning for the thronging visitors to join her. Taking her stand on the wooden porch grants her a commanding presence over the crowd. She stands tall, exuding a quiet strength as she gazes upon the gathered women.

"My dear sisters," she begins, her voice carrying the weight of both conviction and compassion, "I know you're not here to listen to my ramblings. You've come to meet the brave soul whose story has brought us together. It is my honor to introduce my cousin, Louisinette. Her fight is our fight. Justice for her is justice for us all!"

The crowd—mostly middle-aged women—erupts in a fervent cheer, applauding and stomping their feet. Their excitement resembles the rapture of a rock concert audience, reverberating with an electrifying sense of unity. A younger woman in her twenties, clad in a pink madras headwrap, steps forward, pointing to the men scattered within the group. "We're not all women here," she declares, her voice filled with pride. "Some of our men have joined us, leaving their fields to stand with us today!" She gestures to the males among them, tapping the red-and-blue scarf wrapped around her neck—the colors of Haiti's flag.

The women cheer louder, their solidarity swelling. Claudette beams, pulling Louisinette forward with a tender touch to address the gathering filled with passion. Overcome with emotion, Louisinette falters, her lips trembling as she searches for words. Her gaze meets Céline's, whose warm, encouraging smile recalls a cherished mantra: "I believe in you, and we share this mission."

Steeling herself, Louisinette steps forward. "Sisters," she begins, her voice shaking but determined, "I cannot express how deeply grateful I am. Your support means more than I can put into words. Together, we are *strong...*" Her voice breaks as the haunting memory of her trauma flashes across her mind. Gritting her teeth, she cries out, "Dalambert must pay for his crimes!" The words burst forth like an unstoppable torrent, her voice raw with anguish and defiance.

The crowd roars back in solidarity: "HE MUST PAY! HE MUST PAY! HE MUST PAY!" Their collective outrage ripples through the air, a deafening proclamation of long-suppressed pain and rebellion. Overwhelmed, Louisinette staggers and collapses into Céline's waiting arms, tears streaming down her face. Ludovic rushes in, wrapping an arm around her shoulders, steadying her.

Céline steps forward, her composure sharp and unyielding. "Sisters and brothers," she begins, her voice cutting through the commotion like a clarion call, "Louisette is not alone. Many of you have suffered in silence, enduring pain at the hands of husbands, lovers, neighbors—people who should have protected you. Today, we stand together to say: enough! No more! We'll make sure they get what's coming to them. And so, I ask you..." She pauses, scanning the crowd, her penetrating gaze locking onto one face after another. "Are you ready to take this fight to Saint Louis?"

A tidal wave of sound crashes: "YESSSSSSS!"

Seizing the momentum, Ludovic takes Louisinette's hand, guiding her forward. "As a man," he begins, his voice steady and earnest, "I feel shame for the crimes committed by some of my gender. But I also believe most men stand with you, ready to fight alongside you for justice. The few who commit these heinous acts must face the consequences, for their unchecked violence scars not only their victims but our society as a whole. So, to plan our next step in this fight, our next meeting will be held privately in Saint Louis this Saturday."

A worried voice from the crowd cuts in: "Why secretly?"

"To protect Louisinette and the plan," Ludovic explains. "If her presence becomes known, the criminal may flee, and we'll lose our chance for justice. You will all travel together, but Céline and I will meet you at La Rivière-des-Barres to ensure your safe arrival. It's a long road, but I know you'll make it."

Standing tall and unyielding, Louisinette absorbs the energy of the crowd. Fear still lingers, but it is eclipsed by a newfound strength. Women and their male allies surge forward, shaking hands, offering words of encouragement, and pledging their unwavering support. As Céline and Ludovic engage with individuals, answering logistical questions and strategizing for the journey ahead, a sense of determination envelops the gathering.

With the sun climbing higher, the crowd gradually disperses, each person heading home with a renewed sense of purpose. Louisinette watches them go, standing arm in arm with Céline and Ludovic, her heart swelling with the belief that together, they are unstoppable.

$$Chapter\ 22$$

Even in the tropics, where machismo reigns supreme, outright cruelty among men is rare. While they seldom express their deepest love, passion, and admiration for women in public, Haitian men are renowned for their steadfast commitment to family and responsibility—a cultural legacy passed down through generations. Yet, Dalambert's story veers into a far darker realm, one that starkly contrasts with these traditional values, due to the position of esteem he occupies in society.

Gédéon Dalambert is no ordinary man. By trade, he is a sought-after agronomist whose expertise frequently places him in consultation with local farmers. His arrival in Saint Louis—on assignment as a government official tasked with promoting modern agricultural techniques—was meant to last five years. Yet, his transfer soon becomes permanent as he ingratiates himself with the town's affluent elite. Through charm and calculated bribery, Dalambert not only extends his stay but elevates his social standing. Wealth, prestige, and unchecked access to indulgences, both refined and debauched, cement his image as an influential figure in Saint Louis.

A once-celebrated bachelor from the southern Haitian town of Miragoâne, Dalambert's past is riddled with a complexity that mirrors his current life. Beneath his polished exterior lies a man enslaved by his desires, concealing the devils that lurk in the shadowed corners of his soul. While he flirts freely with willing women, no one suspects the darkness that festers within him.

Soon after settling in Saint Louis, Dalambert sets his predatory sights on Colette, a young woman whose beauty is as celebrated as her virtue. A Creole enchantress with deep-set hazel eyes that can disarm the coldest of hearts, Colette has remained unscathed by the advances of Saint Louis's many Casanovas. But there is one weakness many Saint Louis women share: an affinity for out-of-towners. Gédéon Dalambert, with his black Jeep Wrangler and polished French-tinged Creole, epitomizes the allure of the exotic. To Colette and her family, he seems like the ideal suitor, a man whose title and wealth promise an escape from the grip of poverty.

Underneath his dignified facade, however, Dalambert is a man of many faces. Married to six women and father to ten children in the Miragoâne region alone, his reputation as a womanizer is celebrated by some and whispered about by others. Yet, even his seemingly endless string of conquests fails to quell the darker urges that define him. Colette, unaware of the storm she is inviting into her life, becomes his next victim—not in love, but in the twisted game he plays with lives and trust.

At first, Dalambert channels all his charm and cunning into Colette, adorning their modest apartment with lavish furnishings and showering her with rare, expensive goods from Port-au-Prince. Bewitched by her new life, Colette pledges undying devotion, vowing to uphold their union in joy or sorrow until death. Vowing to etch herself into Dalambert's heart, she exudes unwavering pride and fidelity, her youthful smile glowing with amber warmth and sincerity—a sincerity that every man dreams of. Every man, that is, except Dalambert.

Cunning as a camouflaged coral snake, he never marries her. Their relationship lasts just three years, during which Colette bears him two children. One quiet Sunday morning, he vanishes without warning, never to return to the rented house she had envisioned as their forever home. Whispers soon spread: before his transfer to Saint Louis, Dalambert had fathered at least six children with multiple women in Hinche on the central plateau.

Shattered by betrayal and scandal, Colette flees the town. She retreats over the mountains to the safety of her parents' ancestral home, a secluded village near the valley of Forje along the banks of La Rivière-des-Barres. Yet in Saint Louis, such stories are all too familiar. For the townspeople, another woman exploited and discarded by a powerful man is hardly newsworthy. For Dalambert, however, each conquest only fuels his warped sense of power. Over the years, he has come to revel in his promiscuous impunity, seeing every new victim— even an impoverished *restavèk* girl—as a mere sideshow in his secret, Machiavellian theater of exploitation.

<u>*Chapter 23*</u>

At around three o'clock in the afternoon, Céline and Ludovic arrive at the northern fringes of town after crossing La Rivière-des-Barres. Though their faces appear groggy, a renewed energy courses through them after such an eventful morning. Street vendors at the riverside's bustling open market immediately rush toward them, perceiving them as affluent city folk. Ludovic purchases a bag brimming with ripe mangoes, while Céline secures a handful of her favorite shelled, roasted peanuts.

Behind them, the vendors trail like a flock of fluttering birds, each eager to outpace the other in pursuit of a sale. Their jostling and persistent calls create a whirlwind of chaos, slowing Céline and Ludovic's progress toward downtown. In synchronized determination, the pair presses forward, their pace fast and steady.

A half mile later, the clamor fades into the background as the road veers toward Morne Desgranges, where a local slaughterhouse operates amidst a flurry of activity. Meat cutters work feverishly, striving to meet the demands of late-arriving country folk eager to secure last-minute bargains. Perched atop a high-backed metallic chair, a bulky, red-eyed overseer bellows orders at the exhausted workers. "Move faster, you lazy *vagabonds!*" he shouts, his vulgar language unfit for women or children to hear.

"How much faster can they go without slicing off their fingers?" Céline murmurs, her concern laced with indignation.

"He doesn't care," Ludovic replies, his voice barely above a whisper, and his tone is somber. "And they wouldn't dare show exhaustion—not unless they're ready to lose their jobs."

The overseer's tirade continues unabated until a tall woman dressed in a white garment strides over and tugs at his shirt sleeve, attempting to pacify him.

Disheartened, Céline and Ludovic resume their walk, passing an assortment of quaint houses on their way to Ti-Rivyè, a creek meandering through the northern outskirts. Instead of crossing the creek, they follow a narrow path running parallel to it, leading them to the shoreline where the stream empties into the ocean. The sandy trail dissolves into clumps of grass as they reach the beachfront, and the pair sinks onto the sugar-fine sand.

The ocean breeze cools their sweat-dampened faces as they sit side by side, gazing out at the vast expanse of water. To the east lies the petite bay of Nan Figué, where fishermen stand in a neat row, poised to haul in their afternoon catch. Directly ahead, the turquoise waves ripple in mesmerizing undulations, cresting into white foam that gently laps at their aching feet. Nearby, a group of women sings as they wash clothes by the river delta, their melodies blending in perfect harmony with the rhythmic cadence of the waves.

"Remember the gentleman I introduced you to at the play last night?" Ludovic asks, breaking the gentle rhythm of their walk.

She sighs, pausing for a moment of recollection. "I met more than one gentleman. Which one?"

"The playwright—Jean-Mara. He's one of my best buddies nowadays."

"Ah, Jean-Mara," she murmurs, her expression brightening as memory settles in.

"He lives nearby, you know," Ludovic continues casually.

"Where?" she stutters, her eyes darting around with curiosity.

"We just passed his house, back on the southern end of Desgranges."

Céline pauses, regret shows on her face. "We should've stopped to say hello."

"I thought the same. But it's too late now. Besides, Jean's a sweet talker. He'd have dragged us into an endless discussion, and we need to get home. We've been out since daybreak."

"You're right," she agrees, nodding. Then, with a hint of longing, she adds, "But we must visit him someday. He has that magic touch—the kind of words that send our people soul-searching."

"You bet he does, *chérie*," Ludovic replies with a chuckle. "He's got a gift."

Céline's eyes sparkle with mischief as she seizes on the word. "*Chérie?* Is that what I'm called now?"

The way she says it—her voice touched with a playful, sensual lilt—makes him think of a furtive meow.

"Sorry," he murmurs with a sheepish grin, "I meant Céline! But I dream of the day I'll be able to call you that."

She frowns briefly, then surprises him with a smile—an evocative combination of sternness and softness. "Words like *chérie, mon amour...* they carry weight, Ludovic. They take on a whole new dimension."

"And sometimes, that dimension could be for the better." He leans in, lips just a breath away from hers, but she turns abruptly, avoiding him.

"Ludovic," she calls out, pointing toward the bay, "look at the fishermen! They're laughing so much—must be a great catch!"

She springs to her feet and races toward the water, leaving Ludovic stranded mid-gesture.

"Céline!" he groans, amused but exasperated. "I'm not some naïve kid you can fool. Don't treat me like a snake charmer trying to tame a python. Do I look like a Céline-swallowing python to you?"

Laughing, she tosses him a glance over her shoulder, her movements beguiling. "Why are men all the same?"

"We're not," he counters with mock indignation, rising to follow her. "Each passion, every emotion, is uniquely aimed—targeted toward just one person."

"Of course," she teases, turning to face him, "and the depth of that passion must always be vetted, measured, weighed…"

"And mutually understood," he interjects, stepping closer.

"Mutually inclusive?" she quips, arching a brow.

"Precisely," he says with a grin. "And when all calculations are correct, the result must manifest itself."

"In what form?" she challenges, still keeping just out of his reach.

"In the warmest embrace," he replies, his gaze brimming with admiration.

Céline hesitates, her playful facade slipping just enough for a moment of vulnerability to show. "*Assez…* enough!" she shouts, though her tone lacks conviction. Her face contorts into an exaggerated mask of displeasure.

"Why the sudden turn?" Ludovic asks, baffled but amused.

"Because this conversation is entirely out of place," she says, though the trace of a smile lingers on her lips. "Let's go."

"As you command, mademoiselle," he replies with mock formality. With a slight bow, he steps aside, letting her take the lead. Together, they walk side by side, the playful tension between them palpable yet comforting.

By the river's mouth, they pull off their tennis shoes, rolling up their pants to wade across. One of the women washing clothes by the bank catches sight of Céline. "That man is surely a good shepherd, mademoiselle," she calls out with a twinkle in her eye, her flowered dress cinched at the waist with a foulard. Céline grins, waving back at the smiling women gathered near the water's edge. Yet, as they wade through the cool, flowing stream, a quiet unease begins to settle within her. Ludovic's words—assertive, tender, and of undeniable charm—linger in her mind, stirring something she isn't ready to face.

They cross the river in silence and continue along the shoreline, the rhythmic lapping of the waves providing an unwanted accompaniment to the tension between them. Céline finds herself grappling with a strange urge to present a version of herself she holds no belief in—a persona she fears might be beyond her reach. She puckers her lips faintly, as if dismissing an imagined rebuke from the voice of her own conscience. Sensing her unease, Ludovic makes the sensible choice to hold his tongue, allowing her space. The silence between them becomes weighty, unspoken thoughts swirling in the salt-tinged breeze.

After a while, Ludovic slows his pace, grimacing and leaning to one side. "*Ow,*" he murmurs, feigning a misstep. "A sharp stone."

"What's wrong, Dodo?" Céline rushes back to him, concern softening her voice. Without hesitation, she slips an arm around his shoulders and uses her other to steady his waist.

Hearing her call him Dodo sends a spark of joy coursing through Ludovic's chest. For the first time, she's let slip an affectionate note, a tiny window into her guarded heart. "It's nothing, *ché...*" he begins, but the rest of the word—*chérie*—catches in his throat. He dares not push too far. Wrapped in her supportive embrace, Ludovic can feel the tender warmth of her touch and the elegance of her form. Céline, sensing the shift, grins slightly, unsure of what to make of the moment. Yet, for a brief instant, she lets herself lean into the comforting rhythm of their shared connection.

Reflecting on their evolving friendship, Ludovic feels a pang in his heart at the frankness of Céline's words. He wonders when their bond might transform into a deeper, love-filled connection. She has genuinely captured his heart, but her uncompromising demeanor continues to baffle him. Unlike anyone he has met before, Céline's fierce dedication to social justice outshines the romantic inclinations he often finds in others. She is not a typical young woman from the tropics—she is exceptional, her convictions soaring beyond conventional notions of love. Ludovic realizes he must tread carefully, cautious not to jeopardize what they already share. His natural prudence, marked with self-doubt, advises him to keep his feelings in check.

In silence, they make their way along a sandy pathway that eventually threads into a trail. Skirting a bed of sticky cacti, they cross a shallow stream running parallel to the northern outskirts of Saint Louis. Home lies ahead at last.

<u>C h a p t e r   2 4</u>

As the seaside huts come into view, the landscape shifts to a tableau of well-tended backyards, shaded by dense almond trees and bordered by manicured banana gardens. The duo cuts across the pathway, entering the backyard of an old man named Célestin—a common practice in Haiti, where neighborly passageways crisscross private yards, linking them to the town's Main Street.

"*Bonsoir*, Uncle Célestin!" Ludovic greets as they approach a massive almond tree under which the elderly man rocks in his chair, savoring the cool afternoon breeze.

"I'm fine, my son," the old man replies, his frail voice quavering. He raises his head and hands, as though reaching for a face he can no longer clearly discern. Age has robbed him of sharp eyesight and clarity of mind, a fate inevitable for all, yet one the poor are fortunate to reach.

"I'm happy to see you, Uncle," Ludovic laughs. "You don't remember me, do you?" Céline stands in silence behind him, observing the exchange.

"Of course, I do!" Célestin replies with surprising vigor. "You're Malbranche's boy! *My*, how you've grown—quite the handsome young man! But who is this lively little *négresse*?" He shifts in his rocking chair, squinting to get a better look at Céline.

"I'm Céline, daughter of Monsieur Jean-Foreste Bodin," she interjects, cutting off Ludovic before he can respond.

"Ah, I see," the old man murmurs, nodding.

"How's your health, Uncle?" Ludovic asks, his tone turning serious.

"I lost control of it years ago," Célestin replies with a wry smile. "One day is good; the next, not so much. But the Good Lord keeps watch over me."

"You're right, Uncle. God is our ultimate lifeguard," Ludovic says. "By the way, where's Virgile? I haven't seen him in town since I returned in May."

"That fellow is like a night owl these days. Before dawn, he's already up and gone. People say he's involved with a young woman in Chenno, behind La Pierre Gorge. She's the elder daughter of Célimène, the mambo there."

"I thought he was engaged to Francilia," Ludovic says, perplexed.

"That's old news, my son!" Célestin chuckles. "Francilia ran off with another man from Graçette. Young folks today are reckless with their love lives—one day a couple, the next it's RRI!"

"What's RRI?" Céline asks, her curiosity piqued.

"Revoke and Replace Immediately!" Ludovic replies with a hearty laugh. Céline bursts out laughing, clutching her stomach to contain her mirth.

"I'm serious," Célestin insists. "It wasn't long ago that Virgile said he was going to propose to Francilia."

"Is that so?" Ludovic asks, trying to suppress his amusement.

"You better believe it," the old man replies with a hint of sadness in his voice.

"Graçette is in the third rural section, isn't it?" Céline asks, tilting her head slightly.

"*Oui, ma belle mademoiselle!*" Célestin's eyes widen. "How do you know such a thing?"

"My parents owned land there once," she says, her smile softening with memory.

The two young companions exchange a knowing glance, realizing how late it has become and how much farther they still have to travel. "Goodbye, Uncle Célestin," they say, smiling as they prepare to leave.

"Goodbye, my children. Go in peace, and may the Good Lord always guide you. Love you both to the moon and back!"

"Thank you, Uncle!" they reply, their voices filled with warmth.

Feeling inexplicably refreshed, though they haven't yet quenched their thirst with fresh water, Ludovic and Céline stroll past a carefree hedge of hibiscus, so ubiquitous in the islands. They wade through tall grasses into an empty lot on the right side of Main Street. An old mango tree casts a cool, tranquil shade over a group of children jump-roping at the center of the lot. The space serves as an informal courtyard for the adjoining house, a charming little thatched-roof cottage.

"*Bonsoir*, Aunt Nini," Ludovic calls out to a middle-aged woman seated on a low, splay-legged wooden chair, her arms working with a steady beat to pound maize in a mortar.

"*Bonsoir*, my pair of beautiful children," Aunt Nini replies with a smile, pausing her labor to watch them as they pass.

"How's your husband and the kids?" Ludovic asks with genuine concern.

"The children are fine, by the grace of God. But my husband…he's struggling with a bad knee. He has an appointment to see a specialist at the missionary hospital in Bonneau," she replies with a sigh.

"Sorry to hear that, Aunt Nini."

Before they can exchange further pleasantries, the children in the lot spot Ludovic and Céline. They race over in total elation shouting, "Dodo! Dodo! Dodo!" With a broad grin, Ludovic pulls a handful of chunky silver coins from his pocket, giving a fair amount to each of the eager youngsters. After several minutes of laughter and chatter, the young friends resume their walk, crossing Main Street. Ludovic waves to neighbors he seems to know at every turn, and they wave back with cheerful familiarity.

"It looks like you could run for president of uptown Saint Louis du Nord," Céline teases, half-joking, half-intrigued. "How do you know all these people?"

"I grew up in this part of town. My grandmother lives just down the curve of this street, in the cul-de-sac. Her name's Clairmantine. I've always lived downtown, but every weekend, you'd find me at my grandma's. I also idolized one of my uncles, my dad's younger brother, Abner. He's a poet who spent years—decades, really—living in Canada."

"Where is he now?"

"He's back home. A few years ago, he decided to return. Grandma's not in good health, and having him around makes her so happy. Before he came back, she was lonely—just her and her maid in the house."

"That's…unusual," Céline remarks, her brow furrowed.

"Folks in Vertus think he's crazy."

"Why?"

"They can't fathom why anyone would leave the comfort of Canada to come back here and face the daily struggles of life in Haiti."

"I know plenty of Haitians living in Europe and North America who dream of returning home. Maybe your uncle is living out that dream."

"The sad truth is, most people here—whether in Saint Louis or across our fabled country—believe life outside Haiti is nothing but a bed of roses."

A handful of row houses down, they pause at a modest brick home with an enclosed terrace. A teenager perches, legs akimbo, on a high-backed cherry-wood chair, her face buried in a French novel.

"*Bonsoir*, Royo," Ludovic calls. Céline stands quietly beside him.

"Dodo!" the girl squeals, leaping from her seat. Her long black hair, tied into tails and adorned with multicolored barrettes, bounces like jump ropes as she runs. In seconds, she unfastens the gate, throwing it wide open to welcome the visitors.

"*Manman*, Dodo is here!" she yells, bolting inside with swinging arms, her enthusiasm scattering the calm. In her rush, she collides with a half-open door, sending her book tumbling to the ground. The pages splay open like the wings of a fallen bird.

Céline, curious, stoops to pick up the book and its bookmark. A quick glance reveals the title: *Le Sourire Captivant de Jean-Robert* (The Captivating Smile of Jean-Robert). She smiles to herself, slipping the bookmark carefully back into its place. Royo, oblivious to her book's fate, dashes ahead, still calling for her mother.

Ludovic and Céline follow the girl's trail through a narrow hallway that opens into a graveled courtyard. At its center stands a deep well surrounded by neighborhood children, who race to pump water into their jugs. Their lively chatter ceases abruptly when they notice the visitors.

Royo makes her way into an outdoor kitchen, her hurried movements startling a mother hen nesting in a corner. The bird clucks in protest, flapping her wings to shield her chicks.

Céline and Ludovic linger by the kitchen door, waiting. Moments later, Royo reappears, accompanied by her mother, who greets them with a radiant smile. A silky blue headscarf loosely frames her face, while her cow-skin sandals, the smooth, tanned leather making a gentle clap against the gravel with each step.

"*Zazou!*" Ludovic cries with excitement, spreading his arms wide to embrace the two women.

"Méloria told me last week you were in town, but I didn't believe it," Zazou says, her voice warm and teasing. She coos like a dove, holding Ludovic tightly while Céline watches with quiet awe.

"I'm sorry, Zazou," Ludovic says laughing. "Yes, I've been here since May…just too busy with my father's projects to visit sooner."

Zazou turns her attention to Céline, her eyes sparkling with mischief. "*Bonsoir, ma belle chabine,*" she says, lowering her voice in mock flirtation while casting a playful glance at Ludovic. "Is she your new princess?" she teases, adjusting her aquamarine scarf over her bushy, silver-threaded hair. Her navy-blue apron, tied at the waist, shifts as she moves.

"No, we're just friends for now," Ludovic stammers, the words stumbling awkwardly from his lips.

Céline remains silent, declining to respond. Instead, she takes Royo's hand and leads her toward the back of the kitchen, leaving Zazou and Ludovic to their conversation. They stop beneath the shade of a grapefruit tree, its branches laden with fruit, near the well's cooling presence.

"You like to read a lot, don't you?" Céline asks, handing the French novel back to Royo.

"Yes, I read all the time, especially during the summer months out of school when there isn't really much to do around here."

"What do you mean 'there's not much to do?'" Céline questions, her tone a mix of curiosity and concern.

"Of course, we have plenty of activities, but Mom won't let me participate. There was a picnic last week at the beach in Cap-Rouge. I begged her to let me go. She refused, saying I'm too young. Besides, my father isn't here. He's never here." Royo punches out this last statement with a deep pout, her features suddenly older, marked with sadness. "My older brothers are not in the summer house this year, also."

"Where are they?" Céline asks, ever curious.

"They all live in Miami now with my dad. I have yet to meet my own father, my dad, face to face since I was born. And my brothers recently joined him there." Royo's eyes glisten with unshed tears, and she turns away in an effort to conceal her emotions.

It is a sad, continuous trend in these outlying regions of Haiti, even for families with property and possessions. Many wives are left to raise their children alone as their husbands travel to distant lands seeking work. The absence of steady employment opportunities forces many to live apart indefinitely, straining familial bonds.

"Haven't you spoken with him on the phone?" Céline inquires, resting a comforting hand on Royo's shoulder. She strokes the girl's braided hair with a tender touch, as if trying to mend the invisible cracks in her heart.

"I've never had a chance to talk to him."

"How so?" Céline's voice grows even softer, sensing the emotional weight of the conversation.

"I'm not sure he keeps a phone at the place he's living. When I was younger, my mom told me he used to live on a remote Bahamian island, where only migrant workers were allowed. But nowadays he's in Miami. It looks like he goes every way around the world, except for the one..."

"Which one?" Céline prods, though she knows the answer.

"Except for the road that leads him home to us." Tears threaten to spill, but Royo waves away Céline's offered tissue, signaling her determination to endure the moment unassisted.

"Why doesn't he come to visit your family?" Céline asks.

"Zazou told me that if he comes, he can't return to Miami. He doesn't have the necessary legal papers that would allow him to travel to and from that country. Meanwhile, I keep waiting here like an un-watered flower ready to shrivel, ultimately wither, and die."

"Have you talked to your mother about how you feel?"

"What good does it do? This would increase her suffering, furthering her everlasting solitude." Bookish and precocious, Royo steps to a bed of crotons lining a concrete fence. She snaps a stem, crushing it in her hand, the sap trickling like the sorrow etched across her face. She gazes toward the east, her eyes tracing the dull redness of the tropical sun sinking behind the mountains.

"My life has one color here—gray. Soon nightfall will inevitably make its way here, silencing the bustling sounds of tap-tap horns and cheerful voices. *Manman* and I will retreat to our lonely quarters, wrestling with our bitterness in the shadows of sleep, longing for the first rooster's crow, heralding a new day. One as hopeless as the last." Finally, tears spill freely, tracing clear lines down her cheeks.

"I was at the wonderful play last night in the *Salle d'Oeuvres*," Céline says, attempting to shift the conversation to a lighter note. "It was very interesting."

"I know. Jean-Mara, the organizer, is my older brother's best friend."

Before Royo can say more, Ludovic's voice cuts through their poignant exchange. "Céline, we'd best get going before darkness falls." He stands by the porch, his tone a mix of urgency and care.

Zazou approaches, her expression a blend of maternal concern and warmth. "Downtown is a long way away. Dodo, you should hurry to take your pretty lady home before her parents go bananas!"

"Zazou, you'll never change. You're just like my mom— forever overprotective, with the same incredible sense of humor," Ludovic replies, his smile infectious.

Everyone laughs a little, the tension lifting for a moment. Royo hands Céline two bags filled with green grapes, and the pair begins their journey back, leaving behind the bittersweet echoes of a family longing for unity.

<u>*C h a p t e r   2 5*</u>

Early the following day, Céline sets off in her parents' black Jeep, heading to Habitation Laveaux to visit her cousin Athénaise. Freshly back from France after completing an internship following her political science degree at *The Sorbonne*, Athénaise has much to share. Despite the early hour, the sun already pushes through the cottony clouds on the far horizon, spreading its first orange beams across the land. A few commuter vehicles dot the road, ferrying passengers bound for Port-de-Paix, the central hub of Northwest Haiti.

As Céline maneuvers along the foothills of Morne Miguel, she notices the figure of a young woman walking briskly eastward, her silhouette softened by the dusty morning haze. Slowing her speed, Céline draws closer and recognizes the familiar gait—it's Solitude, her housemaid, on her way to work. Céline halts the Jeep, rolling down the passenger-side window, a warm smile lighting her face like the cashew-colored glow of the rising sun.

"Solitude! Where are you off to so early?" Céline calls out, her voice edged with curiosity.

"Mademoiselle Céline, I'm headed to work!" Solitude replies, her tone cheerful despite the hour.

"This early?" Céline glances at her watch, her brow contracting in surprise.

"Yes, I can't be late. You know how your mom is!" Solitude says, her eyes brightening as she recognizes Céline. Her blue-

and-white garment is crisp and neat, her muslin sash cinched tightly at the waist. She removes her fletched straw hat, revealing hair that dances rebelliously over her broad shoulders. With practiced ease, she begins coaxing the stray locks into place, her fingers moving like seasoned performers at the *Salle d' Oeuvres*.

"Where's your house?" Céline asks, her eagerness heightened.

"Just past the almond trees at the bottom of the hill," Solitude replies, smoothing the last strand of her whimsically coiffed hair.

"And your husband? Is he home?" Céline inquires, frowning a little at the realization that she has yet to meet him.

"No, he's off to a day job in Rémoussin."

"Come on, hop in. I'll drive you to work!" Céline insists, her tone playful yet firm.

"That's kind of you, mademoiselle, but I'm used to walking."

"*Non, non, maintenant, j'insiste!* No, no, I insist," Céline chuckles, motioning for Solitude to climb aboard. With a quiet laugh, Solitude obliges, sliding into the passenger seat with a touch of flair. Céline pivots the Jeep in a tidy U-turn and drives Solitude to her parents' house. She lets her housemaid inside with a warm smile but refrains from going in herself, retaking the road back to Habitation Laveaux.

By now, truckloads of travelers and street vendors begin to crowd Main Street, joined by countless children locked into servitude, trudging their way to the bustling marketplace. For every small group of walking kids, Céline stops to offer them a ride in her Jeep. Some of the weary youngsters, wary of strangers, shyly decline her kindness. Others leap aboard without hesitation, their laughter ringing out as the vehicle rocks with their youthful glee.

As she crosses the Saint Louis River, Céline spots a group of elementary school children on an excursion near the hospital at La Pointe, about five kilometers south of town. She waves, and instantly a dozen small hands flutter back at her like captive butterflies set loose. "Me! Take me!" they shriek, sprinting toward the Jeep until their teacher's whistle cuts the air. With a smile that crinkles the corners of her sun-weathered eyes, Céline leans out the window. "Ah, little tigers," she laughs, voice thick with apology, "this old beast can barely carry its own rust, much less all your glorious noise! Next time I'll bring the bus— and your teacher's permission slip!" Many of the children recognize her; they live in the alleyways near the town square, not far from Céline's home.

Instead of driving on, Céline pulls over, watching the children march in single file until they disappear behind the twin rows of mango trees lining the dusty highway. Turning off the ignition, she steps out, wandering toward the riverbed where the cool water rushes over smooth stones. She lets the cycling waves lap against her bare toes, their touch a fleeting comfort.

Her thoughts, however, are far from serene. Louisinette's harrowing ordeal on that fateful night floods her mind. She finds herself retracing steps, the shadows of that tragic moment superimposed on the present. Céline moves along the riverbank, her eyes scanning the landscape for any sign of the site where the crime occurred. She stops at a shallow passageway, certain the assault took place on the south bank, mere feet from where she now stands.

The morning sun climbs higher, casting harsh light over the barren riverbed stretching toward the delta. The north bank's banana groves sway lightly in the breeze, while the eastern hilltop glimmers with golden rays. But here, by the water's edge, Céline finds nothing to confirm the scene etched in her memory. Frustrated and heavy-hearted, she returns to her Jeep, starting the engine with a resolve to leave the haunting river behind.

As she drives south toward Habitation Laveaux, the scenery shifts. Rural communities flank the dusty highway, their homes humble and worn. Scores of children, ragged and despondent, sweep the porches of houses that are not their own or stand listlessly at courtyard kitchens, wielding brooms with mechanical motions. Their tired, vacant expressions weigh on Céline, each a silent testament to a life of unchosen toil.

The road rises as Céline ascends a low hill, its slopes lined with dense banana groves clustering in abundance. At the hill's crest, she pulls aside to allow a commuter vehicle to pass, heading north toward Saint Louis. From her vantage point, the expanse of Laveaux opens before her, nestled in the valley below. To the west, a breezeway stretches toward the shoreline, where the rhythmic crash of heavy waves echoes across the land.

To the south lies a sprawling courtyard dominated by a massive building—a Catholic-run elementary school. Beyond that, the village of La Pointe shimmers like a desert mirage, its distant edges blurred by the haze of the rising sun. Céline veers left, her jeep giving a soft rattle as she approaches a grand set of wrought-iron gates, their black paint glinting in the morning light. These gates, imposing and majestic, dwarf even the ones that guard her own family's estate.

Two shirtless boys, clearly *restavèk*, sprint forward to open the gates. The Jeep glides through, its tires making a muted crunch over a marble-gravel alleyway flanked by an array of tropical wildflowers. Their vibrant hues and intoxicating scents envelop Céline, accompanying her like an unspoken welcome until she pulls up to the grandiose facade of an imposing mansion.

This sprawling multi-room residence is a striking homage to the 18th-century colonial era. Its architecture immediately evokes a sense of time suspended, a deliberate effort to preserve the elegance of a bygone age. Wide-open porches and patios encircle the mansion, supported by slender alabaster-white columns rimmed with gold, their upright forms adorned with intricate arabesque designs. From the ceilings dangle porcelain pots bursting with orchid flowers, their delicate petals cascading like living jewels. The scene is a visual feast, a haven of cultivated beauty designed to charm even the most sophisticated visitor.

To the right of the mansion, double French doors open onto a porch paved in veined black-and-white marble. This leads seamlessly to a turquoise granite and quartz pathway that curves toward a freshwater well nestled in the heart of the courtyard. Nearby, a stocky man, his face obscured by the tilt of his wide-brimmed hat, tends to a lush vegetable garden stretching toward a wooden fence in the distance. The rhythmic hiss of water from his hose is faintly audible above the bubbling sound of the fountain at the yard's center—a masterpiece of pink-veined marble and reinforced concrete. Its silvery-golden spray arcs skyward, catching the sunlight in dazzling bursts before cascading back into its granite-framed basin.

The courtyard itself is a veritable Eden. Groves of soursop, custard apples, and grenadines bend beneath the weight of their ripe bounty, their branches bending as though offering their fruits to the earth. Vibrant beds of scarlet roses and golden jasmines surround clusters of lemon-scented verbena, their intertwined fragrances merging to create an atmosphere so heady and surreal it feels almost otherworldly.

Céline steps out of her black jeep, pausing to let the blending scents and salty ocean breezes play across her face. Molded by the refined opulence of her uptown upbringing, she feels a familiar stir in her heart—a subdued but undeniable passion for beauty in its most fanciful forms. Removing her Coco Chanel glasses, her amaranthine eyes scan the courtyard, drinking in its splendor. For a fleeting moment, awe fills her, a dazzling emotion she didn't realize lay dormant.

However, this sensation is short-lived. A group of school-aged children shuffles into view, breaking the spell. Their white calico garments flutter in the breeze, but the details tell a harsher story: many are barefoot, their feet dusty and calloused, and a few boys wear tattered trousers and stained undershirts, streaked with sweat and smudged with road dust. The dozen children halt abruptly when they notice Céline standing on the final step of the front porch, her poised elegance an unmistakable contrast to their ragged forms.

"*Bonjour*, mademoiselle!" the children chirrup in a unified cacophony, their voices like baby mockingbirds. Céline, delighted, hops onto the final step but turns to face them. Their innocence and bright, dovish faces are impossible to ignore; the sight brings a warm tickle to her soul.

Suddenly, like a gust of wind, a young woman about Céline's age bursts through the front door and onto the porch. The children scatter instantly, like wildfowl taking flight at the first sign of danger.

"Céline, *ma chère cousine!*" the woman calls out, her voice brimming with joy. Tall and slender, with a fierce energy and a touch of poignant naiveté, she radiates both charm and theatricality. Her feline eyes flicker beneath mascaraed lashes, while her golden hair snarls in the gusting winds, seeming almost to resist the confines of her sharp, oval face.

"Athénaise," Céline replies with an enthusiastic laugh. "Look at you—still the same!"

"And you, Cousin! Still just as radiant," Athénaise counters with a dramatic flair, clasping Céline's hands. "You can't imagine how thrilled I am to have such an unexpected visit. Truly, I'm honored."

Her tone and mannerisms remind Céline of her cousin's unique character: exquisitely sweet, yet fiercely energetic, existing in a surreal aristocratic bubble. Athénaise's red-rouged lips and refined air seem designed to obscure any trace of African lineage. A true quadroon in the most historical sense, Athénaise embodies the elegance of their shared Bodin heritage but wears it differently from Céline, who embraces her mixed roots with pride.

Athénaise leads Céline down a hallway with gleaming mahogany floors, opening onto a veranda exuding artful grace. A polished cherry-wood coffee table surrounded by cushioned chairs and blanket-covered futons invites lounging. At the center of the table, an enormous stainless bowl overflows with bunches of green, red, and purple grapes, alongside strawberries the size of billiard balls. Around the edges of the veranda, orchids striped with every hue of the rainbow spill their delicate blossoms, perfuming the charming courtyard below.

Seated at the table like true aristocrats, Céline and Athénaise face a fringe of elderberries intermingled with radiant mandarin trees. Céline picks up a strawberry, rolling it between her fingers but declining to eat it. "Tell me, Athénaise, whatever happened to the promise you made me last week?" she asks.

"I don't know what you're talking about," Athénaise replies, shifting in her cherry-wood chair as she adjusts her golden hair, pinning it back with a pair of sleek, black lacquered combs.

"The visit you were supposed to make to my house."

Athénaise lets out a theatrical sigh. "*Pitit*, girl, I totally forgot! I'm sure you've heard about what happened between me and Marc."

"No, nothing at all," Céline says, her brow knitting with concern. "What happened?"

"How could you not have heard?" Athénaise says, quite astonished. "We broke up."

Céline's eyes widen. "No! What happened?"

"He left me for a chippie named Lonise—a brunette, I'm told." Athénaise shrugs, her voice trembling with uncharacteristic humility. Céline stares at her, disbelieving.

"But you two were so in love! When I met you last year at Bruno's party, you seemed inseparable."

"Yes, we were, but it didn't last. We clashed on everything. Marc rejected my values, accused me of being a carbon copy of my parents—clannish, aristocratic. He befriended everyone, from the market vendors to the shantytown dwellers, ignoring his parents' objections. He said I was living in a fog, refusing to see the world as it is."

"Why would he say such things to you?" Céline asks gently, peering into her cousin's tear-filled eyes. In a flash, a golden-furred poodle darts out of the breakfast room adjacent to the veranda.

Athénaise's voice falters. "He thought I inherited my parents' grotesque prejudices. He said I needed to change. But I thought he was the one who needed to change." Tears spill from her green eyes as she strokes the golden poodle that has leapt onto her lap, licking away the salty streaks on her cheeks.

Céline leans forward. "Cousin, he might have been right. Have you ever questioned why we live so differently—so comfortably—while most of our compatriots struggle just to survive? Do you think our lavish lives are providence, or something we should share?"

Athénaise's head snaps up. "Are you saying you agree with him?"

Céline hesitates, choosing her words carefully. "I think he freed himself from the fog of bigotry that bewitched us. There was a time I was ignorant too…"

Before Céline can finish, a group of young girls appears along the path to the main gates, headed for the shoreline to buy seafood. One stumbles, falling onto a bed of vincas, crushing the delicate flowers. The child's forehead bruises as blood trickles down her creamy face.

Athénaise leaps from her chair, striding into the garden with an air of fury. "Get out of my sight!" she roars, kicking the girl out of the vincas. Tears streaming, the girl struggles to her feet, rejoining her frightened friends near the gates.

Céline watches in stunned silence, her hands gripping the edge of the table. The warmth she felt for her cousin moments earlier vanishes, replaced by a cold unease. The stark contrast between their values feels insurmountable.

"Why did you do that?" Céline asks, her voice trembling.

Athénaise shrugs, brushing a lock of hair from her face. "She crushed my vincas."

Céline's heart sinks. She turns away, staring out at the garden, wondering how two people so close by blood could be so far apart in spirit. She then steps closer to comfort her fiery, volatile cousin, though her voice carries the weight of an unspeakable disappointment. "Athénaise, I feel sorry for you…

you need help!' Her words are as much an attempt to soothe as they are a quiet indictment.

Distracted, Céline's gaze follows the injured girl as she limps away, her tattered garments streaked with peat moss from the flowerbed. Céline's heart aches, a quiet rage simmering beneath her calm exterior. The young lady struggles to comprehend how Athénaise can show such boundless affection for her dog while harboring intense hatred for the poor children who only live to make her happy. Céline fights the urge to scream, swallowing a deep distaste for her cousin that she can neither express nor ignore.

And yet, Céline's compassion for Athénaise is genuine, born of an understanding that her cousin is a victim of a pernicious ignorance. Athénaise's cruel mannerisms, her self-centered outlook, and her inability to see beyond her gilded world all stem from a life cocooned in privilege. She has been raised in an atmosphere where her every whim is met without question, her moods studied and catered to by an endless retinue of *restavèk* whose own humanity has been stripped away in service of her comfort. Her obtuse refusal to see important matters is a perfect testament to her deeply unreachable insensitivity. Not once in her foggy imagination has it occurred that these people have human thoughts and feelings.

Having lived with the ability to buy and own whatever her heart desires, Athénaise rides a golden unicorn on a dazzling one-way street, forever lost within the frenzied world of the splendid, puerile uptown girls. Her prejudices are not merely inherited; they are woven into the very fabric of her being. She believes the world exists to flatter and serve her, her narrow understanding of love buried beneath layers of unconscious selfishness. To Céline, it is a tragic reality—Athénaise cannot fathom that the people around her have inner lives, emotions, or dreams.

When she makes her spectacular entry into the world of courtship, she runs across an array of eligible bachelors lining up like fuzzy flesh-tone slippers at her glowing feet. Love, for her, is less an act of giving and more a currency she trades to maintain her social standing; and it is hard to conceive that a woman with such a loveless outlook could be an honest partner in the arts of affection.

Her choice of Marc, the son of a wealthy businessman from Jacmel, reflects this transactional view of relationships. To Athénaise, Marc was not a partner but a strategic move, a trophy to confirm her place in the rigid hierarchy of wealth and status. She likely saw his affection not as a gift but as her due— his victory in a race she controlled from the start.

Céline, however, sees the emptiness lurking beneath her cousin's glittering facade. Athénaise floats through life on a velvet cloud, insulated from the struggles of the world, unaware of the pain her ignorance inflicts on others. In this moment, Céline is struck not only by her cousin's callousness but also by the profound loneliness it must bring. Athénaise may hold the world in her hands, but her heart remains a barren field, untouched by the true warmth of human connection.

Exasperated, Céline rises abruptly, snatching the keys to her Jeep. Athénaise, caught off guard, tries to mask her irritation. "Cousin, you're not leaving already, are you?" she asks, her voice strained with suppressed anger. But Céline has already moved toward the breakfast area, where two women are busy dusting the plastic-covered furniture. The servants pause their work to greet Céline, nodding politely before returning to their tasks, as Athénaise hurries after her retreating cousin.

The two women walk side by side through the narrow flower-lined alley, an uneasy silence stretching between them. Both are too consumed by their mutual resentment to bridge the growing divide, yet they exchange fragments of empty conversation in a half-hearted attempt to restore civility. Reaching the main porch, Céline leans in to deliver a quick farewell kiss to her cousin before heading to her Jeep. Without a backward glance, she starts the engine and speeds away, leaving Athénaise standing on the steps, her composure a brittle facade.

<u>*C h a p t e r   2 6*</u>

In the still, shadowed hours of early morning, Louisinette shifts around in bed, seeking gentler thoughts to calm her troubled mind. She turns sideways, then back again, but no position offers comfort. The coarse fabric of the bedclothes scratches her skin as she shrugs them aside and rises on tiptoe. Passing through the doorway to the children's room, she pauses, listening to Victorin's heavy snores in the background, his oblivious rest a jarring contrast to her inner unrest.

Sliding to the front window, she peers through its cracks. The moon's milky beams caress her careworn face, tricking her into believing it is dawn. Yet the muted darkness of the cottage reminds her that the day's light is still far off. With a sigh, she tiptoes back to bed, where she lies staring at the ceiling, praying to God for either the haven of sleep or the strength to resist the unwholesome images that claw at her night after night.

In one week, she leaves for Saint Louis. The thought steels her resolve, even as it tightens her chest with fear. How can she tell Victorin? The risks are insurmountable, yet so is her growing conviction that silence betrays herself and others who rely on her. For now, she feels subdued, held captive by her own reluctance.

At dawn, sunlight filters faintly through the window cracks, brushing against her lids and waking her groaning body. Victorin is already outside, leading their hungry burro to graze. She rolls to one side, her stomach churning from nausea, both physical and emotional. Yet, one thought overpowers the rest: she has to tell Victorin, somehow, about the journey that will change everything.

Startling, Louisinette hears the rush of footsteps and the low murmur of voices in the courtyard. She moves cautiously to the wall, pressing her sleep-deprived eyes to the crack in the window. There is Victorin, talking with his cousin Jean-Noël—a chubby boy in his late teens, wearing a well-worn brown hat and leaning against the backyard's apricot tree, hands buried deep in his pockets.

"I need to get up, or I'll miss another chance to talk," she mutters, steeling herself. Ignoring the aches that protest against her sudden movement, she races outside, side-stepping the children asleep in the other room. She pushes open the back door, the early morning's cooling breeze brushing against her unkempt hair. Standing on the steppingstone, she greets Victorin and his apprehensive young cousin.

"*Bonjou*, Jean-Noël. How's the family?" Her smile is warm but commands authority.

"*Bonjou, bel kouzin!* Hello, my pretty cousin! By the grace of God, everyone is okay, *wi*," Jean-Noël replies, jerking a hand from his pocket to adjust his hat.

"What brings you here so early?" Louisinette asks, her attention shifting discreetly to Victorin standing by the apricot tree.

"I'm heading up the hill to Gaspard with Victorin," Jean-Noël answers, his voice tentative.

"What for?" she asks, her wide eyes locking on her husband.

Victorin laughs, cutting in before the boy can stammer a reply. "Baby, I told you last week—there's going to be a *mazinga* on Monsieur Cérile's farm. We're clearing the fields for September planting, just before the rainy season ends."

"Jesus, Mary, and Joseph, you're going all the way to Gaspard to work for free?" Her voice rises, her disbelief streaked with anger.

"What do you mean by work for free? It's a *mazinga*," Victorin counters, his tone light, brushing off her concern.

"Did this *grandon* Cérile have a sudden change of heart?" Louisinette challenges, her voice dripping with sarcasm. "Not long ago, he made you and your cooperative boys work for an entire week without pay. And now you're going up there again—to be used as slaves?"

"Come on, darling," Victorin protests, his tone exasperated but still affectionate. "Don't even go there. I'm not working for Cérile. I'm helping the boys who keep an agreement with him."

In the morning stillness, a rooster crows on the other side of the fence, prompting a flurry of motion as a brood of chicks and hens scatter into the yard. Glowering, Victorin casts a sharp glare at the fowl before turning toward Louisinette. "Honey, you forgot your duties; you'd best start the day before we face a revolt from our chickens!" he teases. Laughing without mercy, he lands a quick kiss on her lips. Jean-Noël, standing nearby, joins in the laughter so loudly it almost frightens the already spooked birds away.

Throwing a playful arm over Louisinette's shoulder, Victorin guides her toward the house, their steps light and easy. She clucks her disapproval, mimicking a grumpy old hen as they amble inside. A minute later, she re-emerges carrying a canister filled with dry maize. Scattering it at the birds' feet, she watches as they greedily snatch up the edible grains before they even touch the ground.

"These chickens aren't the only ones needing food. You two can't go to work on empty stomachs either. Jean-Noël, come sit here," she says, gesturing to a low wooden chair. "I'll fix you a decent breakfast."

Grinning with cheerful compliance, Jean-Noël takes the seat. Using the moment to her advantage, Louisinette turns to Victorin. "I need to speak to you. There's something serious you must know." Grabbing his arm, she guides him indoors, asking him to wait in the room while she retrieves coffee powder from the silver chest. She then steps outside to the small outdoor kitchen, blowing at the cook-fire to hasten the coffee's readiness.

Jean-Noël shifts in his chair, glancing toward Louisinette as she works. "*Mèsiwi,* my cousin. Life gets harder every day for folks in this valley," he says, tipping his hat onto his lap.

"Looking at you, one would never notice it." Louisinette chuckles, her tone light but observant. "Your face is full and round like a *grandon*'s!"

"Don't tease me, cousin," he replies, a smile tugging at his lips. "Life is tough here, *wi,* but by the grace of God, you see my face glowing. As I was tellin' Crizo last week, if things don't change soon, our family is going to face real trouble. There's almost nothin' left to eat."

"Is Crizo your new *anmourèz?*" Louisinette inquires with playful curiosity. "She's a pretty girl, *wi.* Plenty of boys in the valley are eager to court her, I hear. Her big sister Annaise was just as lovely before she left for Port-au-Prince."

"You mean, she's not pretty anymore?" Jean-Noël asks, feigning shock.

"I'm not saying that. But you and I know how men in the city operate. If she lets herself be mistreated, she's doomed."

Jean-Noël nods, his voice dropping to a confidential tone. "Last week, Crizo told me Annaise got engaged to a man who speaks Spanish. She said he's madly in love with her—so much so, he wants to marry her right away."

Louisinette's eyes widen. "Say what? That's why Crizo mentioned going to Port-au-Prince last week. When did she tell you this?" Leaning in, she hangs on his every word, her love for familial gossip lighting up her expression.

"Cousin, keep this to yourself. You know how much superstition fills this valley. Nobody wants to spread news too soon."

"That's true," Louisinette murmurs, nodding. Her voice softens as she reflects. "But people here, especially Ti-Nèg, always seem to make big promises they can't keep. The moment they let hate take hold of their hearts, even their most faithful pledges fall apart…"

While they are talking, Louisinette finishes brewing the coffee. She pours it into a larger aluminum kettle, beckoning Jean-Noël to follow her inside. By the time they enter the modest living room, the children are already awake, playing hide-and-seek. Ever the attentive husband, Victorin has tidied their beds. Wasting no time, Louisinette gestures for Jean-Noël to sit near the silver chest. She disappears into her bedroom for a moment and returns with a black lacquer Japanese tray. Upon it, she places a *boukousou* sandwich filled with creamy peanut butter, along with a steaming cup of milky coffee.

"Yours is in the room, honey," she says to Victorin before turning back to Jean-Noël. She walks to the bedroom, Victorin trailing close behind. Inside, she hands him his breakfast on a smaller tray and gestures for him to sit beside her on the edge of the bed.

"I have to go to Saint Louis next Saturday," she announces, her tone steady with conviction. She cuts a piece of the *boukousou* sandwich, dips it into the milky coffee—prepared just the way he likes—and with a light touch presses it to his lips.

"Why are you going to Saint Louis?" he asks, chewing thoughtfully.

"Do you remember what Céline was talking about?"

"What thing? Was it about trying to change people's minds about their *restavèk*?"

"Well… yes and no. What I'm going to do in Saint Louis is related, but it's not quite that. It's about something from over five years ago. Next Saturday, I may finally have the chance to face that awful man…."

"Baby, NO. That's too dangerous! You could get yourself killed, thrown in jail—or worse—start something you won't be able to either win or stop!" His voice trembles, his entire body tense with emotion.

"I understand the risks," Louisinette says softly, her voice steady despite the tears forming in her eyes. "But, Victorin, I can't be at peace until I find justice. For a while, I thought I had my pain under control, thought I was free again… until Céline came to see me."

"That woman again!" he shouts, his voice rising in frustration. "How dare she drag you into this! How can you two dream of finding justice in this unjust country? Dreams like that always vaporize at dawn, leaving only false hope."

"I know what you mean, baby," she replies, her voice cracking. "But you don't understand what's been happening inside me every night. I've never shared my nightmares with you because I didn't want to disturb your peace. But when I wake up, and Lamizè stands before me at the start of each day, it tears me apart. Justice may be difficult, but I have to try. If I let this chance pass me by, my suffering will never end."

Tears spill freely down her face as she leans into Victorin, seeking comfort in his warm embrace.

"*Chérie,* you know how much I love you. I'd die for you without hesitation. But taking on the fat-bellied rich men and their powerful families? That's a risk too dangerous, too unsafe. I can't let you walk into that."

"Baby, I won't be alone," she insists, her voice laced with quiet resolve. "My friend Céline will be with me."

"What? Just two women, up against a pack of wolves with human faces, their jaws dripping with blood and violent hunger?" Victorin's voice trembles with fear and disbelief. "And don't forget, Céline is one of them. Nothing will happen to her—she knows that..."

"No, baby, it's not what you think!" Louisinette interrupts, her voice low and firm. "Last week, while you were away in Barlatier, Céline came up here with a fine young man named Ludovic. They promised to help me. They told me this fight isn't just mine—it's the fight for countless women like me in this country, women who've been victims of unspeakable violence.

"I took them to the mountain, to my cousin Claudette's house in Jean-Claire. From there, she led us to Fond Philippe. When we arrived, we found a huge crowd—a whole field full of people, young and old, ready to stand up for women's rights, especially us peasant women. It was incredible! And they're not stopping there. Hundreds of men and women from the mountain and valley will be heading to Saint Louis with me and my friends this Saturday. I won't be alone!"

Victorin's eyes widen in amazement; his jaw slackens. He begins to see the possibility of justice flickering in the distance like the first light of dawn. "Really?" He lifts his face skyward, as if seeking reassurance from Jesus, Mary, Joseph, and the heavens. Then, turning back to his wife, he gazes at her with awe and tenderness. "I have to come with you. I'll be by your side. We can leave the kids with Crizo!" he declares, grabbing her hands and kissing them. "I'm so proud of you, Louisinette."

Her heart warms at his support, but she shakes her head gently. "I'm grateful you're happy, honey. But Crizo—and many of our neighbors—are going, too. The entire mountain and valley are coming together. This isn't just my journey; it's everyone's."

"What about Dantilia?" he asks after a pause.

"She wants to come, but I'll convince her to stay. Someone has to protect our boys, and she loves them like her own. She'll keep them safe."

Bittersweet sensations course through Victorin's heart. Skeptical as ever, he now feels somewhat disarmed. There is little more he can do to dissuade Louisinette from her resolute quest for justice in Saint Louis. Accepting this, he resolves to become her staunchest supporter, offering unwavering moral and logistical aid, the kind befitting a devoted husband. Taking the final, satisfying bite of his *boukousou*s and wich, he feels a surge of renewed strength, like a warrior preparing for a decisive battle in a historic struggle.

Louisinette lies prone, her undone, shaggy black hair spilling copiously across Victorin's chest. For once, she is neither crying nor engulfed in sorrow, unlike so many nights before. Done with his food, Victorin slides the tray to the other side of the bed. Wrapping his arms around her, he gazes deeply into her luminous eyes, as though rediscovering her innate beauty. Memories of their past lovemaking surface, filling him with certainty that those tender moments will return.

"I love you more than anything," he whispers, his voice unwavering with conviction. In this moment, he is content—sure of his love for his wife, their shared bond, and their place in the brighter dawn he eagerly anticipates: a day of justice, reason, and greater human rights for all.

When Victorin and Louisinette step outside, Jean-Noël has already finished his breakfast and is playing with the boys, who are thrilled to have his familiar company. At the sight of Victorin, Jean-Noël halts, grabbing his hat from the top of the silver chest, ready to leave. The children clutch his pants, unwilling to part with their lively companion. With a firm but gentle tone, Louisinette calls them to her side. They comply with hesitation, their morning's excitement giving way to obedience.

As Victorin pushes open the back door, the golden glow of the relentless Haitian sun greets them, illuminating the surrounding hills with buoyant light. Between the tree-covered headlands, the sharp ridge of Morne Gaspard stands sentinel in the distance, where the first rays of dawn part the lingering embrace of the night. On the ground, the dew surrenders to the sun's warm caress—a slow dissolve of silver into thirsty earth.

Victorin grabs his machete and a sack of dry fronds, striding eastward toward Gaspard. Jean-Noël hurries behind him, the effort evident in his labored breaths as he tries to match Victorin's brisk pace.

"Good day…Cousin!" Jean-Noël grunts, at last finding his rhythm. The children, unable to suppress their attachment, attempt to follow, but Louisinette tightens her maternal hold. When she finally releases them, they dart like rabbits to the back door. But it is too late; by the time they leap into the open air, Victorin and Jean-Noël have already vanished beneath the vast canopy of the overgrown cacti and coffee fields, leaving only the promise of their return.

<u>*Chapter 27*</u>

Saint Louis hums with festive energy. From Rivière-des-Barres at the northern entrance to the Saint Louis River at its southern end, homes are freshly painted, their walls gleaming in glowing hues. Blue and red—the proud colors of the Haitian flag—dominate the streetscape. The townsfolk, fierce patriots to their core, refuse to bow to the central government's "Haitian Salvation" campaign, which parrots hollow promises: Believe in God and the Church, and your worst problems will cease to exist. This relentless flood of reactionary, papalist rhetoric does little to sway the people of Saint Louis, whose steadfast resistance to such propaganda remains one of their defining traits.

For them, faith is entwined not with submission but with celebration. The town is abuzz with preparations for *La Saint Louis*, the grandest religious festival in the northwest province, held each year in honor of Saint Louis Roi de France. It is August, the blazing finale of summer, and all the island's roads converge on this energizing coastal town. Here, rivers flow mysteriously upstream, vultures and eagles soar unchallenged, and men carry their secrets with heads held high, unburdened by guilt as long as they remain hidden.

On this Saturday morning, Céline is roused by the lilting sound of a banjo drifting through her window. Across the street, a troupe of troubadours and a lone jongleur stroll by, their rainbow-colored overalls shimmering in the sunlight.

Their music dances through the air, an ode to the festival's unfolding vibrancy. The banjo player leads the group, accompanied by three singers whose voices meld into a tapestry of high-pitched melodies. The lively procession ambles away from the main square, heading toward Chez Ramo, a shadowy haunt tucked near the shoreline, infamous as a magnet for pleasure-seekers. Fresh "girls" from the Dominican Republic and Port-au-Prince are shuttled in weekly, catering to the town's nocturnal appetites during this celebratory frenzy.

Curious, Céline throws open her window curtains, her eyes catching the folk musicians' colorful spectacle. Their serenade delights her, a rustic harmony cutting through the buzzing streets. Inspired, she fishes a twenty-dollar bill from her purse, secures it with a rubber band, and tosses it down to the performers. The money flutters into their midst, sparking a raucous cheer. Neighborhood children, drawn by the commotion, gather in growing clusters beneath her window. The singers, emboldened by Céline's generosity, raise their voices to new crescendos, their chorus blending with the rhythmic strumming of the banjo.

As Céline leans into the window, her long tresses cascade over the panes, catching the sunlight like threads of spun gold. In this fleeting moment, she becomes a Haitian Rapunzel, radiant and alive, basking in the rustic charm of a morning serenade.

"Mademoiselle Céline, *breakfast is ready!*" echoes Solitude, standing in the entryway to Céline's bedroom.

"Oh, I forgot," Céline responds, pulling her hair away from the window to clamber from her unmade bed. Grabbing a fluffy brown towel from the hall rack, she hugs Solitude, binding her tresses on top of her head with gusto.

"What's new? It's the same storyline every day…you *forget!*" Solitude chides and teases her. "Hurry up, before your food gets cold!"

Céline has no time to dawdle; she has scheduled for today a most urgent meeting with her Ludovic. Twenty minutes later, she emerges from the bathroom, refreshed from a quick shower. Making it to the dining room, she sees that her food is nowhere in sight. Grimacing, she figures Solitude must have taken it to the kitchen. Going in, she discovers her warmed-up breakfast there—it is her favorite Haitian omelet, served over a buttery baguette and fresh-squeezed grapefruit juice. In few quick bites, she wolfs everything down.

"Why are you in such a hurry?" asks Solitude solicitously.

"I have to go uptown for a meeting; it's growing late."

"*Yeah right,* those troubadours outside stole your mind." Chuckling, Solitude exudes an aura of servant's wisdom; she loves to kid around.

"Oh, they're too funny! Where are Mom and Dad?"

"They went uptown, I think."

"Where did they go? It's so early."

"Well, I don't know. Earlier when I first came, I overheard your mom talking with someone about a fancy party to be held tonight. All the very important people in town will attend. You know, it's a holiday! By the way, arriving here this morning I met more than a half-dozen groups of musicians. The last musical group is stationed near the river pass, coming up as they saw me approaching."

"What did you do?"

"I ran away, as fast as I could!"

This made Céline chortle. "*Poukisa,* why?"

"They wanted money, which I didn't have. And they never take no for an answer." The maid then turns her face sideways.

"Mademoiselle Céline," she utters timidly, "I'm waitin' for my holiday bonus. *La Saint Louis* is fast coming. I'm counting on you to buy me some lovely clothes items for my kids…" Having started off in a cheerful manner, Solitude suddenly trails off in embarrassment, lowering her soft voice and tilting her head.

"Don't worry, things will be squared away. Go to my bedroom, peek inside the top drawer of my biggest dresser. There's a brown manila envelope, just bring it back downstairs to me."

The housemaid breathlessly races upstairs, and in less than a minute bounds back downstairs with the envelope. Just when she is about to hand it to Céline, the doorbell rings. As they glance over to the window shades, there stands Ludovic, wearing his trademark white t-shirt and blue jeans.

"It's your handsome young man, mademoiselle," Solitude titters.

"Really? Keep the envelope." Puffing, Céline scurries to the gates, pushing the back door open along the way. "See you later, Solitude."

"When are you coming back? Need to know when, *mademoiselle,* even if you're late again, in order to reheat your food!" the maid squeals, ripping open the manila envelope and pulling out a pair of fifty-dollar bills.

She is overjoyed, reaching to give her mistress a big hug for the gratuity, but by this time Céline is gone.

<u>*Chapter 28*</u>

The minuscule span of Saint Louis's topmost elite mirrors the thin layer that constitutes the upper classes of Haitian society. Nestled in their stunningly furnished provincial homes, they remain oblivious to the abject poverty engulfing millions of their compatriots. This group—composed of coffee exporters, local merchants, and heirs to the remnants of a bygone landed aristocracy—relies mainly on inherited wealth as a financial safety net, while clumsily trying to position themselves as guardians of an antiquated social order.

Self-conscious of their limited influence, they resign themselves to being second-class bourgeois, content with exploiting the labor of their *restavèk* and lower-class subjects. Their ambitions rarely extend beyond immediate material gain, and their intellectual pursuits are often guided by opportunistic arrivistes, devoid of humane awareness, much like charlatans such as Dalambert.

To this elite, wealth is not merely possession but ostentatious display—lavish parties in meticulously groomed courtyards, where marble-graveled pathways wind through exotic gardens tended by underpaid servants. Their gatherings mix American "dirty dancing" with contrived voodoo rituals, blending superstition with superficial piety. These displays, far from honoring African heritage, reveal a hollow mimicry, bereft of genuine spiritual depth.

Yet, despite their access to modern comforts, they remain mired in gregarious excesses and deep-seated superstitions. Their beliefs often surpass the desperation of the downtrodden, like Emilus the shoe-shiner or Ti-Marie-Suzette-Sonnen, the homeless girl on the street corner. For them, *La Saint Louis* becomes the grand stage to flaunt their existence—a curious blend of privilege, insecurity, and misplaced grandeur.

It is within this morally repugnant reality that these recalcitrant lumpen-bourgeois stand ready for yet another Ultimate Bash of Pointless Extravagance. Tonight, Madame Lucette Dominique Proilleur, a *marabou* with the hue of a milky coffee, whose elegant posture is hard to ignore, celebrates her twenty-ninth birthday. She is married to Fénélon Proilleur, an eccentric dinosaur twice her age who inherits the fortunes of his father. They own a vast portion of the shallow plains off the north bank of La Rivière-des-Barres.

Lucette is a quintessential example of fame springing from sheer providence alone. She has no formal education and can barely read in broken French even at the developmental level. She only conserves her natural beauty—an innocent demeanor, skillfully managed *à la* street-smart styles— to camouflage the ill-mannerisms dwelling beneath her skin. Her eyes are an incredible, purplish-blue; when they twinkle, they bring on the lustful urges of most men, desirable and otherwise. Being neither tall nor short, in formal gatherings she towers over Monsieur Proilleur, who is chubby, myopic, and somewhat anal-retentive, with a dull sense of masculine chivalry and civility.

Like all young women in Lucette's predicament, it is money, not love, that formulates her social *parvenu* status; once the status of Madame de Grand Salon is attained, her attentions soon turn to the hunt for an infinite, temporary love. Since Lucette lacks the intellectual hook to catch *cet amour provisoire sans fin,* this ever-tentative love, she begins to display her flawless figure, courting those unafraid of venturing forth into her fatal love-nest. Thus, Dalambert shortly becomes one of her secretive yet ardent lovers.

Lucette is extensively versed in playing her role as a *nouveau riche,* a corrupt aristocrat traveling to Port-au-Prince every Christmas, suitcases filled with American dollars, hiring a half-dozen maids solely to chaperone her around the downtown district. From fancy footwear to elegant velvet dresses, she buys new clothes without even trying them on, as a way to suppress the disquieting gloom which pervades her unhappy soul.

However, she is the first one to laugh at her own fears, concealed pains, and social clumsiness. She will show coyness at the first sound of a rustling leaf—a shrewd skill, reminiscent to that of surreal histrionics performed by minor uptown sluts. Money will solely purchase affection, not mutually inclusive emotions or love. In essence, she feels nothing for Monsieur Proilleur—the man who has brought her into high societies, but also a person she appears ready to transform into a miserable Shakespearean cuckold.

Proilleur spends most of his time traveling abroad on business trips. To fill the void, the emptiness in his young wife's soul, their living room has to be regularly transformed into a replica of decorative grandiosity. Every month, Lucette finds an excuse to throw a lavish party at their sophisticated, copiously *chic* mansion. As for all small communities, in the regal backwaters of Saint Louis, the secret love affair between Dalambert and Lucette has long been *un secret de polichinelle*—an open secret, so open that word has reached Proilleur's ears. But he shrugs it off, saying he will not hire a private detective to watch his wife's every move. He trusts and loves her instead.

Lucette has spent an entire year preparing for tonight's posh birthday party. She has spent thousands on three whirlwind trips abroad, buying fancy and exotic commodities including sets of Coco Chanel glasses and fine, cozy, opulent colognes—crowd-pleasers with the magic to force bourgeois in splendid gatherings to perk their noggins skyward, sniffing the air like tame baby hounds. Lucette plans on distributing these luxuriant gifts secretly to some of her close associates during the night, the ones who, with a theatrical show of kinship, might hand them back to her as presumed birthday presents. But it is probable that few of her supposedly "good" friends will return the items. Despite such social backstabbing and friendship blackmailing, she cannot seem to understand that her money will buy neither happiness nor true friends.

An untold number of farm animals will be slaughtered for the event. Lucette's wealth and beauty will be exhibited and paraded for all to see, and the whiny, hopelessly spoiled aristocrats from downtown and uptown alike will be able to settle in, enjoying another night in a rich man's paradise.

*****

Céline and Ludovic, avoiding Main Street by taking a sandy trail near the shoreline, arrive at Ludovic's grandmother's house in Vertus. The colonial mansion, with its large red bricks and wide-paneled windows, is enclosed by a heavy wrought-iron fence. Ludovic's grandmother, however, is nowhere to be seen. Instead, the housemaid sits quietly on the concrete terrace by the back door, peeling lima beans from their pods into a plastic bowl, preparing for the midday meal. The expansive backyard, shaded by carefully trimmed almond trees, stretches toward a thatched-roof cottage in the far corner. There, Céline and

Ludovic enter to find Jean-Mara and Jessie waiting for them with a mix of impatience and excitement.

"Here you are, at last!" Jessie cries with excitement, leaping from her chair to give her friends warm double-hugs. Her exuberance is contagious, but Jean-Mara, ever composed, greets them with his usual discreet smile. Yet, it's clear he is pleased. "I told Jessie you'd be here. Patience pays off," he says, running a hand through his tousled hair before handing Céline a three-page draft. "This is the outline for tonight."

Without a word, Céline takes the paper and begins scanning it with intense focus, her eyes scrutinizing every detail. Ludovic leans over her shoulder, reading along, his casual demeanor in sharp contrast to Céline's furrowed brow. "We need to be there by nine o'clock?" Céline asks, her voice trembling with nerves.

"I'm worried about the timing too," Jessie admits with a sigh, mirroring Céline's unease.

"Why're you ladies so anxious?" Ludovic asks, his boyish grin radiating confidence. His tone carries the fervor of youthful determination.

"I think it's too late. By the time Louisinette and her group get there, Dalambert might already be gone," Céline reasons, searching Ludovic's face for his usual agreement.

"No, nine o'clock is better," Ludovic counters, his hand instinctively brushing Céline's neck in a reassuring gesture. "Lucette is his secret lover. He'll stay long after most of the guests leave."

Jean-Mara interjects thoughtfully, "We need to wait for more guests to arrive. A larger crowd will amplify our impact."

"I get it now, but I thought the plan was to confront him when fewer people were around," Jessie says, her hesitation palpable.

"No, we want to corner him in front of his cronies," Jean-Mara explains in a firm tone of voice. His words resonate with conviction.

"We also need to anticipate their reactions," Céline murmurs, her voice betraying a flicker of fear. "I'm scared to death."

Jessie, emboldened, places her hands on her hips. "You knew this was part of the deal, girl. I'm ready for whatever happens. *Que sera, sera.*"

Céline sighs, her apprehension bubbling to the surface. "I'm only nervous because my parents will be there. Otherwise, I wouldn't care."

"So will mine, and Jessie's too," Ludovic adds. "Their presence is our best shield. They can vouch for us if things spiral out of control."

"Exactly. Their influence might help Louisinette walk away unharmed," Jean-Mara says with a dry chuckle. His gaze meets Céline's, as if seeking her approval. "We need to prepare. Things could get messy tonight. I saw Claudette on Monday. She's ready, and so are her women."

"You went all the way up there to meet her?" Céline cries out, her surprise evident.

"Yes, my lady," Jean-Mara replies with a wry smile.

"Did you see Louisinette?" Céline presses.

"No, she'd already left by the time I got there."

Rejuvenated by the update, Céline speaks with newfound determination. "Jean, you'll stay with Louisinette and her crowd—however large it is. Ludovic, Jessie, and I will be inside the party, gauging the situation."

"Jean, wait for my signal before you act," Jessie says with a commanding voice.

"It's a plan!" they declare, their voices united in purpose.

Chapter 29

Consensus has been reached; the group walks out of the cottage, ready to face the uncertainty of the next few hours. Jean-Mara makes his way north toward Ti-Rivière, going to the community of Desgranges where he lives. Jessie heads toward Nan Gwo Twou to see a friend. Meanwhile, Céline and Ludovic remain in the courtyard. They stroll over to the tallest of the almond trees adjacent to the house, where Ludovic leans against a thick tree trunk, and Céline stands next to him, her head tilting toward his chest.

Shaking, she lingers, contemplating the ocean winds welling out from the beachfront colonial house. The thought of going home to face her parents fills her with dread. She knows what she is about to undertake could drive a wedge between her life of privilege and the uncertain path of social and political resistance. Her parents' reaction, especially when they see her at the forefront of the charge against Dalambert, remains an unsettling question.

Sighing, Céline imagines her godmother Aunt Marguerite's disapproving grimace when confronted with her bold actions. She adores her parents, and she possesses a clear understanding of their unconditional affection for her. Yet, she cannot abandon her pledge to seek justice for Louisinette. For Céline, this mission is more than a moral obligation; it is a test of her courage and conviction. She knows justice rarely comes without sacrifice, and she is prepared to bear the cost. Tears trickle

211

down her cheeks as she turns to Ludovic, seeking his steadying presence.

Céline finds growing comfort in Ludovic's companionship. His reassuring touch and unwavering support ground her in moments of doubt. He stands behind her, his hands moving in slow circles over her shoulders—the steady pressure of his palms softening her tension like warm wax. Though she remains silent, she draws strength from his calm demeanor. Despite her internal struggle to keep his romantic feelings at bay, she cannot deny how much she values his presence.

"It's okay, Liline. We'll be fine, and so will Louisinette and her friends. There are moments in history that demand action," Ludovic says softly, his voice imbued with quiet determination. "You brought this cause to us, and we embraced it wholeheartedly. We're doing this because it's the right thing to do, and because people like us—those with privilege and access—have the power to influence real change. Think of Jacques Roumain and Jacques Stéphen Alexis. They, too, came from privilege and used their voices to fight for justice. Change doesn't come without risk, but it's a risk worth taking."

Céline's breath catches midair as his words slip under her skin, burrowing where her pulse thrums loudest. She leans against him, finding solace in his strength, his tender voice, and his firm faith in their shared purpose. His conviction steadies her, as if a flicker of hope has ignited within her soul.

She begins to grasp that life is about stepping beyond comfort zones and embracing the unknown. Growth comes through risk, and those willing to challenge the status quo are the ones who create lasting change. Miracles rarely come to the disenfranchised like Louisinette; progress is achieved through organized efforts and the solidarity of compassionate allies. Céline knows that only through such determination can people like Louisinette and her neighbors hope to claim justice and dignity.

Wrestling with these thoughts, Céline twists around in Ludovic's arms, pulling back her hair that drapes over his shoulders but remaining locked in his embrace. Tilting her head, her rainbow-flecked blue eyes sparkle in his rapt gaze. Her arms loop around his neck, overeager—the kiss lands half on his forehead, half in his eyebrow, a smudge of affection. Ludovic stiffens, then melts, her misaimed tenderness flooding him with unexpected heat. He doesn't anticipate such a gesture from her—tentative yet disarming. His chest tightens as he wonders if she feels even a fraction of the affection he harbors for her.

"Lornise, is the food ready?" a voice shrieks from inside the house, shattering the fragile bubble of intimacy between them. Céline steps a bit away, while Ludovic continues leaning against the trunk, head facing the house's back door.

"Not yet, madame. It took me two hours in Nan Figué this morning to find the barracuda fish you wanted. Oniace, the head of the fishermen, was only selling catfish and red snappers when I got there. A woman from Cap-Rouge purchased his entire catch in one bid. I had to wait for the next round of catch," the maid answers, strolling like a brown-streaked wild goose wrapped in a flimsy red madras, moving in rapid footsteps to the outdoor kitchen where the food is being cooked.

Ludovic shakes his head at her once she sees him standing by a tree near the outdoor kitchen, and he laughs. "Tell Grandma I'm here!"

Startled by his chortling presence, almost invisible in the spreading tree shadows, Lornise races into the house to fetch Ludovic's grandmother, who walks outside into the courtyard.

"Hey, Dodo! How long have you been here?"

"About an hour. I hunted all over for you when I first came," he lies.

She doesn't notice, simply happy to see her grandson. "I had to go to Marché Mercredi, helping Aunt Margo for tonight's Grand Bal at the Proilleur's."

"Really?" His eyes widen as he looks over at Céline, who is listening with an utmost air of interest.

"Yeah. You should see the many people going in and out of Aunt Margo's home. About a dozen maids and *restavèk* were busy cooking, cleaning, and transporting materials next door to Lucette's mansion, where workers were hurrying, putting up the giant tent for the fiesta," Grandma says, exposing ruddy, raw cheekbones where her wrinkles stretch under huge gales of laughter. Her housedress lofts and billows above her cow-skin sandals as she moves in long strides to meet Ludovic under the almond tree. "Who is this pretty lady with you today?" she cries upon reaching the tree.

"This is Céline Bodin, a friend from the downtown area."

"Are you the daughter of Jean-Foreste?" she coos, glad to see her. Shyly, but wanting to say something more, Céline nods her head. Céline felt her cheeks flush under the older woman's keen gaze. Unsure whether to speak or merely nod, she offered a polite smile and let Ludovic take the lead.

"I've known your parents a long time. Your dad owns a coffee depot in one of the great halls right up the street. Why don't you guys come in? Dodo, I have fresh squeezed grenadine in the fridge, your favorite drink."

"Yes, Grandma. We'll get some."

Old gossiper that she is, Grandma waits for them to go inside; in a quick gesture, she calls out to Ludovic. He leaves

Céline on the steps, as off to Grandma he goes, heaving a patient sigh.

"I know what you wanna know," he whispers in a muted tone.

"Tell me the truth: is she the one, the final one?"

"I don't know, Grandma. I can only hope so. I'll let you know."

"You'd better cherish this young woman; she's the classiest girl I've ever noticed you with. Oh, and she's lovely, too."

"I'll see you tonight, Grandma." He then hustles into the house to join Céline, who's standing by the fridge, her fingers brushing the cool glass of the grenadine bottle. She wonders if Ludovic's grandmother likes her or if her nod and shy smile have betrayed too much nervousness. Pouring the juice into a glass, she catches her reflection in the chrome and smooths a stray lock of hair.

An hour later, they step down from the front porch and merge into the flow of Main Street, heading south. It is late morning on Saturday, and the street is bustling with life. Most pedestrians are peasants returning from the market square, their baskets heavy with produce.

Three houses down, they encounter a perky teenage girl wearing a bleach-stained garment and balancing a banana-frond pannier filled with papayas on her head. She strolls toward them, her eyes bright with hope. Before she can offer her goods to Céline, Ludovic pulls ten *goud* from his wallet and presses it into her hand. Overwhelmed with gratitude, the girl's face breaks into a radiant smile, and she bursts into laughter, her voice ringing like a bell through the midday air. Céline takes two papayas from the pannier, nodding for the girl to keep the rest. The girl skips away, her laughter trailing behind her like an unseen melody.

As they continue south, they pass a long line of peasant women gathered in the front yard of Aunt Pauléma, a gray-haired matriarch in her late sixties who reigns over the local tobacco trade. Little boys, some no older than ten, cling to their mothers' khaki dresses while chomping on oversized tobacco leaves. Céline shakes her head, her brow furrowing. "Dangerous habit," she mutters, her voice barely audible over the chatter of the crowd.

Ludovic offers a quiet chuckle but says nothing.

Eager to escape the oppressive heat of the late morning sun, they turn onto a back trail winding toward the seaside. The din of Main Street fades behind them, replaced by the rustle of almond leaves and the rhythmic crash of waves in the distance. From here, they head south toward downtown, their steps definite. Though the exact challenges ahead remain unclear, they press onward, ready to confront the lion's mouth of danger among a crowd of strangers and allies alike.

Chapter 30

Three o'clock in the afternoon: Louisinette and her growing group begin descending from the mountain villages. Their ranks swell as even more people trickle in, joining them as they progress along the way. Their journey takes them east of the Acajou River, near the shallow passageway of Lavomie. They're on the road to Forje village, which serves as the gateway to the valley floor. From there, their line stretches all the way back to Dédé Sapotille. This is where a one-thousand-pound boulder squats on the cliff's lip—balanced on a child's handful of pebbles, its bulk cocked toward the river basin like a fist unclenching. Claudette and Louisinette stride forward, shoulders squared against the wind. Behind them, Victorin matches their pace—and Crizo, her knee-length skirt snapping like a battle banner with every step.

Crizo's eyes flash and glimmer in the midday's harsh sun. Jean-Noël hands her his large, shielding straw-poked hat to keep her ebony face shaded. Louisinette, motioning toward the flowing water ahead, stops to instruct everybody how to cross. With feverish strides they wade through the shallow water, advancing along a narrow trail. Then, they reach a giant fig tree at the entry of Forje. There, they decide to halt their march and wait for sundown under sheltering trees.

The tiny village of Basen Tounen lies just yards away. From the milling crowd, silhouettes of naked children flash in the river basin, while roadside vendors haggle with buyers at little

217

crossroads meat stands. News of their "secret mission" sweeps through the area like wildfire. Soon, peasant women and children pour in by the hundreds from Graçette, Barlatier, Morne Mérice, Nan Fon, and other smaller villages, adding "people fuel" to their ranks.

Mixed emotions and raw feelings surge unbounded. Many folks wish to march on; but Claudette, fearing a surprise visit from the local authorities, tells them to wait in a most skillful move. Louisinette, on the other hand, is growing tense. Hair wrapped tightly in her favorite blue headcloth, she leans on Victorin, plumbing the depths of his strength, to appease her fears. She and Claudette keep searching down the trail, looking for Jean-Mara, who told them not to move beyond this point. Only some members of the sprawling crowd know the entire story of Louisinette's rape and Dalambert's role in it. Many of them think they are only marching today for women's rights and better living conditions. Sellers returning from Saint Louis slow their way through the mountain passes upon reaching the crowd. Some of them simply give up on their original destination to join Louisinette and her thronging, rebellious folks.

The huge herd of people now numbers in several hundreds. The few men with them, including Victorin, decide to form a civil brigade, forming a cordon around the perimeter of the crowd to create some sense of order. By late afternoon, thunder rumbles from the east, and Louisinette takes it as a bad sign. With a commanding stride, she approaches Victorin, who stands at the tail end of one long line talking to a small group.

"*Chéri*, my head is…spinning," she pants, losing breath, gawking around like a buzzing fly trapped in a spider's web.

"It'll be okay, honey. Tonight's our night. There's no thunder or lightning that can break or disturb this moment. It's now or never!" Victorin proclaims with expansive authority and unlimited self-assurance. Holding his wife fondly by the shoulders, he kisses her lips to calm her down. Now, he seems more determined than his wife.

A young man, carting a bottle of *kleren*—the popular Haitian rum—strolls to the giant fig tree's trunk. He raises the bottle toward the eastern mountain, where thunder continues to rumble, roar, and roll. Seeking Granbwa's protection, God of the Forest, he sprinkles seven droplets of rum onto the tree. He then calls upon the African gods for immunity from what common folks call "Saint Louis's wild dogs"—the town's police.

Just minutes later, the thunder subsides; the ballooning gray clouds vanish, revealing the blue ridge of Morne Zombie in the distance. By six o'clock, the sun's last piercing rays sink into blurs behind the mountain, leaving only faint traces of sunglow that scatter in golden spots across the mountainsides. The oppressive heat gives way to a cooling breeze, soothing the mounting tension. Beneath the giant fig tree, people stand or squat on the thick undergrowth, their murmurs fading into the rhythmic chirping of crickets as twilight descends.

Suddenly, Crizo appears, jogging up to Claudette and Louisinette, her breathing labored. "I saw a man in a trench coat walking this way," she gasps, her voice barely above a whisper.

Louisinette and Claudette exchange alarmed glances, their eyes scanning the dense plantation undergrowth. "Where?" they demand in unison, their voices hushed but urgent.

Crizo points eastward, but before she can elaborate, Claudette raises a finger to her lips, silencing her. This is no time to incite panic; the crowd, already restless, needs no further provocation.

The group settles again, their collective resolve evident as they await Jean-Mara's return, the mystery of the trench-coated man adding a new layer of tension to their already fraught mission.

"There, under the banana grove," Crizo replies, her voice taut, pointing emphatically toward the shadows. Then, a familiar figure emerges from the trees: Jean-Mara, weaving his way through the undergrowth. Taking the most discreet path possible, he moves swiftly, his footsteps muffled by the rustling foliage. The crowd's murmur grows as he approaches—a tide of whispers breaking against his path. When he finally reaches Louisinette and Claudette, daylight bleeds its last across the horizon, and the air thrums with the crowd's impatient energy.

"Jean…" Claudette blurts, her tone a mix of relief and reproach.

"Sorry I'm late," Jean mutters, shrugging off his trench coat and slinging it over his shoulder. His gaze sweeps over the gathering crowd, a flicker of awe and unease crossing his face. "I wasn't expecting this…" he breathes, almost to himself.

"What do you mean?" Louisinette asks, her voice tight with worry as she studies his expression.

"This…" Jean gestures broadly at the sea of people. "This is far more than I anticipated. If we march into town like this, we'll face trouble. La Rivière-des-Barres is where the authorities will try to stop us. And with a crowd this large, tensions will explode into violence. It's too dangerous to proceed as planned."

"What do we do, Jean?" Louisinette's voice quivers, her hands gripping her headcloth as she pleads for guidance.

"We'll have to adjust. Our original plan to stop in Desgranges is no longer viable. The authorities will see us coming and move to contain us there. We need to split into two groups. One will take the back roads through Barlatier and Morne Mérice, passing through Ti-Rivière to Bois Chandelle. From there, they'll descend into Marché Mercredi. Ludovic and Céline will meet them at the foot of the hill. Claudette, you'll lead that group."

Claudette nods, her calm demeanor masking the fire in her heart. "Let's move. Stay together, and stay quiet," she instructs, her voice firm yet reassuring.

Jean continues, "The second group follows me down to the riverbed. We won't cross until we reach the river's mouth. From there, we move along the shoreline to the back of Marché Mercredi. Once both groups are in position, we wait for the signal to converge on the party."

Victorin offers to join Claudette, but Louisinette grips his arm firmly. "No. I need you with me," she insists, her voice leaving no room for argument.

Within minutes, they form two columns of intrepid feminist warriors, advancing painstakingly west. Claudette leads one column, crossing the river to ascend a pebbly path winding toward the hillside. The other, led by Jean-Mara, Victorin, and Louisinette, lingers briefly, watching the last members of Claudette's group vanish beneath the banana groves across the river. Then they march on, not a word passing between them as they pick their way along the riverbed.

At the edge of Basen Tounen, startled villagers on both sides of the riverbank look on, bewildered by the vast procession unfurling before them. As the last vestige of daylight dissolves into evening's shadows, the valley plunges into darkness. The voyagers step cautiously, hands resting on their hips; no one dares break the heavy silence.

While Claudette's group navigates the back roads, the valley floor teems with politically charged figures drawn to the mission's cause. Vendors at makeshift stands, lingering for last-minute buyers, pause to watch the scene. Some, moved by the fervor of the crowd, close shop and join in, bringing their animals and wheelbarrows into the fold.

Jean-Mara, energized by the moment, marches ahead with a theatrical flair. His trench coat, adorned with golden buttons and velvet pockets, sways with each stride. Twirling a hibiscus twig, he strikes at drooping banana leaves, his movements purposeful yet tinged with nervous energy. Flanked by Louisinette and Victorin, he exudes a charisma that seems to propel the group forward.

Louisinette follows a short distance behind, her lips pressed in solemn silence. With each step toward the looming confrontation, memories she once buried resurface with agonizing clarity. The long-suppressed thirst for justice and retribution courses through her veins, mingling with a growing unease. Although racked with hesitation, she pushes forward, each step an act of will against the emotional storm within her.

By the river's mouth, the trail frays, its last traces swallowed by the white sands of Lestè Déré. The group veers southward, accompanied by the rhythmic crashing of ocean waves, their path weaving through beds of cacti as they strain to converge on Marché Mercredi. Midway to their destination, they pass a seaside shantytown where a small cluster of women, suspecting the significance of this quiet march, wave ragged scraps of cloth in a poignant gesture of respect for the group's noble cause.

In the cooling night breeze, the immense procession maintains an eerie silence. They abandon their single-file line, reorganizing into staggered rows of five to minimize attention—resembling parishioners on their way to a late Saturday evening mass.

As they near their goal, the group skirts a red mangrove at the town's seaside edge, where cottages cling like barnacles. Wide-eyed children gape as the villagers march past, stone-faced, their silence a wall against the whispers. Not once do their footsteps falter.

Moments later, Jean raises a commanding hand, signaling the group to halt. In scattered bursts, the marchers take shelter beneath the thick canopy of a sprawling sea-grape bush, its broad leaves concealing them from sight. The crash of waves against the nearby shoreline reverberates in the cool night air, but the true source of tension lies in the heavy apprehension simmering within the group—an unease about what the next hour may bring.

Jean steps forward, scanning the shadowy path ahead before instructing Victorin and Louisinette to maintain order in his absence. He moves ahead as planned, making his way toward Ludovic and Céline, who wait for him at the foothill on the town's eastern edge. There, Claudette and her group are expected to join them.

Navigating Rue Camille, a narrow lane stretching from the shorelines to Main Street, Jean treads carefully, passing a lone boy preoccupied with his slingshot in front of a rickety cottage enclosed by whitewashed palisades. He crosses Main Street, slipping into Derrière Rue—the Back Street—snaking along the foothill's edge. His keen eyes quickly catch sight of an unusual gathering: a line of people dressed in white, walking arm-in-arm, their movement reminiscent of a solemn church procession.

Suddenly, the hushed stillness is interrupted by the rustling commotion of two girls darting from a nearby backyard. They call out to Jean in urgent, whispered tones. Without hesitation, he turns on his heel and strides toward them, his mind racing with questions as the mission grows ever more complex.

"Who are these people?" Jean asks the girls, his curiosity piqued. In an instant, he recognizes them as his cousin Nativida's youngest daughters.

"They're from Latiroli," the taller one explains, her voice trembling. "Out tonight protesting the beating of a *restavèk*." The younger girl clings with a protective grip to her sister's ankle-length floating garment, her wide eyes betraying both concern and innocence.

"Where's your mom?" Jean inquires, glancing around the dimly lit surroundings.

"She's inside," the girls reply in unison, their voices soft and childlike.

Smiling to reassure them, Jean takes their tiny hands and guides them through the cottage's half-open front door. Inside, a tall, slender woman with freckles dotting her face stands near a clay jar at the far end of the room. She fans herself with a tattered hat, batting at the relentless flies buzzing in from the backyard kitchen.

"Jean, what's going on?" Nativida asks, her tone a mix of curiosity and anxiety.

"I'm not sure," Jean replies, masking his own urgency. "I'm heading downtown and saw a lot of people in the streets, all dressed in white." He pauses, hoping his vague mention of a crowd will cover for his own approaching group. "Who are they?"

"I heard my neighbors say they're from the southern edge of town," Nativida explains, her voice stained with irritation. "They're protesting the unfair beating of that girl Amélie, the servant of the Morons."

"Do you know where Amélie is now?" Jean presses.

Frowning, Natividá shakes her head. "I've no idea."

"Manman, they say she went back home to her parents in La Plate," the older girl chimes in, her timid voice breaking the silence.

"La Plate?" Jean mutters, raising an eyebrow. "That's far, behind the mountains. Amélie must be someone remarkable to stir up such an uproar." He hesitates for a moment, then adds, "Listen, I have to meet a friend downtown, and I'm running late. It might be very dark by the time I make it back, so I need to leave now."

As he reaches the front door, Jean stops, turning back with a more serious tone. "Say, whatever strange noises you hear outside, keep the girls indoors. Do you hear me?"

"Yes, cousin," Natividá replies, her voice shaded with worry. Her arms wrap tightly around the girls, pulling them close to her as though shielding them from unseen dangers. Her mind races, imagining werewolves, prowlers, or riot police in the night. Unaware of Jean's true mission, she assumes he is warning her about the crowd in white—a thought that aligns all too well with the chaos brewing near Lucette's mansion, just two blocks away in the heart of town.

The air hangs heavy with tension, thick with anticipation of the multitudes converging not for a party, but in pursuit of long-overdue justice.

As Jean steps out of the house, the street lies deserted, its silence punctuated only by the faint strains of music and echoes of laughter drifting from the mansion. People in the neighborhood know all about the gala but have closed their doors, conveying their distance from such ostentatious events. Minutes later, Jean arrives at the ivy-clad concrete walls enclosing Lucette's home. The sounds of gossip, music, and cork-popping surge to an almost oppressive crescendo, enveloping the area.

Jean hesitates, a quick scan of his surroundings, and then he leaps forward. He knows Ludovic and Céline aren't inside yet—it's just shy of nine o'clock. Avoiding the guarded back door, he veers east, following a narrow path flanked by darkened cottages. As he passes the last house, the silence breaks.

"Jean-Mara!" Céline, Jessie, and Claudette call out, their joy unconstrained by fear of being overheard. Ludovic stands a step ahead of them, his watchful eyes fixed on the path. They've been waiting beneath the cover of banana trees, along with the Claudette's boys, Manuel and Daurélien.

"What took you so long?" Ludovic teases, though his voice betrays relief.

Jean waves off the question. "We need to talk," he says brusquely, signaling the group to draw closer. Claudette instructs Daurélien to return to the trailing crowd to help keep order and calm.

The remaining group presses against an avocado tree's trunk, its roots knuckling up from the soil. Above, the leaves dapple the ground with restless shadows. "Where's Louisinette?" Céline's voice splinters on the name.

"She's with the others, waiting under the sea-grapes by Nan Borben. Everything's set," Jean reassures her, though his own nerves are evident.

"We need a meeting point between here and there to merge with a smaller group before advancing," Ludovic suggests.

"Good idea," Claudette agrees, her gaze gone feral, unblinking, muscles coiled to bolt. She summons Manuel, who bounds back to join them, ready for instructions.

"Manuel's coming with me," Jean declares. "The rest of you, stay here until he returns. Once we're at Madame Bathel's house—right across from the Big House—I'll send Manuel back to bring you."

Claudette grabs Jean's arm, her voice quivering. "Are you sure? This is too important to leave anything uncertain."

Jean places a steadying hand on her shoulder. "Trust me. We've planned for this." He looks to Manuel. "Let's go."

"Be careful, Jean," Céline's voice is a match struck in the dark—brief, bright, gone.

Jean hesitates at her words but then nods, his impatience clear. "Is our man inside?" he asks over his shoulder.

"Oh, yes," Ludovic confirms with a smirk. "He's in a blue velvet tuxedo, bright red necktie—looking every bit the overripe fool. Last I saw, he was whining into his glass with Céline's dad, my dad, and their clique."

"Dodo!" Jessie scolds. "This is serious."

Ludovic grins and, leaning forward, plants a gentle kiss on Jessie's forehead. "We'll be okay, Jess. Trust me."

As Jean and Manuel disappear down the trail, the group steels itself, each bracing for the moment their plan collides with fate.

Chapter 31

About ten minutes later, Manuel returns; without exchanging a word, the small group of young adults sets off, following Manuel down a shadowy alley that snakes toward Main Street. Behind them, more than a hundred people move like silent phantoms, their footsteps muffled by the gravel and dirt, as if the earth itself conspires to keep their mission secret.

Céline, her nerves fraying with every passing second, clings tightly to Ludovic, her fingers spasming against his arm. She leans on him as if his steady presence alone can shield her from the waves of dread crashing through her. Each step feels heavier than the last, the air thick with the weight of what lies ahead.

The narrow path leads them to the rear of Aunt Marguerite's home. The house looms in the darkness, its shuttered windows giving no hint of life within. Yet, the sudden, sharp barking of dogs erupts, slicing through the tropical night and sending shivers down the spines of the marchers. The noise causes their procession to falter, but the group presses on, undeterred. Their resolve remains unshaken as they trail Manuel along the graveled walkway flanking the house.

Within moments, the group emerges onto Main Street, where the dim light of gas lamps casts flickering shadows. Waiting there are Jean, Louisinette, and Victorin, standing at the forefront of their own contingent. The sight of them uniting the two columns into a single force sends a ripple of determination through the gathered crowd. Now numbering some two hundred strong, they pause, a formidable presence on the quiet street, ready to storm Lucette Dominique Proilleur's house party and claim their moment of reckoning.

Inside the sprawling mansion, the party pulsates with energy, crescendoing with each passing minute. The elite guests gather in clusters of four at massive mahogany tables, their polished surfaces glinting under the chandelier's glow. Haitian Barbancourt rum and aged Bordeaux wines—red, rosé, and white—are abundant, forming the centerpiece of the lavish feast. While some guests lounge on the terrace, their animated chatter and bursts of laughter spilling into the night, others linger inside, drawn to the wine cooler where Lucette holds court.

Dressed in a silvery ballerina outfit paired with striking red-velvet gloves, Lucette radiates an effortless allure, casting beatific smiles at the latecomers filtering into the magnificently adorned living room. Italian Renaissance artwork lines the walls, each piece reflecting an air of cultured extravagance. In the corridor leading to the veranda, a gold-framed portrait of Lucette and her jolly husband, Fénélon, beams a glowing welcome to the arriving guests. The atmosphere is further enlivened by the rhythms of a well-known Saint Louis disc jockey, who spins tracks from Jazz Des Jeunes, Raoul Guillaume's Jazz Guignard, Jazz Choucoune, and other celebrated Haitian bands of the 1940s.

As the night deepens, Fénélon's absence stands out, a detail unnoticed or deliberately ignored by the revelers—Lucette no less, whose attentions are divided among her secret admirers. Proilleur's predictable routine plays out at every grand fiesta: he never makes it "alive" past ten o'clock. Lucette, knowing her husband's weakness for alcohol, ensures his early departure by serving him with her own hands a generous dose of warmed Barbancourt rum, heated with utmost care to match his peculiar preferences.

At 9:30 p.m. sharp, Fénélon at last emerges from the master bedroom, stuffed into an ill-fitting formal black tuxedo and bowtie. His entrance is cautious, as if testing the waters. He shuffles toward Lucette, who is still engrossed in greeting guests. The whimsical sparkle in her demeanor dims the moment she spots her husband, but Proilleur, ever the oblivious fool, seems not to notice. He grins awkwardly, trailing a single step behind Lucette in an almost servile manner, casting himself as a faint shadow of her radiant presence.

The absurdity of his appearance completes the picture. Fur-lined bedroom moccasins protrude beneath the hem of his tuxedo, glaringly at odds with his formal attire and catching the fluorescent light beams. His left-hand fidgets inside his jacket pocket, while his right adjusts the owl-rimmed prescription glasses perched on the tip of his nose, ready to slide. The glasses, like a stage prop, amplify his bumbling, eccentric aura, rendering him the quintessential image of a hapless wealthy nerd.

Tonight, as always on Lucette's grand Birthday Bash, Proilleur attempts to embody the role of the dutiful husband. Yet, even in his fumbling efforts, his presence is a mere footnote to the dazzling spectacle orchestrated by his wife, whose command of the room—and the night—is absolute.

Meanwhile, out in the courtyard, newly arriving guests take their seats one by one under a sprawling almond tree rooted in the center of a brick terrace. Dalambert and his entourage of "good" friends recline in elegant fashion at a table laden with the finest rums and an array of ripe tropical fruits. Positioned near the back entryway, Dalambert ensures Lucette's exotic features remain within his watchful line of sight. His flushed face betrays his delight as he cradles a cup of Kremas, a creamy, sweet alcoholic indulgence cherished at Haitian celebrations.

Tonight, Dalambert's Kremas is a bespoke creation commissioned by Lucette herself. Extra-powdery green lime zest infuses the concoction, along with the bold flavors of raw cinnamon, nutmeg, and anise. A generous splash of pure vanilla extract and the juices of raisins and currants enrich the condensed evaporated milk base, perfectly blended with white rum to sweeten the heart of Lucette's "secret" lover.

From her station at the entryway, Lucette often pivots, her eyes narrowing to catch a fleeting glance from Dalambert. He grins each time their gazes meet, a smug affirmation of their clandestine affair. Yet, when he notices the quiet awareness among his table companions, he quickly adopts an air of decorum, engaging in a spirited political discussion with Céline's father, Monsieur Jean-Foreste, and three other prominent members of the local "dinosaur clique." These include coffee speculator Gérome Maurepas, the opulent landowner Louverture Pierre-Jean, and Ferdinand Louisincou, a real estate broker notorious for his exclusivity and aversion to mingling outside his nouveau riche circle.

By 10:30 p.m., Fénélon Proilleur—inebriated but clinging to ceremony—rises to his feet. With a clumsy flourish, he takes Lucette's hand, instructs a manservant to shut the front door, and escorts her to the indoor banquet table. The table, a masterpiece of craftsmanship overseen by Mademoiselle Rosaline Duverger, reflects her mastery of Haitian gastronomy and her attention to refined detail. As the guests—both inside and out—transition to the banquet, anticipation builds for the evening's highlight: the formal toast honoring Lucette.

Each cavalier takes his seat beside his dame, save for Monsieur Dalambert, whose commitment to a libertine lifestyle has left him unattached. He claims a seat directly opposite Lucette, their glances charged with silent meaning. Despite her husband's presence, Lucette's longing gaze toward Dalambert betrays her discontent, seeking in her lover the solace her marriage cannot provide.

Beyond the banquet table, three small marble steps ascend to a makeshift dance floor perched atop a raised terrace below the mansion's wide-open back door, inviting the cool night breeze. Dalambert's attention shifts momentarily to a bottle of five-star Barbancourt rum, Haiti's strongest. A wicked thought dances in his mind: Lucette's audacious indecency might just ensure Fénélon is under the table after two grogs, leaving the rest of the night entirely his.

As is customary in these gatherings, Dalambert is slated to deliver the formal speech. Proilleur, desperate for a moment of recognition, suggests to his wife that he speak in Creole instead, ensuring that none of the audience misses a single word. Yet, as before, Lucette flatly rejects the idea, delivering a sharp jab of her elbow beneath the table as a final, dismissive reply.

Moments before the speech, Dalambert, the self-proclaimed sexologist with his rustic eccentricities, rises from his seat, adjusting his blue suit and gleaming red necktie. His gaze lingers on Lucette before sweeping over the room.

"Bonsoir, belle Lucette and our distinguished guests! Tonight, we are once again reunited in this lovely mansion of the Proilleurs to celebrate in our own version of paradise, an unforgettable—"

Before he can finish his sentence, a thunderous crash reverberates through the courtyard. The sound shakes the walls and startles the room into a shocked silence. The front gates have been struck with such force that one nearly buckles from its hinges. A second blow follows, then a third and fourth, each more resounding than the last.

Then comes the ROAR.

An enraged chant rises into the air, swelling with indignation: "Dalambert assassin, Dalambert assassin, ASSASSIN!"

Pandemonium breaks loose in the dining hall. Guests jump from their seats, their faces frozen in shock and terror. Lucette clutches the edge of the table, her painted nails digging into the mahogany.

Proilleur, the supposed host of this opulent soirée, stumbles to his feet, his bowtie askew and his face drenched in panic. Weaving through the chaos, he shoves the front door open and steps into the night.

His mansion is surrounded.

Before him stand Céline, Ludovic, and a well-organized mob, their faces alight with righteous fury. At the forefront is Louisinette, flanked by Céline and Ludovic on either side. Behind her, Jean-Mara and Victorin hold their ground, their presence like unyielding pillars of support for the determined woman between them.

Proilleur freezes, his breath catching as he takes in the overwhelming scene. His body trembles, and a sob, soaked in drunken despair, escapes his lips. "Dodo…Mademoiselle Céline…what…what is the meaning of this?" he stammers, his voice cracking under the weight of disbelief.

Céline steps forward, her composure taut with suppressed rage. Without a word, she pushes Louisinette to the front. "Tell him what you came here for, Louisie," she says, her voice vibrating with the conviction of long-awaited justice.

"I want…no, I demand…that Dalambert come outside right now," Louisinette declares, her voice sharp and unwavering. "I won't wait another second."

"Wha—whatever for?" Proilleur asks, the beads of sweat on his forehead gleaming under the flickering lantern light.

"If you don't send him out right now," Louisinette warns, her voice a low growl, "we will come inside and drag him out by the neck."

"Give me…one minute," Proilleur pleads, his face pale and drenched in desperation. He stumbles backward, tripping over his own feet before breaking into a panicked sprint toward the backyard.

As he retreats, the mob surges closer, their voices rising to a crescendo, echoing off the mansion's towering walls and shaking its foundations. The chant for Dalambert's reckoning climaxes, piercing through the night air: "Dalambert assassin, ASSASSIN!"

In the midst of the chaos, Proilleur finds Dalambert hiding near the veranda. His voice cracks into a frantic scream. "Dalambert, it's you they want! For God's sake, Céline and Ludovic are with them!"

"Who's with them?" scream both Monsieur Jean-Foreste and Madame Bernadine, their ashen faces stricken with terror. The disbelief in their wide eyes is matched only by the fear draining the blood from their cheeks, leaving them paler than the midnight moon.

Monsieur Malbranche, Ludovic's father, rises from his seat, his brow furrowed with concern, and strides toward the commotion at the front door. Céline's parents, wide-eyed, follow closely, their apprehension mirrored by the guests now frozen in collective shock. All eyes remain fixed on Dalambert, who squirms under their scrutiny, visibly shaken yet unrepentant. The reason for the crowd's fury remains a mystery to most of the attendees, but not to Dalambert, whose guilt radiates like a smoldering ember.

Lucette, seated nearby, clutches her wine glass, trying to piece together the situation. Her mind flits to possible explanations. Perhaps a misunderstanding over land, she reasons—Dalambert is, after all, the region's renowned agronomist. Land disputes often erupt into chaos in Haiti. But then, Dalambert's trembling voice cuts through the thick, oppressive silence.

"I...I did a job in Barlatier last week," he stutters, his voice rising in pitch. "Must've upset them."

His eyes ricochet off walls, faces, exits—anywhere but here—searching for a lifeline. Panic seizes him as he yanks a concealed pistol from beneath his jacket, the motion clumsy and frantic. Gasps ripple through the room as Dalambert, teetering on the edge of reason, appears ready to lash out. Before he can spiral into full-blown chaos, Lieutenant Florantin Milord, a young and composed officer with the Haitian Army—and another of Lucette's admirers—steps forward.

"Put it down," Milord commands, his voice calm yet authoritative.

Dalambert hesitates, but the stern glare of the lieutenant, coupled with the collective murmurs of disapproval from the guests, forces his hand. Reluctantly, he relinquishes the weapon. Stripped of his feeble sense of control, Dalambert now resembles a cornered animal, his eyes wide and flickering, his breath shallow.

At the door, Malbranche and the visibly shaken Jean-Foreste push it open, only to come face to face with their children. The sight halts them in their tracks.

"Dodo, my son, what in God's name is this madness?" Malbranche growls, his voice a mix of confusion and fury.

"Papa," Ludovic replies, his voice unsteady but fearless, "we are here tonight to seek justice for Louisinette." He steps aside, pushing the young woman forward. Louisinette, though shaking, stands tall, her gaze locked on the older men.

Céline's parents gasp, the sound serrated with shock. Bernadine seizes Céline's arm, her fingers digging in as she desperately pleads with her daughter to abandon the mob. Jean-Foreste's face contorts with a volatile mix of fear and anger, his hands balling into fists.

"Justice for Louisinette?" Jean-Foreste's voice quakes as his stare flickers between his daughter and the crowd. "What does any of this have to do with Dalambert?"

The name hangs in the air like a curse. The mention of their former *restavèk*—someone they've spent years trying to forget—shatters the carefully maintained veneer of their social standing. Louisinette's mere presence is an affront to their prestige, her story a festering wound they've refused to acknowledge.

Céline's voice rises, steady and unwavering. "You know exactly what he did, Papa!" Her tone slices through the tense atmosphere. "He raped her, threatened to kill her if she ever spoke a word. And when she became pregnant, you and Maman cast her out—discarded her like trash! You sent her away to the mountains, to places she had never even heard of, to suffer alone."

Jean-Foreste's face flushes a deep crimson, his jaw tightening as he struggles to absorb the indictment. Bernadine's grip on Céline's arm falters, her hand dropping limply to her side. Across the threshold, the crowd murmurs, their voices a mixture of righteous fury and sorrow. Louisinette stands silently, her presence an undeniable testament to the truth that has long been buried.

Tears glisten in Céline's eyes, but her eyes remain fierce, inflexible. "Tonight, justice will no longer be ignored," she declares, her voice resonating with the weight of years of unspoken pain. "Not for Louisinette, not for anyone."

Scratching his head in disbelief, Malbranche seems utterly stunned. "What is it, my dear Céline? Have you lost yourself to this peculiar cause?" he asks, his voice tinged with both confusion and disbelief.

"Don't worry, Malbranche; I will deal with my daughter!" Jean-Foreste asserts forcefully, his tone cutting like a blade. But the surrounding crowd draws Céline back into its embrace, defiant and unbending.

"We want Dalambert! We want Dalambert!" The crowd's chants roar like a storm gathering force, a quake of voices shaking the air. The growing mob, now bolstered by fresh ranks filtering in from the two massive groups behind them, threatens to overwhelm the mansion, surging with the relentless energy of justice long denied.

Malbranche, sensing imminent danger, bolts inside and rushes to the backyard. With urgency etched on his face, he commands the remaining guests to exit through the front of the mansion before they are engulfed by chaos. "Go! Now! If you stay, you'll face total annihilation!" he shouts.

Panic takes hold. Guests spring from their seats, their polished façades shattered by fear, and scatter like frightened woodland creatures. Trapped like a caged animal, Dalambert clings to the young officer, his trembling frame a dead weight on the man's shoulder. His eyes scythe through the crowd, hacking at the illusion of escape.

On the back steps leading to the terrace, Lucette stumbles. Her legs buckle beneath her, and she nearly crashes face-first into the cold concrete floor. Her sodden husband, Fénélon, dives, wobbling himself as he struggles to steady his sobbing, tear-streaked wife.

<u>*Chapter 32*</u>

Within moments, the once-opulent courtyard is transformed into a chaotic arena. The frightened guests spill into the front yard, their faces masks of terror as they come face-to-face with the roaring crowd. The demonstrators' chants and cries surge to a fever pitch, the air thick with righteous fury. For a fleeting instant, it seems the mob is poised for a fatal charge.

Sensing the tipping point, Céline and Louisinette raise their hands high into the air, their commanding gestures slicing through the cacophony. The crowd, as if obeying an invisible tide, falls silent. Under the moon's cool glow, an eerie hush descends. For one long, tension-filled minute, the world feels suspended, quiet enough to hear a single pin drop.

This is the moment Louisinette has dreamed of—endured endless pain and hardship for. She stands unflinching, her body a monument of resolve, as immovable and enduring as an underground boulder. Her face, chiseled with determination, hardens as she takes measured steps toward Dalambert, each one closer to the man who robbed her of so much.

As if summoned by an unspoken command, the crowd shifts, following her like an ocean wave bending to the will of the wind. They stay within arm's reach, a living shield ready to defend her should the powerful elite attempt to silence her with force.

The movement's leaders—Céline, Jessie, Ludovic, Jean-Mara, Claudette, and Victorin—stand tall, their solidarity a fortress against the oppressive forces they confront. The crowd's watchful eyes fixate not only on the terrified Dalambert but also on the finely dressed elite guests. For the masses, these figures embody a lifetime of disdain and injustice—a contempt as deep and palpable as the night itself.

"Tonight," Louisinette softly begins, "I come here to demand justice. I'm a rape victim *nobody* paid any attention to when I was sexually assaulted. The criminal threatened to kill me if I went and told my story to others. In the process, the rapist forced a baby into my young body—a child who reminds me every day of that horrifying evening, the worse night of my life. I was only sixteen. I'd been a household slave, a *restavèk,* since I was almost a babe…serving without disobedience a group of people who happen to be the best friends of the maniac who penetrated me, leaving me to die from bleeding that night aside the Saint Louis River.

"My dignity was the only thing I had to remind me that I was still a human being; all else was taken away from me. That night, I felt *so* useless and *so* dehumanized. I had no one to turn to while a river of blood was running out of the forbidden part of my body. Life is too cruel, and the savage, barbarous world we live in gives me no chance for justice…because it is a world controlled by heartless, well-to-do maniacs constantly on the lookout, on the hunt for vulnerable people like me. It is a filthy world, a world harboring and honoring criminals like Dalambert, *the brutal monster who raped me!*"

Her voice breaks. Unable to continue, the poor victim weeps; but her sobbing is no match with the moaning and groaning emanating from the wealthy partygoers gathered on the front lawn. Lovingly, Céline caresses Louisinette's shaking shoulders, using an embroidered handkerchief to dab at and wipe away her tears. In the house, Lucette collapses into the quivering arms of her devoted husband, who somehow manages to carry her to bed. But on the front lawn, emboldened and empowered by this historic moment, Louisinette staunchly walks the last three steps over to where Dalambert stands, shaking and trying to hide, nothing more than a petrified and humbled coward.

"Tell them what you did to me. *Tell them.* If you don't, I'll order the crowd to take you on…they're *furious,* and they're hungry for *your meat!*"

"Can't you use your authority on her, officer?" the quaking, guilt-ridden fool demands of the Haitian soldier, who glares at him with nothing but aversion and rancor, and who also sees the golden opportunity to rid Dalambert of Lucette's secret game. Dalambert does not look as if he understands the nobility, the ferocity, or the seriousness of this highly significant moment; his infamous arrogance blurs any such subtle reasoning, or the lack of same.

"What do you *want* me to do? Shoot her? Shoot *them?*" the young officer mouths, leaving Dalambert behind. The other guests as one being also desert him, including Céline's awe-stricken parents, who now feel nothing but unadulterated shame for ever having been this man's friends.

Louisinette reiterates her command for Dalambert to "tell them," adding to it a stern warning: "You have thirty seconds to start confessing your crime."

Humiliated, Dalambert falls to his knees, begging without shame for mercy, whining his confessed guilt. An unsympathetic Crizo, abruptly leaping from the crowd, strikes him with a bludgeoned baton. Her harsh blows knock him over; blood trickles from his scalp and out of his mouth.

Distressed by this sight, Proilleur, emerging from indoors, thrusts himself into the crowd, beseeching pardon for Dalambert.

"Fénélon, don't you know you're one of his victims?" Jean-Mara challenges, his voice carrying above the din. The drunken Proilleur stumbles, clutching at members of the crowd and disoriented partygoers alike, his face a picture of bewilderment.

"What do you mean? What is all this? Why?" Proilleur's voice quavers, but Jean-Mara's response slices through the fog of his confusion.

"The whole town knows he's one of your wife's secret lovers. You're just lucky you're not in your usual drunken stupor tonight."

A vise-grip on his bicep, the officer spins Dalambert around. Cuffs glint—cold promise against his wrists. "Under arrest, you bastard," he declares, his voice a thunderclap against the murmuring crowd.

"Not so fast," Céline cuts in, her commanding presence halting the officer mid-motion.

"Why?" the officer asks, his tone irked yet curious.

"Simply arresting him lets him escape true accountability. You must promise us, officer, that this man will never again set foot in Saint Louis and that he will serve his sentence far from his next potential victim. He owes the world more than just handcuffs."

Dalambert stands defeated, his once-pristine suit reduced to filthy tatters. He looks nothing like the grand agronomist of Saint Louis but rather a broken man, stripped of dignity and power. The officer hauls him away, his cries drowned out by the jubilant roar of the crowd.

"Victory, victory is ours! Justice is served!" the crowd thunders, their voices uniting in a triumphant anthem as fists pump into the air and tears of vindication stream down weathered faces. At last, the weight of unspoken truths has lifted, and justice strides into the heart of Saint Louis.

243

Chapter 33

Upon break of dawn the following morning, Céline awakens, her body heavy but her spirit alight. Memories of last night's coup cascade through her mind, and she recognizes it as an irreversible victory for women's equality. Yet, the triumph is bittersweet; her parents' disappointment looms large, their likely inability to forgive her casting a shadow over her elation.

"So be it," she murmurs, resolute. She feels no shame for standing on the right side of history. In her heart, she knows last night offered oppressed women, particularly the *restavèk*, a reason to hope—a glimmer of light promising a better tomorrow. Most importantly, her dear friend Louisinette has finally found the poetic justice she was denied for so many years.

Céline heaves herself out of bed, still in her nightgown, and glides down the elaborate staircase for a refreshing morning shower. After dressing, she makes her way to the kitchen. The house is still, her parents asleep in their master bedroom. Solitude is absent. Céline glances at her wristwatch: 7:30 a.m. She prepares a simple breakfast—two slices of multi-grain toast slathered with butter and strawberry jam, paired with a steaming cup of Earl Grey tea sweetened with organic honey. As she sips the last of her tea, a renewed sense of purpose stirs within her.

With her lace-fringed leather purse slung over her shoulder, she steps out the back door, the fires of a new day burning bright within her. The streets of Saint Louis are slowly awakening. Passing the town's main dispensary, she sees patients waiting for their early appointments. She waves at them, and they wave back with warm smiles, recognizing her as a leader in the extraordinary events of the previous night.

Crossing the small bridge on the town's southern fringes, she heads west along a pebbly street that leads to Ludovic's family home. At the gate of the two-story house with polished mahogany double doors, Ludovic waits in his tropical jogging outfit of black shorts and a white t-shirt. Spotting Céline, he beams her a smile, one as buoyant as her own. In a swift motion, he unhinges the latch, swinging the metal gates open.

"Morning, Liline," he greets her, his voice laced with affection.

"Good morning, Dodo," she replies, her spirits lifting even higher as she steps through the gate.

"You managed to surprise me," Ludovic teases, a grin spreading across his face.

She bursts into laughter. "Oh, come on now—how so?" Though deep down, she knows he wasn't expecting her this early.

"Dodo, I couldn't sleep a wink last night. My mind was spinning with thoughts, running through my brain like water through a sieve."

"Like what?" Ludovic asks, tilting his head with mock seriousness.

"What do you mean, 'like what?'" Céline retorts, a smirk curling her lips.

"Liline, I couldn't rest either," he confesses, his voice softening. "I kept thinking about the people last night—the fire in their eyes, their firm determination for justice. And Dalambert," he adds with a scoff, "his cowardice was almost laughable. The moment he realized his so-called friends had deserted him, he crumbled like clay."

As Ludovic steps closer, he plants a light kiss on her forehead—a gentle, familiar gesture of his affection and respect. "I'm so happy for Louisinette," Céline says, her voice brimming with emotion. "Now she and her family can hold their heads high and say that justice is possible, even for someone like her—a *restavèk*."

"Not happier than I am," Ludovic replies, his smile steady and warm. "At least now, people who think they can exploit the vulnerable without consequence will have to think twice. It's a step forward for equity."

Feeling a newfound lightness, Céline wraps her arms tightly around his waist. "Do you remember what you promised me by the river?" she asks, peering up at him, her eyes sparkling with mischief.

Ludovic shakes his head playfully. "No, which river are we talking about?" he jokes, though he remembers every detail of that day.

"Don't play coy. Bassin Joseph. Our first walk there," she presses, her cheeks flushing slightly.

"Ah, yes!" Ludovic chuckles. "I promised you a canoe ride downriver. Are you ready for it? The weather won't stay this good forever."

Releasing him with a laugh, Céline steps back, her expression a mix of excitement and disbelief. "Yes, I am…oh, I can't believe I just said that!"

"Canoeing with you—it's the dream I've carried since day one." His voice roughens, as if the words have been waiting years to escape. He then settles his hands on her shoulders, the weight of them like fallen leaves catching on a branch. This time, she doesn't pull away; instead, she leans into his touch, her soft moan betraying her growing comfort in his presence.

"Let's go!" he says, his grin widening as he takes her hand, hoping to mask the slight blush coloring her cheeks.

They hold hands, walking like true lovers toward Ludovic's convertible Jeep Wrangler, parked in front of the house as if it had been waiting for this moment. He drives east onto Main Street and then south toward the river. Reaching the riverside, he steers the Jeep under the shade of a sprawling sapodilla tree. With a nimble leap, he exits the car and circles to unlock Céline's door.

They follow a hidden dirt road that winds up the hillside, tracing the town's edge as it meanders toward breathtaking views. Scattered cottages dot the landscape, nestled among the greenery like treasures inside a tropical snow globe. Ludovic knows nearly all their inhabitants.

He points out a charming blue cottage, its courtyard adorned with clumps of pink and blue vinca flowers. "That's Josafa's place," he remarks. "He's leading a team of local farmers into the mountains today."

Off in the distance, Josafa's towering silhouette is visible, rallying his crew with commanding gestures and gung-ho cries that echo across the morning air. Hoes slung over shoulders, the farmers advance in a disciplined line, their determination unmistakable even from afar.

"Look at them," Céline observes, her voice soft but unequivocal. "They're so committed."

"Not only that," Ludovic replies, "they're way more disciplined than our last-minute crew was when we stormed Proilleur's party."

Céline bursts into laughter, the sound rippling through the quiet grove. A flock of wildfowl, startled by her gaiety, erupts noisily from the branches of a young mango tree. Surprised, Céline jumps and stumbles into Ludovic's arms, her laughter dissolving into breathless giggles. Her body presses against his chest, and his arms instinctively tighten around her.

For a moment, the world seems to pause. Beneath the mango tree's heavy branches, with its unripe fruit swaying in the breeze, they stand entwined. Ludovic's gaze locks on her luminous hazel eyes, tinged with hues of indigo, and his fingers trace the delicate curve of her chin. Strands of her golden hair dance in the wind, brushing his face like whispers of the sea. Emboldened, he lets his hands rest lightly against the fabric of her flowing dress, brushing the warmth of her cinnamon-kissed skin beneath.

Céline shivers, her blush deepening as she draws back. Yet she stops short of pulling away. There, under the morning light, she offers him a tentative smile—a wordless invitation that speaks of both innocence and courage. Closing the gap, Ludovic presses a gentle kiss to her lips. It is soft, exploratory, and laden with unspoken promises.

After a while, Ludovic pulls her hands into his. "Let's keep moving," he says, his voice warm and steady.

Hand in hand, they follow the road until it curves downward to a river basin, where birch canoes rest on sandy shoals. Céline pauses, taking in the emerald mountains that cradle Saint Louis in their quiet embrace.

"How peaceful it is up here," she murmurs, her voice filled with awe. "I wish the entire country carried this kind of beauty and tranquility."

Nodding affirmatively, Ludovic holds her close, his arm snug around her waist as if to shield her from the world's imperfections. Her blush has faded, replaced by a serene glow, and in his eyes, she sees a reflection of her own quiet joy. A joy that, oddly enough, brought to mind a memory she hadn't touched in years.

"You know, when I was in Scotland, there was this girl named Richlicia who reminded me a lot of your sister. She was from Cape Verde and spoke some Creole," Céline recalls but continues, "Every morning, I'd watch her walk to the school cafeteria, and she'd always stop to chat with me. She went back to Cape Verde a year before I returned, but her profound nationalism struck me deeply. Haiti was always in my heart, but it was her steadfast patriotism that made me question staying in Glasgow. Today, I've been thinking about her. I'd like to find Richlicia, to thank her personally."

Humming softly, Ludovic feels no threat from the memory of this other girl; his only concern is Céline. "Really?"

"Yes. Because of her, I returned home—and because of that, I have you in my life. Coming back gave Louisinette the courage to confront Dalambert. Her inspirational story of survival and justice shows how people across the world are interconnected by values that honor human dignity. The tragedy of children in servitude is a global issue. It's only through a united struggle, waged by honest citizens everywhere, that we can someday eradicate human trafficking and childhood enslavement."

"We share the same dream, my sweet love." Ludovic's voice is soft, filled with unspoken emotion. For the first time, he calls her love. She does not flinch or object, instead tilting her face upward, as though seeking the consolation of his lips.

"I love you, Céline…more than words can express," he whispers, drawing closer to her parted lips. This time, their kiss is deeper, longer, sealing the bond between them.

"Me too, *mon amour*," she breathes, her words barely audible yet brimming with affection.

Standing entwined by the riverside, they hold each other as if time itself has paused. When they finally pull apart, they make their way to the nearest canoe by the water's edge. Ludovic gently scoops Céline into his arms, placing her in the front seat with care. Grasping a pair of wooden oars, he hands them to her.

"Watch me, sweetheart. Each pull against the current pushes the boat farther along the river."

"I'm scared, Dodo," she admits, her voice quivering a little.

"Let me guide you first. Don't start until I tell you," he assures her.

"*Oui, mon cœur.* Yes, sweetheart," she exhales, her eyes locked on his. Turning her head just so, she murmurs, "My love, take me to paradise—a place where our joy will last forever. Promise me this: you will never leave me."

"I'm with you always, 'til death do us part."

Bound by love and hope, the pair rows with unhurried strokes down the river. They are two Haitian souls, lost in the rush of the water, the promise of new adventures, and their shared devotion to each other and their beloved homeland.

THE END

<u>*Epilogue*</u>

Louisinette's story echoes the lives of millions of children across the globe, many trapped in deplorable conditions. Though slavery was officially abolished in Haiti over two centuries ago, a form of modern-day servitude endures, and children remain its primary victims. Most of these children, whose fundamental rights are flagrantly violated, come from impoverished rural communities. In Haiti's hinterlands, where poverty reigns supreme, parents often lack the basic necessities to provide for their children—offspring who never asked to be born—leaving them vulnerable to exploitation.

Predators from urban centers prey on these families, luring them with false promises in exchange for free labor. These children, known as *restavèk*—a term derived from the French phrase "*reste avec*" meaning "stay with"—are often promised an education. But in most cases, that promise is never fulfilled. Even when some lucky children are offered schooling, it often occurs in makeshift, unregulated night schools. Instead of learning, *restavèk* children endure exhausting labor from dawn until dusk, carrying out household chores under conditions of extreme abuse.

The schooling they might receive, if any, happens in archaic environments that lack resources and fail to foster cognitive development. Exhausted from ceaseless labor and the physical and emotional torment inflicted upon them, these children are ill-equipped to thrive. Tragically, *restavèk* children are not just exploited by strangers; many are enslaved by friends or relatives who are supposed to provide care and protection.

A United Nations report on child labor in Haiti revealed that, before the devastating 2010 earthquake, an estimated 250,000 children were living as *restavèk*. Of these, two-thirds were girls, many of whom suffered sexual abuse at the hands of community members or even within the families they served. Given the worsening poverty following the earthquake, it is likely this number has increased significantly, highlighting the persistence of this crisis.

Despite their indispensable contributions, *restavèk* children are often undernourished—even as they prepare meals for the households they serve. Stripped of the joys of childhood and denied a proper education, many remain in servitude until they reach the age of eighteen, as documented by UNICEF. These young adults, deprived of the skills and confidence to navigate an already unforgiving world, often fall into cycles of poverty and despair, joining society's marginalized fringes.

This story was written to raise awareness of the harsh realities faced by children in servitude, not just in Haiti but worldwide. While Haiti may seem emblematic of such exploitation, it is far from the only nation grappling with these atrocities. A report by the Walk-Free Foundation, an Australian-based human rights organization, estimates that 29.8 million people globally, many of them children, live as modern-day slaves, trafficked and subjected to horrific abuses.

There are countless Louisinettes in the world—children who desperately need rescue from the suffocating grip of their oppressors. Human intelligence is the most valuable and underestimated resource of any society, especially embodied in its children. Turning a blind eye to slavery or involuntary servitude, particularly child enslavement, is not just a betrayal of these children; it is a profound disservice to our shared humanity.

253

<u>*G l o s s a r y*</u>

A la mizèpou lave kay tè = Mopping a house with a dirt floor is quite a challenge.

Au revoir = Goodbye

Basso profundo = Low tone of voice

Beau Garçon, = Handsome boy

Bonjou = Good morning in Creole

Bonjou bel cousin = Morning pretty cousin (in Creole)

Bonsoir = Good afternoon or evening

Bonsoir ma bellechabine = Good afternoon, my pretty lady

Bon vivant = Someone who loves to live in luxury, who has a refined taste

  for superb food and drink

Bouche-en-bouche = Mouth-to-mouth

Boukousou = A local bread made out of cassava flour

Camionette = A pick-up truck or minivan used as a conveyance for local transportation

Cet amour povisoir sans fin = This temporary love without end

Chéri = The masculine version for the word darlin.

Chérie = The feminine version for the word darling

Cocottes = concubines or female prostitutes

Cuisinière = A female chef or cook

Dans la gratitude = Live in gratitude

De touspoils et sans poils = Of all hair, without hair

Dinstinctive grandeur et beauté inestimable =Unique splendor and of beauty of great respect

Djanm = Firm

Djïouba = Nighttime festivity in the countryside

Fresco = Frozen drinks

Goud = Haitian currency, the equivalence of twenty cents

Granbwa = The god of the forest

Grandon = Wealthy landowner

Justicier = Lawenforcer

Kleren = A traditional rum

Kowosòl or Korosol= Sour-sop or guanabana, a tropical fruit with edible pulp and a large

seed. It is related to custard apple.

Kremas = It is a sweet and creamy alcoholic beverage very popularin *Haiti*. Kremas or

Cremas is usually served on special occasions like a wedding reception, a

special gathering. Kremas is made from creamed coconut, sweetened

condensed evaporated milk, and rum.

Landòmi = A nocturnal snake

Lingua franca = A mixture of French and Creole commonly used by the Haitian elite

Ma chère cousine = My dear cousin

Maestro = A chief or a conductor

Malanga = A popular vegetable whose roots are eaten like yams

Manbo = A female voodoo priest

Mango monben = A variety of mango

Manman = Mother (in Creole)

Mazinga = A cooperative, agricultural work

Mèsianpil = Thank you very much

Mèsiwi = Thank you

MètKalfou = Master of crossroads

Moun la vil = City people

Nat = A mat made out of dry banana stem straps

Non, non, maintenantj'insiste = No, no, now I insist.

Onèrespè la sosyete = Honor and respect to you all

Piskèt = Minnows or freshwater or saltwater fish

Pitit = Girl!

Poukisa = Why

Raison d'être =Reason for being

Restavèk = Children in forced servitude

Secret de polichinelle = Open secret

Soirée = A fancy, private party, traditionally at a lavish mansion

Tête-à-tête = Anintimate or private conversation between two individuals

Timoun = Children

Ti-nèg = People, a word commonly used to describe untrusted people

Ti chéri = sweet boy

Twa-de = Peanut butter over cassava, an important commodity in Haiti

Très stupide = Very stupid

Wi = Yes

Wi mesye= Yes sir